4-8-12

To Stacy
Braaiiins —

PaxCorpus
Ryan S. Fortney
Edited by: Anastasia Rivera
Cover art illustrated by: Leah Moore

© 2012 Lulu Ryan S. Fortney. All rights reserved.
ISBN 978-1-105-46975-6

Without limiting the rights under copyright reserved above, no part of this publication may be reproduced, stored in or introduced into a retrieval system, or transmitted, in any form, or by any means (electronic, mechanical, photocopying, recording, or otherwise) without the prior written permission of the copyright owner of this book.

This is a work of fiction. All the characters and events portrayed in this book are fictional, and any resemblance to real people or incidents is purely coincidental.

What would you do if, six years after the apocalypse, your shattered memory began to return? Piece by piece, everything that happened and the tale of your survival unfolds right in front of you and at the exact same time, the past repeats itself.

What if the lines between real and unreal began to blur and all you could do is hold tight and hope the ride's not too bumpy?

Would you stop the process before it's too late? What if you couldn't?

This is PaxCorpus.

Acknowledgments

This slice of page is dedicated to all of those people that helped me through this. Without you I'd still be sitting around drunken and slumped all alone in a ball of depression, with only an idea and a scratchy little prologue.

To my Dad, for not only supporting me one hundred percent of the way and then some, but for being an amazing voice actor and producing all of those awesome little cuts from the book itself.

To my Mom, for just being Mom. Through rough patches and tribulations, no matter what, you're there.

To Ed "Pumpin' and Thumpin" Shaffer. You brainstormed with me, hell, you work with me. And little did I know your reverse psychology actually worked. I'm not sure how much of a friend you consider me, but this is my testament to you – You're one hell of a guy. Publish that book already.

To all of the others that read the rough copy of this and gave me some feedback, thanks – You're all FIRED. Stacy, Uncle Doug, Rob (and his Sister, I suppose!), Sara, Angel, Mike and whoever else I may have missed with this insert. I'll get you with the sequel!

And to that maniacal person who won't be named. You opened me up, you made me bleed and you took me for a ride through something euphoric. Until you stopped me dead in my tracks, pulled out my heart, slammed it on the ground, beat it with a hammer and tormented me for eight months – I thank you. I've come to the conclusion that this story might not exist today, if you hadn't completely destroyed me.

**Because of you.
This is all
because of you.**

Muffled voices of a man and a woman slip through the cracks of comatose consciousness, arguing left and right – "Where are we taking him?" she asks.

"Harrisburg," A deeper voice responds abruptly, then hesitating for a moment, "I've got an idea..."

"Why not just leave him with the rest of the forsaken?"

My lungs constrict and tighten, ready to implode. An invisible hand grabs my heart and squeezes with all of its might. I wanna scream, but not a muscle moves.

"He's going into cardiac arrest, administer the sedative!" The woman's voice bursts through my eardrums like an Earth shattering sonic-boom.

A quick sting to my neck, like a hornet, then extreme cold bursts through my veins. Grey meets black and they swirl together; dancing back and forth behind my eyelids as they tether and snap, spinning, swirling, washing away and here we are –

0

Ground Zero

Looking to my left, I see rioters and looters pushing office furniture through the window of a glistening high-rise. To the right, you see the dead ripping flesh from bone, with the entrails of someone you hadn't known, hanging from their gnashing teeth. A blurred cloud of panic and chaos erupts from the volcanic streets of Manhattan. Behind you, the deafening sound of chopper blades, lifting and dropping in unison, with the bellowing sound of a ship's horn breaking through each millisecond of a pause.

The scenery is smudged water color, red and grey, bouncing off the top of skyscrapers. Something you've never really taken notice of, thinking to yourself, with the stench of foul eggs tickling at your nostrils. The roads and sidewalks littered with twisted and over-turned vehicles, military men and their "so-called" crisis situation training being put to good use – the muzzle flash of a hundred guns going off in the distance, once again, pondering the realization that maybe, we weren't prepared for this, no matter how many times we'd trained for it.

Bullets whiz by from all directions. A shred of cloth flutters from your shoulder, the impact throwing you back, leaving a sticky red substance in its crater like shape. Shaking and nervous, you pull a needle from your front shirt pocket and drive it directly into the large blue vein on your wrist. Depressing the pump, you pull it out before you even have a chance to react to the pain.

You crouch, watching bodies drop, then rise, drop, then rise, head swirling – you stop, mouthing inaudible words to an invisible listener, "Make it fucking stop!" Preprocessed meat and synthetically made French fries climb through your esophagus, spilling out of your mouth and onto your brand new, police issue combat boots.

In a book or a dictionary, you might've read that the apocalypse would have been the hand of God destroying all evil. You may have thought that this was necessary. What you don't know or might not have considered, is the fact that maybe God sees evil in all of mankind. If there really is a God – a question you constantly ask yourself.

Out-of-body, watching the back of your head, turning from the crowd in a soulless, milky-eyed trance, he says, "When death sleeps..." The sentence trails away, lost in a catacomb drenched in two-toned shadows.

On both sides of him, shoulder-to-shoulder, a squad of New York's finest yell obscenities, saliva streaming from their mouths, a light shadow of yellow and orange reflecting from their disgruntled faces.

"Fuckin' kill 'em, damnit!" He says, "We got this!"

"Blow 'em back to Hell!" A woman yells, pointing to the crowd with the barrel of her gun, barring teeth and revealing the burning eyes of death-incarnate.

"Why won't they just fuckin' die?!" He screams this question, still firing, hearing bullets pelt flesh like punching a sack of potatoes.

There wasn't really any distinction between the dead and alive, who could've blamed him. Not like he hadn't seen this scenario before. Not like Hollywood didn't shove it down his throat. Seems it's a bit more frustrating in real life. You don't have make-up artists spraying fake blood all over the blacktop. You don't have flashy special effects; controlled fires forming a dotted line through the crowd; fake limbs being torn from fake muscle tissue. You don't have emotionless and desensitized characters.

He could've pretended it wasn't happening, but in the end, the blood would end up on Dante Marcellus's hands – mine.

The pulsing tone echoing in my ears finally dies down. The morphine dissipates. There was nothing fake about this; we were killing indiscriminately – franticly. The outbreak was moving too fast to contain. Anyone who made it to the evacuation zone, made it out, infected or not, we had no way of confirming this many civilians. If they didn't, well, let's just say that Mother Nature's cruel in her selection. Blame is always easier to place on faceless, irrelevant things.

Sitting behind the trenches of piled sandbags and empty shell casings, my stomach swirls around and my heart feels heavy, a frog emerging in the deepest part of my throat. "What the hell am I doing?" the little voice in the back of my head questions, before remembering that it had to be done, no matter what. I was here for a reason; I was called here and it was my duty, along with the rest of the police force and military, to secure as many survivors as possible. Even if it seemed like mass genocide, it wasn't about my feelings. Those would come later, much later.

The first stage of grief is denial. The first stage of Hell is limbo. If you're grieving, you're in a transitional period. But what if you're constantly in denial?

From the burning ember I rise with fists of iron, a smoking barrel in each hand and I say these words, "This is only the beginning."

Intermission

Sweat beading from my pores, the warmth of tears streaking down my face and the barrel of a forty-five glimpsing through the rising flames. Compared to this, the end of the civilized world didn't seem so bad. I had seen the warning signs, heard all of what she had to say, but my stubbornness wouldn't let me see the truth, it couldn't.

Just moments from now, my life, our lives, they'd never be the same. It kinda makes you think, makes you wonder; would you give up tomorrow just to have today? Would you give away your soul just to have something you told yourself you'd never lose, but did anyway? Would you fill that gaping void, deep inside of you, with something, anything, just to forget the pain?

Whatever, it was too late for questions, too soon for answers.

1

The Night Before

Before that fateful morning, it was completely and utterly obvious that we had something greater than a pandemic on our hands. But the public, our government, they ignored it as if it'd just go away with time.

The first Presidential speech involved an address to the nation. Schools closed for a week and people were urged to stay within their homes, avoiding contact with others to avoid infection.

Phase two involved an increasing amount of violence reported in the media – hysteria began. There were even reports of savage murders and acts of cannibalism all across the nation. We, the people, were turning on each other.

Three minutes from nineteen hundred hours, on the night of November fourth, twenty-thirteen, martial law was declared. The military moved in on every major city and town across the United States of America. I sat, holed up in my small, shitty little Manhattan apartment, flipping through channels, trying to find something interesting to keep my mind busy.

But all every channel had were still pictures of the White House or that multi-colored distress signal, which sounded off with that annoying fucking tone and the sounds of numbers dialing, like an old fax machine.

So I stopped on four, the one preparing for the next Presidential speech and I cracked open my last cold beer from a refrigerator powered by generators.

I'll never forget that taste. I guess I was a bit of an alcoholic then.

"My fellow Americans..." The President began, in front of bullet-proof shields. "It has come to my attention that our country, as a whole, is in a state of crisis."

A secret service agent on his left and right and a raging crowd in front of him that spanned for miles beyond the cameras view.

"This will be my final address," Moving the black tie around his neck, back and forth before clearing his throat, "The armed forces stationed in each of your cities and towns will ensure your survival if you follow their directions precisely and evacuate in an orderly fashion."

"What are we?" I ask the television, lighting up a smoke, "Kindergartners?"

"I am asking all law enforcement personnel to please cooperate with the military," Looking stern and important, "We need all the help we can get. Your sacrifice will not be forgotten."

"So he's asking us, no me, to stay behind for a suicide mission?" Out the window, past my unlit table lamp, rested on an empty bookshelf, the streets screech with tires and shouting, little bits of gunfire lighting up grey curtains that hid my presence and the dim light of the glowing television.

"We are dealing with a pandemic. The virus has not been identified but there are science teams all over the world working on a cure, as I speak. To you all, I bid good luck and mark my words, this nation will not fall!" He pounds a fist down on the podium that stands in front of him.

Anger reverberates through the crowd and the booing, screaming ensues.

"Yeah, great." I puff and take another sip of my sweating bottle of beer.

He begins to move away from the stand and the camera shifts slightly. In the background, one of the secret service men, his face twitches and arms shake violently, unnoticed by both the President and the other agent. Another split second goes by and he's pouncing on the leader of the *once* greatest nation in the world, taking a hefty chunk of flesh from his neck as silent screams of pain go unheard by anyone in the audience or at home.

I switch the television off, uncaring and not surprised in the slightest.

"S'pose it'll be a long night, eh Dad?" I speak to a picture of my Father that hangs alone on the wall across from the boarded doorway, the only exit from my seventh story apartment.

On the coffee table in front of me, a black cellphone (that went mostly unused, unless on-duty) vibrates and rings loudly, for the first time in a week. Slamming my beer down, I sigh, reach for the phone with the palm of my hand and after contemplating the words that'll be most likely exchanged, I flip it open and answer, "What is it?"

"It's Jack, you see that shit?!" My only brother, that works the same job as I, shouts into the earpiece.

"Fuckin' hell, yeah, I saw it; don't scream into my ear, *please*."

"I got a call from the station; they want all of us there, now."

"No shit," I smash the butt of my cigarette against an overfilled ashtray, "They really expect everyone to be there, in the middle of this crazy bullshit?"

"I think it's pretty exciting, I've never seen anything like this!" He speaks with enthusiasm.

"Exciting?!" Pulling the phone away from my ear and closer to my mouth, "You think the end of the world is fucking exciting?!"

"Erm," He hesitates, "I didn't mean it like that..." Going silent for a moment.

"Whatever, I'll meet you there."

"Alright, D. Just be careful out there, people are going nuts."

"People were going nuts days ago. This is chaos." I shut the phone and slide it into the back pocket of my only remaining clean pair of uniform pants, adorned with a beer stained and white muscle shirt.

From a hook on the wall hangs a double gun holster that fits beneath my arms and wraps around, holding a Glock machine pistol and a Colt nineteen-eleven, each fully loaded and unused.

The remaining water from the kitchen sink, just inches from the living room, provides a cold splash of water that shocks my buzzed and mind-crushing consciousness into reality. I blink and breathe in a few times, "Alright, alright."

Grabbing my pair of boots, I slide each foot in and secure the laces till the veins in my ankles pump hard.

With a crowbar, smashing against wood, peeling like a banana, I undo the barricade that is the door to my apartment.

"No turning back, this is for the people of the city..." I say to myself as I inch the doorway open, a hallway full of people running up and down, all ignoring each other and making their way out to the streets. "This is absolutely insane."

2

From Memories Unclear

The wind blows against my skin like an ice cube, hair standing on end, as I flick my cigarette onto debris littered pavement.

"Let's get this show on the road!" I say, shivering and rubbing my palms together in anticipation as the rest of the guys shuffle out of the back of an Emergency Response van.

It was late fall, middle of downtown Manhattan and strangely, dead silent. Only the whisper of the air passing by your ears and its faint whistle could be heard.

Twisting my weapon around, back-to-front, I aim upward and click the safety with my index to the "off" position, leading the four members of my volunteered team to the inside of a bank. Jericho, being one of them, stumbles over himself as he emerges last through the door.

"Dammit!" He exclaims.

I point at him in disdain and command, "Keep it fuckin' quiet."

Having lost power during the evacuation, the reception room and all others adjacent sat dark and foreboding.

"Flashlights." I whisper, twisting a knob near the barrel of my gun, illuminating a dark patch of concrete at the furthest end of the teller line.

The five of us twisted around, moved stealthily throughout each room, lights dancing around on the walls, not seeing a single person.

"Man," One of them says, unseen, "I don't think we're going to find anyone in here..."

"What about the vault?" Jericho chimes in.

"Hey," Looking out of the corner of my right eye, seeing its gleaming, circular surface staring directly at us, "Not a bad idea."

Glaring down, with a million locks and cylinders, we approach, as if about to open a gateway containing some mystical secret or treasure. I order the lanky kid with glasses, Steve, to "unlock" the door.

"Right on it!" Enthusiastically saluting me he pulled small drilling tools from a belt-bag securely adjusted to his waist.

The others take guard to the entrance of the building and a small stairwell at the opposite side of the vault room.

Me? I lean against the wall near Steve, light up a smoke, and puff nonchalantly.

Our mission, here and now, was to find any remaining survivors, eliminate any possible threats and assess if whether or not sections of the city could be reused for safe-camps.

Before all of this, the evacuation and my term with the E.R.U., I was a cop, starting out in

Harrisburg, Pennsylvania. Dealing with crooked cops and drug infested streets. Years went by and I don't remember a time that I hadn't imagined being something greater than that guy who'd busted an All-Mart shoplifter. Or perhaps, the only cop in Harrisburg with a clean record – a clean health bill and fit enough for S.W.A.T.

This is exactly what I turned to.

Transferring to Manhattan for training in the Emergency Response Unit, that's where my life truly started. After that, everything pretty much leads to this.

Looking down at the small pistol in my left holster, I remember things even further from the present. A gift my father had left for me on my twenty-fifth birthday – a Colt nineteen eleven, a good luck charm. In his own words, "one of the greatest side arms ever made." But that was after he'd already disappeared, without a trace, leaving my brother and me to our Mother. Having something to do with his career most likely, something he never really spoke of – mostly because he'd always tell us that it was, "top secret" or some stupid bullshit.

And again, I couldn't stop thinking about the here, about the now. We knew it was some type of virus, but we had no idea where it'd come from and no real idea of what exactly it did, other than turn a perfectly normal person into a rotting, cannibalistic, rage-addicted maniac.

Jack decides to interrupt my string of random thoughts, "Dante! Put out that smoke already man, the vaults opening!"

My brother, of course, who'd joined up years after me. Always thirsty for action, with a hint of bloodlust.

I shake my head, tossing my smoke against a wall and lift my weapon upward, "All eyes." I command.

Steve steps backward as the rest of the group approaches, the door sliding open slowly to reveal a blinding red light that poured out, engulfing the room in a vermilion haze.

One-by-one, we enter, standing side-by-side and gawking at the sight on the floor at the other end of the vault. Blood splattered violently across the walls, pieces of bone and entrails strewn all over the place and two unidentifiable bodies lying parallel to each other. The one on the left, having most of his hair ripped from his scalp and a strange symbol carved in its place.

"What in the hell..." I say, interrupted by sudden drips of blood from the ceiling spitting all over my forehead.

Our source of red light was coming from the blood-soaked panels above.

"The fuck are we dealing with here?" Jericho asks, to no one in particular.

I shake my head and run my fingers through the bristles of a barely shaved scalp. "Hugo," A large and completely bald man, fluent in about twenty different languages, "Check out this triangular object here." Sitting there, in between the bodies, it looked as if it were some type of artifact.

He picks it up and holds it with hands together, admiring its many different symbols and writings.

"I..." Eyes wide and confused, "I'm not sure what I'm seeing here. Some of these look Egyptian, but then the writing; it doesn't look like any damn language I've ever seen."

"Well," I ask, "You think it caused these two bastards here, to mutilate and kill themselves?"

"I really don't know Dante," Turning the object over in his hands, "But my guess is that it was inside one of these safe deposit boxes."

"That doesn't exactly help."

His face suddenly turns a faint shade of green and his cheeks puff large. Everything he'd eaten before our trip back to the city ended up in his hands and all over the strange object, which fell clanking to the ground, as he loses his balance and falls.

"Hey!" Jericho ran to his side, "You alright?!"

Shaking violently and bleeding from every pore, the rest of us sort of just stare in unbelievable horror, as his skin wrinkles from head to toe, eyes melting out of their sockets and cheekbones caving in on his mouth.

The ground shakes uncontrollably and in the distance, beyond the building, something screeches and roars, echoing into the night. It was then followed by the moaning and groaning of what could only be described as a quickly moving mob.

I cock my rifle, "Forget him, he's gone."

By the time I finished the sentence; his body had completely flattened out and filled in the creases of the tiles on the floor.

Eyes dilated and fearful, Jack looks up from his kneeled position on the floor, next to a pile of skin and clothing, "The fuck just happened?!"

I point at Steve, then Jericho, "Get your god dammed gear, we're sitting ducks!"

"Aren't you even the slightest concerned with what just happened here?!" Jericho shouted, an inch from my face.

"Not at the fucking moment, Jer-Ich-O!" Pushing him back, "Now MOVE!"

Dashing for the main entrance, everything a blur, I shout, "Jack, get that goddamn door shut and locked, now!"

The incessant moaning and groaning began to grow louder as the remaining four of us took cover behind the teller stations.

"Just keep your heads down..." I motion with my hand, peering over and through the service window at a hundred or so Undead, pressing their mutilated bodies against the glass to the front of the bank. Drool and a black-ish substance smeared across the glass and the one closest to the doorway gnashed its teeth at the handles. "Well shit, how come we didn't see these bastards when we came into Manhattan?"

"There are a lot of different places they could've been hiding," Jericho responds, "That is, if their minds, in their current state, allow that sort of instinct."

"Regardless," I kneel back down, "They haven't exactly spotted us."

"That's reassuring," Jack sarcastically remarks.

Out of the corner of my eye, I see a light flash from beyond the opening of the vault.

"What in the..." I turn my head to focus on what emerged. A shadowy figure of a woman, creeping out from behind the wide open door. She had a strange greyish, glowing aura surrounding her figure, onyx looking hair pouring down over her face and moving like fog into clear view.

Still holding my kneeling position on the ground, I lift my weapon and aim in its direction. Yet my eyes didn't entirely believe what they were seeing.

Everything around me, the undead, Jack, Steve, and Jericho – they all stop moving and time itself pauses.

"What are you?"

It doesn't respond, moving closer, that cold chill of death sweeping over me, as it lifts it's hand and brushes it against my face and down along my chest.

"My love," It speaks with a soft voice, "You don't recognize me?"

"Recognize you?" Confused, I aim higher, toward its head.

"No matter," The figure runs a hand down a thigh extending from her womanly shape, "What took you so long?"

"Back off," I ponder for a moment, "Demon."

I squeeze the trigger and time speeds up again just as the bullet leaves the chamber. The figure vanishes as the projectile passes through nothing but a mist.

"Dante!" Jack yells, "What the hell man!?" His eyes filled with fear. The eager-to-feed, mindless undead on the outside of the building focus their attention on attempting to break through the glass. "What in the fuck makes you wanna shoot off your gun out of nowhere, really?!"

"I..."

Before I can come up with a logical explanation for my actions, glass shatters and spilling onto the floor, come a handful of flesh-hungry fucks.

"Run!" Jack darts for the stairs.

Too late.

In Jericho's attempt to follow, he's thrown to the ground in a pile of broken glass and tackled by at least three of them. He screams in horrible agony as one of the Undead bares its teeth and takes a chunk clean out of his left arm.

"Jesus friggin' Christ!" He grumbles, lifting his weapon with his good arm and fires off a burst into their faces, blood spattering un-shattered windows.

"Steve!" I command with two fingers pointed at Jericho, "Grab him and head for the roof!"

I picked myself up, gun in hand, firing burst-for-burst as more and more of them made their way inside. Another flash goes off in the corner of my eye, same direction as before, as I sprint for the stairwell, pushing Steve and Jericho up three flights of stairs, to a security panel-locked doorway.

Jack stands there, already pounding random entries into its ten-number sequence pad.

"You gotta be shitting me!" I shout, saliva shooting from my mouth, aiming through the rungs of the stairs and releasing an empty magazine, "Just shoot the damned thing!"

"Come on man!" Jericho cries, "I'm bleedin' to death here!"

"I don't how much longer I can hold his weight, Jack..." Steve begins to say, sweat pouring over his head, arms twitching and shaking.

I push past the two of them and shove Jack out of my way. Pistol out of its holster, I aim at the panel and fire a single shot.

The door chimes and its circuitry sparks as the push-bar loosens from its locking mechanism.

"Dante," Jack pushes past me, through the door, "Don't you ever fucking do that again." Giving me a sneer as we hurdle and stumble onto the rooftop, slamming the door shut, just as the undead clamber from behind.

I snap a steel bar from a collection of rusted pipes, wrapped around what looks like an air vent and jam it between the doors handle and the wall that holds it in place.

"Whew." I let out a gasp of air, "Alright, get that man a tourniquet and keep your gun aimed on him at all times."

Steve looks over to me, quizzically, "What? Why?"

"What?" I ask, as if expecting him to know the answer, "You've never seen a zombie movie before?"

Jericho props himself up and coughs loudly before attempting to speak, "You think I'm gonna turn into one of them, huh?"

I nod, "Can't take any chances, sorry." Turning my back to him, I stare up at the sky, churning like a tornado, red and black.

A few moments pass. Jack paces back and forth with his gun over his shoulder, thinking, pondering; of what I do not know.

Steve finishes the wrap on Jericho's arm and makes his way over to me, standing by the edge of the building, tapping me on the shoulder.

"Dante, problem," He says as I turn to him, "Radio's out, no response from command. Something's wrong."

Clenching my fist in frustration, "Hell, that's not what I wanna hear."

Steve looks over the side and surveys the masses, "You really think we're gonna find survivors out here?"

I look to the side, Jericho's condition worsening as he begins to hyperventilate. Jack paying nobody any mind at all, I look to Steve again, "To tell you the truth, no, but I'll be damned if we don't try."

I light up another smoke, taking a single puff and make my way over to Jericho.

"Wha..." Breathing in and out, faster and faster, "What do you want?" He asks.

"Here," I hand him my smoldering cigarette, un-holstering his pistol and placing it in his hand, "Have a smoke."

"Yeah," Struggling to look me in the eyes," I follow."

I give Jack another look, watching him selfishly cower in a corner on the other side of the building's rooftop.

"Steve, about those communication problems..." Hurriedly walking toward him.

He turns to me, face covered in doubt.

"They setup shop over at the Verrazano-Narrows," Placing both hands on his shoulders, "I'll get us outta here. All we gotta do is head there."

I could tell he didn't even really wanna be here. Neither did Jack.

"But what about Hugo, what happened to..."

A shot rings out with the echo of rifle fire and before he can finish what he's going to say, his head turns into a puff of red and his jaw falls severed to the ground.

"Contact!" I yell, "Get down!" Falling to my stomach in panic, vision blurred with blood, I barely see Jack, twenty feet away already doing the same.

"The fuck is goin' on!" He yells.

"Keep it quiet!" I put a finger to my lips, "We got hostiles firing on us."

Looking over at Jericho, still sitting upright where I'd positioned him, "Jericho, wait." I whisper, as he eats the barrel of his gun. "Fuck."

Attempting to gain a bearing on our sniper, I poke my head upward only slightly as another shot rings out and skims past my scalp. Then, over a loud speaker, we hear his words.

"We are ZeroFactor. We are undying. We are the New World Order."

"Jack," I motion toward him, "How's your throwing arm?"

Grunting and shifting around with his arms, he crawls over, flash-grenade in hand.

"This guy's on the top of the building across the street, I take it?"

I nod and begin with my formulated plan. "Position yourself on your back, against the edge here," Patting my hand against concrete, "Toss that flash on the count of three," Pointing at myself, "I jump up not even a second later and double tap the bastard in the face."

"You sure about that?" He asks with a bit of doubt.

"Yeah, no problem," I wink.

With my right arm holding my weapon against my chest and the other hand down like a spring suspending the rest of my body, I prepare, "On one," Staring directly into his eyes, "Three, two, one…"

The grenade whirls through the air. I count out one second in my head and pounce upward, aiming at only the gleam of a rifle scope and tap the trigger twice just as a flash lights up the surrounding area.

Withdrawing my gun, slung around my back, I say, "Good job, told ya it'd be no problem."

Standing up, he looks me in the face with a new kind of seriousness in his eyes, "Alright, I gotta have a talk with you," Grabbing me by the vest, "What the fuck is your problem?!" Suddenly raising his voice.

I grab him by the knuckles of his fists and push back, "The fuck you talking about?!"

Releasing his grip and shouting, "You just got three," Holding three fingers up to my face, "Of our men killed!"

"No…"

"You sentenced us to death volunteering us to come back to this god dammed city!" Swinging his arm backward.

"Now wait a fuckin minute here…"

"And this ain't the first time your carelessness got a bunch of people killed!"

Without thinking, I twist my arm back and meet Jack's jaw with a right-hook, throwing him over in a hunch. He grabs his face and shoots back with an angry, piercing stare.

"You fuckin bastard," Repositioning himself in front of me, "I'll do you a favor and not strike back, but you fuckin' wait, just wait…"

"You wanna take control of this situation go right ahead," Baring my teeth like a rabid dog, "Until then, back the fuck off."

"Alright, asshole," Lowering his voice, "What do you propose we do?"

Breathing heavily and wiping saliva away from my lips, "We head to Midtown South Precinct."

"Ammunition?" He turned away and checked the magazine of his M-Four.

"Exactly." I rip the clip out of my AR-Fifteen and toss it to the ground, loading the only full magazine I had left.

"So," He sighs, "You gonna open that door and just ask the zombies to leave then?"

"They've moved on," Listening for a moment, "I don't hear a thing."

He unlatches the bar from the door and swings it open with the barrel of his gun in front of him, revealing an empty, bloodied stairwell.

"Alrighty then."

3

To Hell and Back

Metal clanking beneath our feet, we make our way down the stairs, back into the main lobby where the action had originally began. The floor all littered with broken glass and windows completely busted out.

"Switch your light back on." Twisting the switch on the end my rifle, once more.

He pushed by and advanced toward the vault.

"Wait!" I turn to the left corner of the room and fire a shot into the head of a lingering zombie, "The hell you goin?!"

Vanishing behind the door to the vault, with the resonating sound of gunfire, I follow.

A flash of orange light bursts into the room as I turn the corner, only to see Jack, with his face against the wall, shivering in fear.

"Jack?"

I move slowly inward, eyes moving left to right, seeing absolutely nothing, at first.

The door from behind swiftly slams shut and locks itself, with time and space slowing down again, like it had before but with different scenery.

"No, not again…"

Black ash twists all around, metal grating of a bridge underneath my feet. Fire raged from the river below and in front of me sat Front Street in Harrisburg. The heat was far too intense, causing me to breathe heavily, staggering as I barely managed to put one foot in front of the other. My assault rifle, replaced with my pistol, felt like it weighed hundreds of pounds and in the distance something came charging toward me.

My brain felt like it was melting from my ears. I couldn't even open my mouth to scream in terror. The four legged beast drew closer and closer, leaping with its long, clawed feet, tongue hanging out and dripping with what looked like blood.

I squeeze the trigger of the pistol as I finally manage to pull it up in the direction of my impending doom, yet before the bullet can even leave the chamber the scenery around me blows away like ash in the wind.

Slamming outward, the bullet drives fiercely into the monster's head. I duck as the momentum of its leap brings it crashing through the wall of the vault I had somehow magically reemerged into.

Jack stood, now, with his back to the wall, looking helpless.

"Good god, what the hell was that?" He says, terrified.

I put a hand against my chest and pant frantically, "Beats the shit outta me."

A barrage of snow whirls in through the new hole in the wall and covers the area in a blanket of white.

"Ready your pistol," I say, "We're getting the hell outta here."

"Fuckin' crazy shit goin on." Ripping the weapon from his holster, "I'm not gonna die here, not now."

"Neither of us are," Beginning to move with revitalized energy.

On the outside, the beast lay dead, with black ooze seeping from its shattered skull. I stomp down with a boot and its bone structure crunches beneath my foot.

"Shit," Jack covers his nose with his forearm and looks away.

The temperature was dropping and a blizzard was settling in on the city of Manhattan, exactly what we needed for our trek back to salvation.

"Let's move."

With three men gone and limited ammunition, this wasn't about to get any easier.

We were definitely in the thick of it and had front row seats to the apocalypse.

4

Picking up the Pieces
Present Day – 2020

"...and that's all that I remember. After almost six years, it's slowly coming back to me, like a nightmare." I say, gripping the steering wheel of a large black SUV, with Raymond and Paul listening intently, ready to poke and prod with questions.

We're on our way to a routine "cleanup." There'd been reports of another outbreak inside of a large abandoned building down by Market Street.

The city's Harrisburg, a war and death ravaged remnant of what it once was, years and years ago. During the six years that followed the events of Manhattan, that I still struggle to remember due to amnesia, we had managed to establish a new form of governing. Something that resembled a large protection "agency," I suppose.

We call ourselves PaxCorpus – scavenging for whatever we can find on the outside; food, water and fuel, with large military aircraft that resemble flying fortresses and we protect the people, no matter the cost.

But the name hadn't even come from me.

A year or so after we'd erected the wall, a sickly and disease ridden man revealed to me that the idea of "PaxCorpus" was my own but that he'd only heard of it from someone who wouldn't even reveal their identity.

Regardless, I ran with it.

Our homes exist within the wall, the undead and whatever else, scatter themselves all over the outside, held at bay, day and night, by our own watchmen.

And this is what my life became. Plagued by amnesia with no recollection of past events, nor any clue as to how I'd managed to make it out of there, to where I am now. All things come with time, I suppose.

"So you've no idea at all what led to Jack's disappearance or what became of the city?" Paul asks, as if he hadn't been listening to anything I'd just told the two of them.

"No," I sigh, "After that, all I remember is coming to on a surgical table in the middle of a military outpost just outside of Harrisburg."

I wince and shiver; something taps my subconscious on the shoulder.

Paul sits back and watches as we pull up to a building surrounded by frightened civilians.

I jerk my foot down on the brake pedal and grab the keys from the ignition, kicking open the driver side door with my boot. Ray and Paul emerge from the other side of the vehicle with anticipation – they enjoy days like this.

With a sort of grace, I pull two nineteen-elevens from a back-holster tied to my belt and announce, "Alright people, back up. We got a job to do here and it'll all be easier if you just go back to your homes."

We'd done this millions of times throughout the years. Go in, neutralize the threat and get the hell out – no problem. Yet today, it was different, something felt a little off… strange.

At the front of the building, the people had managed to construct a shoddy little barricade of wrecked cars and other scraps of metal, in front of two, large and broken automatic doors. As usual, I expected that the reports were most likely inaccurate.

"Okay guys, let's get this shit outta the way, Jules has somethin' special for us tonight." Keeping my mind at home and off of the soon to occur violence.

It has three or four floors and resembles only a shadow of what it used to be, like the rest of the buildings and structures that surround the city. Bullet holes and broken windows remind me of the twenty-thirteen invasion. Which means we had probably used this place as shelter, once or twice, while retaking Harrisburg.

From what can be seen, the inside is littered with trash, dirt and the old, dried bloodstains of those who'd passed long ago. I figure it had, most likely, been an office building at one point in time, meaning there'd be an elevator somewhere in the back. Not that I ever considered the undead smart enough to operate machinery or something like an elevator, but you never know.

We heave the rubble aside, grunting and scraping across the gravel and inadvertently surround ourselves.

"Great," I say, perturbed.

There were more than a few of them. A whole slew of people had died here.

I waltz in, with Ray and Paul following behind, guns blazing and shells clanging against the black and white tiled floor.

"Paul! Ray! Nine and three, now!" I shout, hitting the bloody remains of a woman, in the face, with the butt of my pistol.

Gunfire explodes all around, the gore intensifying; unflinchingly we storm through a pile of bodies.

Out of the corner of my eye, the bowels of a recent victim spill completely out of his gut. On the other side, the upper half of another man slowly crawls his way over to me, dragging entrails like a snail.

"Go back to Hell." I say, aiming a single shot to his forehead.

After they'd all been exterminated, the only sound you can hear is the re-dying breaths and sighs of the confirmed dead.

I light up a smoke and puff. "Good job, guys."

An erratic buzzing vibrates within my eardrum, signaling me to press my finger up to my earlobe.

"Yes?"

"Don't forget about the roof."

"Are you sure about that?"

"We gotta be efficient; else the rest of these people are as good as dead, alright?"

I think for a good thirty seconds and reply. "Fine."

The man talking through the implanted earpiece, just inside of my skull, was the advisor. Always there, listening and reporting – making sure we never fucked up.

The technology was developed and prototyped by the military, years before the apocalypse. In fact, we'd only gained access to it after a larger percentage of the United States military had been wiped off the face of the planet.

I'm still surprised at the fact that not a single nuke fell that day.

At least not from what I can remember.

Although, by the time they decided to do something, at least from what I've heard, it was already far too late. The military was taken by surprise and without a Commander in Chief to give any orders; there was chaos, even in their ranks.

Then of course, they probably filled their medical bays and hospitals with the infected. Who'd have thought movies and literature would be true, eh?

Some never learn.

"Guys, I'm goin' up top, stay here and take point." I gesture, with a nod, that they cover the doorway.

To the back, behind a pile of broken office furniture sits an old, rusted elevator.

"Careful, that thing's only powered by generators and by the looks of it, a piece of shit." Ray forewarns.

"I figured," With a two finger salute, "I'll radio if I run into any problems."

Anyone that desires electrical power utilizes generators, but like the vehicles we use and the aircraft that we fly, they take fuel. Something we all know will eventually run dry, since there aren't many places left, in the United States, with fuel reserves.

I press the call button, the walls shake and ancient machinery rumbles its way down toward me. After about thirty-seconds and some hesitation, the doors open and inside I see an oddly preserved four by six foot chamber that feels almost as if stepping backward in time, as I step inside.

Holstering one pistol, I draw the empty magazine from the other, replacing it with a fresh one and with my free hand; I pull back on its slide.

I give a little wave and the doors slide shut, elevator ascending to the sky.

Their metallic surface shines a reflection of me and for a moment I imagine the person I used to be, before seeing the man that I've become – hair slicked back, a patchy five o' clock shadow, weary eyes and a c-line scar across my forehead.

Older now than I was before; coming to terms with age has never been something I enjoyed. Always imagining myself at eighteen years of age, head full of wonder at the world and the invincibility of youth.

I still deny it, even today.

Six years of war and loss, these things take their toll on a person.

Then I remember a quote, by some person, fictional or non, from the past that I can't even name, "You really wanna live forever?" My answer would always be, "Yes."

There isn't a single part of me that doesn't want to exist and if forced to imagine the opposite – I'd be unable to.

But maybe that just sounds arrogant.

I pull a pair of shades from the front shirt pocket of my coat and slide them over my eyes, expecting a winter's sunset to immediately blind me upon arrival to the roof.

A picture in my back pocket, like the pistol my Father had given me, blesses me with luck – a picture of my fiancé, Julianna.

She kept me relatively sane all these years, amidst the insanity of a post-apocalyptic world. A hell of a nurse, experienced in combat and a fuckin' great cook. What more could you ask for?

Not to mention the fact that she's got a great ass, but that all boils down to personal preference, I guess. Aside from that, she's got long, wavy brown hair, a perky nose, beautiful

eyes and a smile that'll melt your damn heart –
my little Italian angel.

Though, I met her on the battlefield. She'd
taken care of me while I was comatose and
fought by my side 'til we'd finally taken back
my hometown.

Then, one cool summer night, about a year
ago, we made it official. Across the
Susquehanna, over the water, on a moon-lit
night, atop the walking bridge that connects City
Island and Front Street.

Our marriage date is set for October
twentieth and that'll be the day. Fuckin' Dante
gets married, right?

Jack would always say it'd never happen.

My head begins to swim with memories
and hopeful thoughts for a brighter future.

Pistol in hand, I aim at the black and rubber
crease in the elevator doors, prepared for
whatever waits or doesn't wait, on the other
side.

She's one of the only reasons I keep up
with this shit.

A distorted dinging noise sounds off and
the doors open. Immediately, I'm hit with not
only the blinding sunlight but also a strange
sense of déjà vu.

Slowly making my way out to the rooftop, I check my sides and then focus front-and-center.

The past flashes with gritty scenes within my mind – a spot near the elevator structure where a man named Jericho could've taken his life – another, by the concrete ledge, looking down on the city. A wimpy and frail man has his head blown off.

Overwhelmed again and dizzy, something brushes by my shoulder and I quickly snap left.

My reminiscent haze had suddenly gotten the best of me.

"Where are you!?" I shout, not knowing what accompanied me up here underneath the sun.

Something grabs, and then scratches the back of my leg, buckling my knee and I fall to the ground.

"Fuck!" Shouting again, I fire blindly at a shadow that swiftly twists and turns, just out of my field of vision, "Someone get the fuck up here, now!"

Hand pressed against my ear, I fire over and over, dispensing another magazine into the wind.

Feeling sick, something rushes through my veins and I try to speak once more, "I'm hit, god dammit, get your asses up here!"

The pain becomes debilitating, my vision slowly fades and the radio bursts with noise, "Dante! Answer me! DANTE!"

His words slur and fragment into nothingness.

5

Assault on Midtown South
Manhattan – Midtown South Precinct –
2013

A few blocks from the precinct, we trudge through an increasingly harsh blizzard and traverse overturned vehicles and random street fires, all the way up to Thirty-Fifth Street – and up until this point, things had been relatively calm.

Leaning against the wall of a parking garage that sits crumbled and decrepit at the end of a road, I wipe melting snow and sweat from my eyes, squinting and focusing on Jack.

Pointing a few hundred meters away and around a corner, "You see that shit?"

Dark shadows huddle and lurk behind the cover of an overtaken military blockade. You know, the ones with small stone-wall like objects and piles of sandbags, with a tripod holding a light-machinegun.

Only problem, is the fact that these guns weren't there. In their place, sat empty stands and even emptier ammo casings.

"I know their pain," Jack responds, "Wanting release yet hungering endlessly for something, anything."

Placing both of my leather-gloved hands on his shoulders, "What the fuck are you talking about?"

"The air is thick with death, Dante, can't you feel it?" He looks into my eyes, as if in some sort of a trance, "My soul beckons for that same release."

His head snaps back, "Hell on Earth, the walking dead, how's this any different from what used to be?" Coming back down, with a smirk, "Ha ha ha ha ha!" Laughing maniacally

I lower my eyebrows and groan, "Don't make me fuckin' punch you again."

He blinks a few times and shakes his head, "Whoa," Pressing a palm against his forehead, "The hell was that?"

Pushing me back, he blinks a few more times, "Get off of me, man."

Returning to his formal position, he leans out from the corner and takes a look at what I had pointed out earlier.

"Don't go all getting possessed and shit, Jack, the fuck was that?"

"What was what?" He asks, with a strange look in his eyes, still.

Something was going on, something I couldn't quite figure out. Maybe I was seeing things. Maybe he didn't just go crazy for a minute or two.

Whatever.

"So, the undead over there," Turning to me with drops of water dripping from his nose. "That's a problem, right?"

I stare at him a little while longer, waiting for something more to happen.

"And this is where you tell me what we're goin' to do next." Looking at me as if mouthing words to a thick-headed, moron.

"Alright, alright…" I attempt to think of a solid plan, running fingers over my scalp, water falling down against my shoulders.

A lonely and mostly unscathed vehicle sits in the middle of the street across from us – a white Geo Metro.

My combat suit feels heavy, sticking to me like a plastic bag as I shift around to survey the area once more.

"And the precinct is just around that corner, past just a few obstacles…"

I move my tongue over my lips, spitting bitter and metallic tasting snowflakes to the ground.

"Hey!" Jack grabs me by the arm, "What's the fuckin' plan!?" He demands.

I check my pistol; remembering the amount of bullets left in the magazine of the rifle slung over my shoulder – just a few shots shy of being empty.

"Weird, I don't remember firing that many shots…"

Jack clenches his teeth together, ready to rant some more.

"You know, you're a little pushy." I say, jokingly, "Get behind me and follow quickly."

Moving again, we sprint in a crouched position, guns pointed at the ground, infiltrating the enemy stronghold. Cutting through the snowfall like a knife through butter, we splash through puddles and put our backs to a nearby Ford truck, turned over on its side – windshield busted out, blinkers still illuminating the night.

"This is it?" He looks over his shoulder, "We're gonna hide behind a damn truck?"

"Shut the hell up a second."

Through the windows and past the front seat of the vehicle, over the slump of a long, dead and decaying corpse, barely visible, stand four undead.

Jack ducks his head down when he notices what I'm looking at.

"D, we ain't gonna make it to wherever you're leading us, we're done, this is it."

With my finger in his face, "Don't fuckin' call me D."

"Then fill me in dammit, what the hell are we doin'?"

"That little car over there," Sitting a few feet away, "We're gonna drive that right up to the station. These vehicles were abandoned when their drivers went for refuge on foot. Odds are, it works and it's got at least *some* fuel."

"Well then," He blinks a few times and looks in the direction of our destination, "Not as suicidal as I thought."

"Just gotta be careful," I nod.

He nods.

We ready ourselves and I hold out three fingers.

Two fingers; Jack aims his rifle.

One finger; I'm already moving.

Like shadows, we slip by, the soles of our boots hugging slush and blacktop. Looking dumb and confused a few of the undead shift around. Maybe they noticed one of us, maybe not.

Jack circles around to the passenger side and with my thumb and index finger I pinch the handle and open the vehicles door carefully, quietly. The two of us slink inside and lower ourselves to the torn and worn seats.

"Hah!" My eyes light up, noticing a pair of jingling keys hanging out of the ignition. "Told ya!"

"Yea, but as soon as you turn that key, our cover is blown."

"I hadn't planned on keeping it." I say, turning the engine over in a roar, slamming my left foot down on the clutch and shifting into first, then second.

Clutch, shift, gas – we squeal down the road.

With a sharp right, we dodge the barricade, but not the shambling undead hurtling toward us to the left.

One of them lunges at the windshield, catching its legs underneath the speeding car – ripping them out of their sockets.

Yet he still kept at it, scratching fingernails against glass, biting nothing but air.

The front of the precinct emerges, just ahead.

The straggler's skull fragments as bullets pelt it's backside, punching holes in a stream along the hood of the car.

"Shit!" I jerk the wheel to the right, sending the corpse flailing through the air, revealing the aforementioned rifleman perched atop the station. "Fuckin' hold onto something!"

I brace myself.

"The hell you mean!" He shouts, grabbing the leather bar directly in front of him and buckling his safety belt.

"We're goin' in, head first!"

The front of the building stood brown and black, lined with small windows and a tiny little niche of a doorway.

Tiny enough for a Metro.

The windshield shatters, lead ripping through the vehicle and barely missing the two of us. Jerking the wheel again, we tilt to the left, skid through snow and graze a waist-high railing.

Before impact, I see in grey lettering above, "Midtown Precinct South."

"At least it's the right building," I think to myself.

Bursting through concrete and metal, the engine blows out immediately and with a thud my head violently strikes the steering wheel column and darkness fizzles inward.

Intermission Part Two

Sweat erupts from my skin, tilting my head back and my mouth hangs wide open. I see the city – Harrisburg – the highest buildings engulfed in flames, smoke shooting to the sky and again, from where I've been perched, I can see the river, replaced by an inferno.

My eyes sting from the heat, limbs tied down and frayed rope ripping at my flesh. Shaking angrily, clenching my teeth, I tilt my head downward and crush my eyelids together, then up once more, gasping for air.

All around me stand six schizophrenic versions of myself, each holding a handgun, pointing it at one another's head. Then, one by one, I pull the trigger, black clouds spurting out of each cranium.

When the last body falls to the ground, the cold steel of a gun presses against the back of my head.

"Stand."

My restraints vanish.

"I said, STAND UP."

Trembling and almost collapsing, I push myself up and turn to see nothing but the shadow of a woman – something feels familiar.

"Who the hell are you," Asking with my fist wiping saliva from the edge of my mouth.

"I'm the reason you're here."

"And that would be?"

"You dwell on things from the past, far, far too much." She cackles.

"What is this place?" I plead, putting a hand to the barrel in my face.

"You don't recognize it?" She says, curling the fingers of her free hand, "This is home."

"Fuck that. This is some kind of illusion, or nightmare."

"It is what you make of it, Dante," Grinning and parting her hair, eyes gleaming. "I'm coming for you."

The voice disappears along with its speaker, the gun switching to my hand, forcing itself against the temple of my brain. My fingers automatically squeeze the trigger, hot lead penetrating bone, severing brain tissue.

I fall to my knees.

6
The End of Sanity

"Snap out of it!" A muffled and far away voice shouts, "Wake up!"

I come to, thinking I'd be lying in a hospital bed. Instead, what my eyes can see is a large, leather sofa, my own home. Drenched in cold sweat and feeling no pain, I open my eyelids completely and notice the pair of blinds I'd always kept closed, hang open wide.

The evening sun pours inward, cascading through the room in yellow and orange. My surroundings come into focus as three figures, two men and a woman, appear, standing in front of me while I lay dazed on my own couch.

"It's about time you wake up! You been tossing and turning for almost twenty four hours now, sweatin' all over that couch of yours!" This is Raymond, a very religious man, "You're a lucky motha fucka! That wound of yours healed up before we even came within ten minutes of the hospital!"

The large flesh wound that was supposed to be somewhere around the vicinity of my leg, had completely vanished.

They must've decided I was alright to bring home.

"And that woman of yours, you lucky she knows how to cook or I'd be askin' you for special service fees…" He went on and on.

"Hey!" She pushes him by the shoulder, "Don't talk about me like I'm not right here!"

"Alright Ray, shut your mouth." I wrinkle my forehead, "I'm getting a damned splitting headache." Like needles piercing my frontal lobe.

Julianna kneels down beside me, crossing her hands over my chest and she prays for luck and fortitude.

"Dante, I really think it's time you come to church with me," Something she'd always bring up every time I came back wounded or extra-fatigued. "The service is short and the crowds are small, it could really end up saving your life."

Always a reason or an excuse as to why I should attend, even though, at first glance, you'd never mistake her for someone that had any remote interest in fictional fantasy.

I never really needed anything to believe in.

"Jules, babe, you know I don't believe in that crap. Besides, if God," Putting my fingers up in quotations, "Really exists, why would shit like this happen?"

Instead of retorting with some evangelical rant, she storms away into the kitchen.

"You know, you're lucky to have her," Paul chimes in. "And here you go pissing her off. Ain't much beauty left in this place."

"No, Paul, you're just looking in all the wrong places."

He crosses his arms and turns to the side.

"You were almost dead less than a day ago and now you're here after a prolonged nap, telling me the reason why I ain't got any pussy in three years is 'cause I'm not fuckin' looking for it?"

I pull myself up, arching my back and resting my head against the wall, "Do me a favor – save the pity stories and get me my smokes."

"Poor little guy," Raymond adds, "There's more to life than a g-spot."

Giving him a glare, Paul pulls a pack from my suit that hangs on the wall and tosses both the smokes and my lighter at my face.

"Bah!," I snatch my saving grace, "You fuck! Mind the face!" Striking open the zippo, I spark a flame and inhale in ecstasy.

Julianna yells from the other room, "You better not be smoking in my house!"

"Yes, dear!" I reply sarcastically, motioning for Ray and Paul to follow me outside, exhaling as we pass through the front door, with a cold gust of wind that scrapes against your skin.

"So you guys didn't see anything up there?" I puff.

They look at each other in confusion and then back, Paul taking the lead, "No. Wasn't anything but you lyin' there with some weird scratch on your leg."

"And then, like I said, it healed the fuck up." Ray bends slightly, arms crossed; double checking the side of my leg.

Paul shrugs, "You sure you've never been infected?"

"Of course I'm sure, Christ, I think I'd know something like that."

I drop the butt of my cigarette to the ground and stomp out the ashes.

"You said you found some kinda artifact in that bank back in Manhattan," Ray switches to interrogation mode. "I mean, I'm pretty sure that even if you been infected before, without knowing it, that it don't have any kind of rapid healing process. That's pretty fuckin' obvious."

"So what're you sayin'? That thing affected me, aside from what it did to Hugo?"

"Who knows," Turning and watching as the sun begins to set. "Maybe you're tainted." Wriggling his fingers around, "But then again, who knows what those doctors shot you up with back when you came outta that coma."

"Yea, you know, maybe you have some kind of supernatural powers!" Paul jokes, and shoves Ray as if he finds what he's saying completely ludicrous.

"Whatever," Interrupting them, "I'm not infected, nor am I tainted, or whatever the hell you're insinuating."

"Then what the fuck was that all about?" Ray asks in a more serious tone, staring directly into my eyes.

"You got me," Shooting him a cold glare. "But I'm absolutely fine, I give you my word."

We take infection, very, very seriously.

"Alright Dante, I'll take your word for it," He turns to Paul, "How 'bout you?"

"Yea, yea, he doesn't look undead or anything."

"Humph," I scoff.

Julianna's voice shouts from inside of the house, "Get in here! Food's done!"

"Alright, how about we just forget about this, for now," Offering my hand.

The two of them grab hold and shake, simultaneously saying, "Sure."

Back inside, we settle down at an old wooden table, chairs squeaking across non-waxed and splintered floorboards. Ray bows his head over a plate full of spaghetti and a special homemade mountain of meatballs, hands crossed – "Bless us, O Lord, and these Thy gifts, which we are about to receive from Thy bounty, through Christ our Lord, Amen."

I sit with my hands placed on a fork and the edge of the plate, waiting for him to finish as "Amen" comes from only one other mouth; Julianna's.

"Amen," She says, gracefully taking her fork in hand and scooping small amounts of noodle into her mouth, watching the others eat with a slight grin across her face.

Through mouthfuls, in her direction, I mumble, "Is good!"

Then the inner workings of my ear begin to rumble. "Dante, we got a problem down by the Amtrak. An unknown railroad vehicle is heading directly for the wall.'

Swallowing a rather large gulp, I respond, "The hell did you just say?"

"If that thing makes it through, we'll surely lose our communication ability."

And this is what I envisioned happening after they'd built a damn antenna atop an abandoned railroad.

"I fuckin' told all of you guys, don't build that shit there, goddammit."

"Can you please just get your team down there? The others are currently occupied."

"Fine," Slamming my fork down onto the table, wiping sauce from my chin.

"You two heard that, I'm sure, we got a big problem on our hands."

"Yea," Paul finishes his food, "I think we should save the idle chat for later though."

Ray nods, placing his fork upside down on a clean plate, "Thanks for the food Beautiful."

She nods in return to his comment and moves toward me as I stand from the table to grab my clothing from the living room.

An old clock on the wall, past the overhang that separates both rooms chimes nine.

Standing and watching, as I quickly dress myself in an outfit padded with a rubber-texturized armor, she stops me before I get the chance to pull the zipper of a large, oversized and winter-proof coat.

"Dante, please," Her eyes flood in worry and peer directly into mine. "Come back in one piece this time," Grabbing me by the arm.

"You know," I smile, "You've got a helluva grip."

I hadn't even noticed that Paul and Ray were already out the door.

"Jules," Pushing her dangling hair to the side and behind her ear. "There's not a thing I can't handle."

She clenches her teeth in frustration, "Are these peoples' lives really worth all the risk?"

"Yes," Placing a kiss on her forehead, silky smooth skin greeting my lips. "And so are ours."

"Just promise me you'll be more careful." Closing her eyes and tilting her head downward toward her bare feet and loose, white dress pants.

"Promise."

She nods briefly and throws herself into an embrace, covering me with her warmth. My eyes linger around her almost perfectly rounded and curvaceous body, longing for her taste. Glowing, mystical and bright, with an unknown essence, among a deeply shaded grey – everything else blurs and fades between invisible lines when I look at her.

I picture myself shutting and locking the door, leaving Ray and Paul to take care of the serious and impending threat to our safety – everyone's safety.

But that isn't me.

And with a bipolar twist, she says, "I love you, honey," Gently grabbing me by the crotch, in my arousal, "I'll see ya when you get back."

"Yea," Eyes bursting open, "I'll be here!" Grinning as I begin to make my way to the door, "Don't go nowhere."

"Oh," She smiles, "I won't."

"But, you know," Looking back one more time, "You could always come along."

She is, as I mentioned before, quite experienced.

"Not-for-nothin'," Biting her lip, "But I've seen plenty of violence, too much."

I check to make sure that my holster is secure, before finally making my way through the door, Paul and Ray standing beneath a black and heavily clouded sky, delicate little snowflakes beginning to fall.

My mind is still inside of the house, with Julianna.

"Damn, man, what're you doin'?!" Ray swings open the door to the passenger side, "Let's go!"

The air has an eerily dead stillness to it, a calm with which could bring a storm.

Hopping into the driver seat, I catch a glimpse of nostalgia – traffic moving fluidly up and down Fourth Street, making their way into to a long line of slow traffic that lasts for more than a mile.

I blink, sit down, flip on the radio and crank the engine.

"Good evening ladies and gentlemen." A radio spokesman of the Pax Integral says, located around the vicinity of the Capitol building.

We reverse out of a spot surrounded by broken down clunkers and rust, all abandoned and never removed from their resting spots.

"Infection rates are at an all-time low and we expect them to be at a continual decrease, s'long as everyone continues to play it safe…"

My left ring finger clicks on the turn signal out of habit, as I steer onto Bridge Street, the once, small-town commercial district.

"Our forecast tonight calls for a chance of light snow showers with possible drizzling around sunrise…"

A lot of the things broadcasted over this radio system are really just comfortable thoughts, if that makes any sense. We've been trying, for the past few years, to keep some semblance of normality. To create sort of a distraction from what's really been going on – constant attacks from the outside and of course, the every-other-day outbreak that seems to mysteriously occur.

In my own personal opinion though, ignorance isn't exactly bliss.

Passing empty house after empty house, I accelerate down the street toward the eighty-three onramp. We pass a coffee shop with broken windows and a fallen sign. A pile of rubble and ash which used to be some sort of barber shop and at the halfway point, we pull up to a nonfunctional traffic light, just as larger snowflakes begin to fall from the sky.

I slap on the windshield wipers. "Light snow my ass." They streak along with a whine that screams over the hum of the engine.

Before making it to the clear straight-away into the city, I press a finger to my ear and radio back to base, "Can we get eyes on that train? Possibly even air-support?"

He responds, "Working on it, it's pretty close now."

"Keep me updated."

At the four-way intersection is a gas station and two fast food joints, one of them lit up in candle flames.

Not a normal place for someone to live, wrinkling my forehead, as we turn right onto the ramp, slamming a foot down on the gas.

"Yo, Dante! Calm the hell down!" Ray braces himself, with hands on the bar over his head.

Coming down heavier now, the shoulder and the grass that you can see from the road, begin to pile with layer upon layer of white frosting. Like so many snow-storms from the past, I imagine the numerous plows barreling down each road, blocking traffic and creating tunnels of ice, people would drive through, in single file.

Everything that I can remember, all that remains – all ghosts of the past.

This very highway, I'd sit by the ramps so many times and I'd just clock people, never really pulling anyone over.

"You are watchin' the road, right?" Paul asks, noticing I'd become lost in thought.

"Yea, yea…" I sigh.

I take a large chance, pushing the vehicles speed to its limit, but I wasn't about to let a single, giant piece of metal on wheels completely cripple everything we've worked for.

Paul grabs my shoulder from behind. "Slow. The fuck. Down," As we roll up to the section that merges into the bridge over the water.

Sometimes I feel as if I'm the only one that really gives a damn about preserving what little we have left.

Between balls of snow, a black and mysterious figure appears, no features, just a shadow, about a half a mile away, just standing and staring – ominous and foreboding.

"You guys just see that?" I say, but neither of them pays any attention, gazing into the black, wavy water below or watching the road as it quickly approaches with each inclination we make in miles per hour.

A similar feeling, one that I've had before, rushes back like an ocean wave, crashing into the deepest and darkest areas of my mind.

Then a loud crash of noise, which sounds like a highway accident, erupts from the distance and a rumbling shakes the ground that the rubber tires of our vehicle struggle to keep hold of.

Tapping my finger to my earlobe again, "Hey, status report, how much…"

In between two buildings, slightly off to my left and about five miles away past the water, the radio tower, that had been constructed as our central communications nervous system, teeters and collapses in a flurried cloud of dust.

Static suddenly interrupts my speech and then cuts the transmission off completely with a loud crackling buzz.

"Shit!"

"Holy fuckin' hell!" Ray rolls down his window and looks through the scope of his weapon to get a better look.

A buckling sound echoes from the backend, Paul clicks on his seatbelt.

"Hold the fuck on to somethin'!" I shout, foot all the way down, we make it to the halfway point of the bridge before the power-steering gives out and the truck literally trips over itself.

I try the brakes, but they give out completely, as we hurdle through the air like sardines in a tin-can.

My arms cover my face and in a spinning whirl I see Ray upside down beside me and with a quick glimpse in the rearview, Paul holding the ceiling with both hands. Small shards of glass flutter around like ashes and time goes on counting each second like an eternity.

We come down on its roof with a packing thud and an eruption of yellow sparks, sliding against wet pavement, almost directly in front of the Second Street exit.

For a moment, there's nothing but silence and a sharp ringing tone that deafens.

I take a few deep breaths, looking through a shattered windshield and bent steel. Ray and Paul crawl slowly out into the open, obviously in shock and at a loss for words.

Probably wondering when I'd forgotten how to drive.

With the knuckles of my left hand firmly within the grasp of my right, I shatter the side window with the coat-cushioned end of my elbow and quickly roll myself over and out of our, now, upside down transport.

Moaning and groaning as I pull myself up, I yell, "Alright." Slamming my fist against an idly spinning tire, "Comms are down, we're in the middle of a snow storm and now we don't have a fuckin' vehicle!"

Pulling his collar up over his neck, Ray shoots me a glare. "It's your damn fault." Rubbing the back of his head and shaking his legs around.

"Yea and I told you to slow the hell down," Paul adds, rubbing his forehead, "Exactly what were you tryin' to prove?"

"It was tampered with." I attempt to convince them. "The brakes went out and I couldn't even steer the damn thing."

"Really," Paul looks up, "And who the hell would've tampered with it?"

"Your guess," Pulling my pistols from their holsters, "Is as good as mine."

"Well at least we ain't dead." He reaches into the window of the truck to retrieve his rifle.

"We're right here anyway," I point toward Second Street, "I suggest we move down that ramp to Amtrak and fast."

Ray spits a mouthful of blood and flicks the safety of his weapon to the off position, "Fine, let's move."

"Let's hope the people did the smart thing and stayed inside," Clumping one foot after the other through the bone chilling mush and biting wind as the temperature begins to drop.

The two of them follow as I make my way to the ramp, a twisting left curve that would lead right down to street level.

"Hustle up!" I look back for a moment, reaching for and placing a bent cigarette in my mouth.

And so we jog what could have been a quick five minute drive, which would now take us at least fifteen minutes or so.

"This'll lead to Second and straight up to Chestnut!" I shout behind, huffing and puffing as we pass broken down structures and houses. A tall building staring down at us, the railroad tracks that seem to sprawl out all around us and everything else – the dead trees and the light of the moon passing behind heavy clouds.

As we make our way to the turn in the road, a loud screech bellows out among the street to our destination.

"Dammit! I growl. "Now I know that isn't an undead! Move!"

The screech sounded like a woman in distress, but one could only be so sure. The only sound you can hear now is the packing of snow beneath our feet as we run our fastest, weapons forward and turning down Second.

A figure between the steel sights of my two pistols stands screaming. "HELLLPPP!!" Long flowing brown hair, eyes wide in terror, mouth gaping and just behind her, a large, black creature with spider like legs and teeth like a lions; growling and grimacing with a guttural tone.

"Get down!" I command in her direction, as the beast leaps through the air.

The next thing you hear are the sound of bullets pounding from their chambers. Hammers striking hammers. The sound barrier breaking and muzzle flash illuminating the night. I look side to side, two men emptying round after round, adrenaline pumping through my veins, time doesn't slow down but my awareness is heightened and when I look back to the front, I'm firing wildly with fierce anger and determination, squeezing triggers faster than I ever thought I could.

But it's too late.

Bullets shred through its flesh, black blood raining down through the air and its teeth clamp down around the neck of the fleeing woman, ripping spinal cord from muscle and torso. Both the human and the beast die at my feet and I'm suddenly covered in two very different types of blood. Gun smoke billows from each of my hands as we stand in shock, watching as the windows of every building in the street light up and civilians pour out to the sidewalks.

A mixture of evil and death puddle into the snow, melting down to the potholed streets.

And for a moment, in my mind, I'm taken back to the bank. A creature, very much like this one, charges toward me on the walking bridge with unrelenting speed, except this seems more real – more threatening.

"Fuck." Is all I can say.

Paul bends down and pulls an identification card from her back pocket.

"What's her name?" Ray asks, crossing his heart with an index finger and praying.

"Brielle." The plastic slips out of his hands and into the mush. "I know her," Putting a hand to his head. "She was a priestess, an evangelist, a much respected religious figure."

Cries break out from the growing crowd, people yelling. "Why'd you let her die!?"

"We gotta go, now!" I grit my teeth and charge forward.

Paul reaches for my arm but misses by an inch. "What're ya just gonna leave the body here!?"

"We don't have fuckin' time!" Coughing and reloading as the train station draws nearer, crisscrossed metal bent and broken down over its rooftop.

A few seconds later they begin to catch up, Ray yelling, "Get back inside people, it isn't safe out here!" Waving hands and their weapons in the air as everyone stares in disbelief at the three lone gunmen that are supposed to protect the remaining population of the world – or at least Harrisburg.

We arrive at the stations parking lot but everything stands completely demolished, accept for a few of the doors that lead to the boarding area.

The electrical tracks hold no power but judging by the suffocating smell of creosote in the air I imagine that an ancient coal powered train had bashed through the wall, barreling down the tracks and directly into the tower.

We made it, but I feel helpless. Again, someone dies because of my own fuck up. I almost feel cursed, as if I'm bound to lose everything.

What could we possibly do in a situation like this, which we'd been sorely unprepared for?

Maybe I just enjoy beating myself up.

The ice and the snow dangling from my unshaven face trigger a tinge of nostalgia and for a moment I imagine that I'm not even here. Another memory faintly returns from a faraway point in a world that no longer exists.

My family had a little, white-siding house on the outskirts of Harrisburg, before the end, when I was younger, much younger.

Three feet of snow, tunneling around in the backyard, building snow forts and lobbing snowballs at Jack.

Ma calls us inside for turkey and stuffing and Dad sits us down with some hot cocoa and before bedtime we leave milk and cookies for Santa Claus, blinded by glee.

In the morning we'd wake up, bursting with excitement, tearing into the living room and leaving a hurricane of Christmas for our parents to clean up hours later. We sit there around a tree, mesmerized and toying around with whatever we'd received.

Then the harsh reality of things smacks me in the face.

"Jack…" I say to myself.

"Man, this ain't no time to go all wishy-washy and reminiscent on us." Ray walks up behind me.

"Yea, whatever." I turn, giving him an indifferent expression.

From the outside of the large and sprawling, red brick building, darkness looms from shattered windows that once sat adorned with white overhangs. Dead and forgotten fauna scatters itself around the parking lot and the rest of the area – more buildings, maybe what used to be a church, some corporate businesses and an apartment complex.

This though, this transportation center, was older than most other structures around here. No one had ever bothered to pick up the decade old ticket stubs that littered the ground, like everyone left in a hurry.

Well, I suppose they did.

To my right, down below, sit condemned bullet trains. Something I'd ridden when I was younger on a trip to Philadelphia.

I take in a deep breath, "Alright, let's take a look at this shit." Walking in through the door as they follow silently, through a lobby and out again into the area where the train had struck, directly into the four legs of the antenna and the generators that powered it.

There it was tall and black metallic, fucking old as hell, bearing down with its circular yellow light in the center of its face – a coal powered train. Fumes spew out of its smokestack, fire burning in the cabins attached, linking behind for maybe half a damn mile.

Beyond the crackling though, it became apparent as to what we're dealing with – the voices of the dead, shuffling around, scratching at smeared and fogged windows, searching for a way out.

They could smell us and the flames weren't large enough to kill them off.

"You mean to tell me these things all loaded up into a train dead-set for Harrisburg?" Paul scratches his head, ducking beneath fallen pieces of metal and looking upward into one of the faces of the undead.

"Shh!" Ray puts a finger to his lips. "I'm thinkin' there's probably someone or something else 'round here…"

"He's right," I confirm.

Whispering now, "Look, I want you two to head down toward the breach and take care of the situation there. We should have teams arriving at both of these strike points any moment, but we dunno what the hell's comin' through."

Paul begins to move and Ray looks at me, almost concerned, "You sure about that?"

"Dead sure," I nod. "Now go."

He nods, asking no further questions.

They knew what to do. I knew what to do.

We have an emergency plan for situations like this. First, you were expected to neutralize whatever threatened the safety of the people or the integrity of the city's wall. Then, you'd report directly to Headquarters, with no delay.

It was really all we could do now, not having any type of communication with anyone else, at least.

I watch as they disappear behind blinding wind and a white-out, which had increased in intensity since our arrival.

The loneliness settles in, with that small little sense of fear.

With every bit of caution, I make my way to the front of the train, where the conductor's cabin would be.

A waft of rotten flesh slams my nostrils as I pull myself upward and inside, immediately noticing the corpse to the right, against the door that leads to the engine room and cabins for passengers.

My heart jumps and that quick rush of metallic saliva hits my tongue. I nudge the body to the side, half of the face missing, worms and cob-webs where parts of his brain used to be. "Shit." I mutter to myself.

Behind the musty and frost covered window of the door to the undead, stand, single-file, a line of them, waving arms and knocking heads randomly. The leader of the pack smashes its face against the glass, sliding its half bitten tongue across, leaving a trail of blood and mucus.

Holding my gun up with my right hand, the other holstered, I pull on the sliding door, fingers tightening and muscles straining.

I let out a gasp.

Then I notice it, every crevice around the door is welded shut. That means two things –

either zombies know how to use a welder, or this is a trap.

A small vibration hits my eardrum and then a ticking sound. The first thing I see when I swiftly shift around to my right, spinning, fixating eyes on the control board – a timer and a badge – a policeman's badge.

Ten seconds.

7

New Old Alliances

A flash of light and I'm standing within a penumbra – a snow covered tundra, with one small patch of trees and the sun beaming down, large and yellow like a ball of mustard. The skies are clear and you can see for miles, except for the curious looking brink, directly north of my position, crumbling rock spills over the edge.

The air here feels as if it's the final breath before you're gone.

A voice whispers from the shadows of the trees, "Dante…"

The voice, "you've heard it before," my brain tells me.

Drawing my weapons and moving determined to the end of the plane, I see a small dark figure appear like a mirage, wavering in a blur of ripples. The ground stays completely still and doesn't seem to move forward with each of my steps and the trees keep their far away distance, along with the shadow.

I blink a few times and shake my head, a pair of hands grabbing me by the shoulder and again, "Dante…"

Then, suddenly, I'm at the brink, staring down into the darkness of a void, but the grasp upon my shoulder pulls me around and I see a face, long dark hair and a nose, no mouth, no eyes. She pushes gently and I lose my balance, tumbling down and feeling weightless.

My feet align to what seems like a southern position and then the scenery changes – now standing on Fourth Street in front of my home.

"Go get some rest Dante, you look like shit." My advisor says, but his voice doesn't come from the earpiece.

Slowly, I take a few steps up the stone stairway, around the concrete porch to the right, passing the window on my left and to the front door, hanging slightly ajar.

Before I even reach a hand out, the door glides open and a familiar warmth embraces me, but already, I'm hit with that feeling as if something isn't quite right.

"Julianna?" I call out, but no one answers.

The walls erupt in flame, the floor shakes and three sinkholes emerge, carpet and furniture spill downward – something scrapes eerily within.

My first instinct takes me across the room, pounding foot after foot through the dining room, the kitchen and the door by the refrigerator, which leads to the stairs. The ground behind me crumbles and falls away, replaced by ash and brimstone. I grab the railing and pull myself up and suddenly I'm on the second floor, a rooftop and again the sun beats down, spilling red across the sky.

I've been here once before.

A body lays limp and lifeless a few feet ahead of me. Hair covers this person's face but I can tell it's a woman.

"Julianna…" Voice cracking as I move in but before I can see who it really is, the scene melts away like ice and then I'm surrounded by raindrops in a black hole of nothing. I put a hand to my face and I can feel it, scarred and burned.

"What's happened to me?" Asking without an answer.

"What's going on?"

Looking down at the blacktop, I fall to my knees.

"Do you remember when we first met?"

Her voice whispers in my ear.

"You'd just come out of your coma and hadn't the faintest idea of where you were or what was going on…"

I swallow a large gulp and envision myself naked beneath a hospital gown and tripping over my feet as I strain my legs upward and move with her hand in mine.

"I took care of you all that time and to be honest, I was in love before you even woke up."

A window showcases a military camp and bustling men and women, all going about whatever business it is they're tending to.

"The others had bets you'd never even wake up but I knew you would. I knew that you had to."

She plunges a syringe into my arm, liquid blue with a hint of green.

"And we fought, side by side, until we'd beaten those bastards back far enough to enable us to reclaim a slice of this forsaken Earth as our home, once more."

She holds my arms as I stare down the sights of a pistol she'd kept from where I was salvaged, firing slowly down a make-shift target range, regaining my ability.

"To think we'd still be here, the two of us, together, but where do we go now?"

We ride together past the early stages of a wall that would hold Harrisburg together and its people within.

"Where does the future lead us?"

And her voice trails off behind the pattering rain.

Then – nothing.

"Get up!"

"Not again," I think to myself.

"I said, get up!"

My eyes shoot open to the vinyl of a blood-stained steering wheel.

A hand grabs me by the back of the head and pulls me upward, room spinning, bobbing back and forth.

"Who the hell are you?" I mutter with a groan, dabbing my fingers at my forehead.

"Same question, buddy, you one of them?"

An inquisitive woman, pressing the barrel of a gun against my temple.

"Them who?" Asking and pulling my feet to the glass and debris littered floor of the police station lobby.

"You know," Gun between my eyes, "those humanity hating, terrorist bastards gunning people down."

And suddenly my vision becomes clear, once more.

"Meryl?!"

Short, dirty blond hair that curls at the tips.

"Dante?! No way! I didn't even recognize you!"

Puffy red lips and a small, curved up nose.

"Please don't tell me you were the one shooting at Jack and I."

Piercing and accusing eyes.

"Why were you even wandering the streets in the first place? How do I know you haven't joined their ranks?"

Left hand on her hip, right hand still holding a forty-four magnum to my face.

"Gimme a fuckin' break and please get that gun outta my face." I rub a hand over my scalp and sit back for a better view, "You're lookin' pretty good," I flirt. "You never made it back to command, we thought you were dead."

She arches her eyebrows, eyes burning with anger, "More like left me for dead! Assholes cleared outta here in a matter of minutes, I…"

Interrupting her, "If you hadn't noticed, it was fuckin' nuts out there, I'm sure they didn't…" Then I realize Jack hadn't been by my side. "Hey, what'd you do with Jack?"

She backs up a bit, rubbing fingers against her cheek, "Yea, sorry, our fault. He's got a few wounds and he's upstairs. Don't worry though, our medic is taking care of him."

"There are more of you? What? Civilians and NYPD?"

"Yep, pretty much, aside from the medic, some military woman."

"Take me to them." I reach out a hand for hers and she pulls me up, taking me to a narrow staircase that leads circular up to the second floor.

Through a steel swinging door sit, around a table, two men playing cards, paying no attention at all. Across the room, on a black leather couch, Jack, with a peculiar looking woman tending to a bullet wound.

"She doesn't look military," I whisper.

The guys at the table look up briefly, as we pass by, greeting us with a, "Hey," and "Sup."

Middle of the apocalypse, you'd think they'd have a little more enthusiasm.

"That's David and Rob." She points and whispers. "They're a bit shaken up, so forgive 'em if they seem a little cold."

I follow her wiggling behind to the couch, tight and dressed in female issue urban combat pants.

"And this is Nuhm De'Ara."

Covering every inch of her body, she wears black clothing and a pair of shades.

Weird? Yes.

"Nice to meet you," We shake hands. "How's Jack?"

"He'll be fine, Dante." She clasps her hands together.

"And how do you know my name?" I question with a puzzled look on my face.

"I know more than you could possibly imagine." Her voice sounds strong and feminine.

Meryl, whispering again, "I know, creepy, but she's pretty accurate when it comes to firearms and I think you should have a talk with her."

"Sit down, have a seat, you too Meryl." And so we do, watching her take her own, crossing legs and resting both hands on an armrest.

"So where were you when this all started?" Looking directly at me.

"I…" Stuttering for a moment, "I was assisting in the evacuation. The memory is extremely choppy, but I remember all the gunfire, the violence, the gore, screaming, death…"

"And the risen dead." She interjects.

"Yea," I look away for a moment, rubbing a hand on the back of my neck.

"And I'm willing to bet that, not so long ago, you witnessed something more than just a zombie."

I cringe at the thought of the word.

"Something monstrous, something, possibly, demonic?"

I leave out the incoherent vision of Harrisburg.

"Tell me Dante," She begins to speak as I hold up a hand.

"Wait, wait, wait, you're obviously not military. You're some kind of psychic or something." Getting frustrated. "And stop asking so many damn questions."

Meryl giggles, "You'll have to excuse him." She says to Nuhm with a grin. "He's kind of impatient and angry, most of the time. It's normal."

The both of them join each other in a short laugh. I, on the other hand, pull out a pack of smokes and light up a fresh one.

Inhaling and leaning back, "Alright, there's somethin' I should mention." Turning their attention to me, "There was this weird little, triangular-like artifact, in the vault of a bank, alongside two mangled bodies."

They both lean inward.

"Go on…" Nuhm's glasses slide down the bridge of her nose.

"I'm not sure what it did, but I think it has something to do with that monster I mentioned earlier. And possibly the two people that were there before my team had arrived."

Letting out a sigh, she leans her head in the palm of her hand and slides her shades back to her eyes. "That 'artifact' opened a very, very small wormhole. I'm not sure what's on the other side, but it's unstable as hell. Anything and everything can and will come through. You've altered time and space, permanently."

"What?" Wondering why I was being accused.

She coughs and waves cigarette smoke out of her face. "Some believe that whatever comes out of there is simply coming from the darkest, furthest reaches of space. Others, well, they're thinking it's hell."

"And you've heard this where?" I ask.

"I wasn't with this little group the entire time, I've heard of this artifact before, but no one knew where it was."

I stand up, placing my cigarette between my lips, pacing back and forth nervously. David and Rob still sit concentrating on their poker game; Jack unconscious, Meryl and Nuhm watch me as if they expect me to say something more.

"Alright," Placing a hand to my chin. "Let's say I don't believe you. You're crazy and this is all just some sort of mass hallucination. You know, there could be some kind of gas in the air."

"What you saw, you fired live ammunition at it, correct?"

I stop, lean against the wall and stare at the ceiling. "Yeah…"

"I mean, I don't think any of us are hallucinating here, do you?" Uncrossing her legs, "Were you seeing things when you shot innocent people you thought were walking dead?" The anger in her voice rises. "The fact of the matter is, you've got to believe what I say, 'cause there isn't anything else." Standing up and pushing her chair back, "You want to know what I am. I'm an experiment – that's all you need to know."

She storms over with her finger pointed at my face. "If we're going to make it outta here alive, you've gotta listen to what I have to say. The next time we go outside, it'll be different. The city you once knew will be lying in ruins, and this building will be gone…"

"What the fuck are you talking about?" Confused, once again.

"We're standing on ground zero. The longer that wormhole remains open, the more our dimension melds with whatever lies on the other side." Backing off, walking to Jack and checking his pulse. "It could close or it could stay open for the rest of eternity." She removes her shades, eyes shining the brightest blue, like water reflecting the sky. "Where is that artifact?"

I slap my forehead. "Shit, I dunno!" The address had completely slipped my mind; In fact, I don't think I ever knew it in the first place.

"Humph." She crosses her arms and frowns. "That's just great."

"Well, I don't know about the rest of you…" Looking around, seeing an automatic rifle, "But I'm heading for the Verrazano, we were supposed to report back to the men stationed there. You know, once we," Holding fingers in quotations, "Secured the situation."

"That sounds like a damn good plan." Rob stands up, machete strapped to his back, brown hair hanging down in front of his eyes and a twelve-gauge in hand.

"Hell, it's about damn time." Holding a fifty caliber pistol, David stands and holsters his hand cannon, bald head gleaming from the buzzing panels above; He swings an assault rifle around his back.

"Wait!" Meryl barges in between us, hands waving in the air. "Are you kidding me?! We can't go out there!"

I lift a rifle from a wooden counter against the wall and lock-in a full magazine. "We have weapons, we'll be fine," I turn to Nuhm. "Wake up Jack, it's time to go."

"He's nowhere near stable, you four go on ahead, and we'll catch up."

"No," Moving toward her. "You wake him up and you follow us to the bridge."

"Listen, Dante," Meryl places a hand on my shoulder. "He'll be fine, I'm sure he's in good hands. If you're serious though, we should probably get going. Who knows if that team is even still out there."

"Fine," I look over again. "But you better be right behind us."

"As the woman said, he's in good hands." Nuhm points toward the window. "Clear a path for us and we'll be about twenty minutes back."

In a high risk situation, you've gotta do just that – take risks. I'm not sure if leaving him behind is the best of all ideas, but things aren't about to get any better. My own flesh and blood, left to the likes of a strange woman with the bluest eyes I have ever seen.

My eyes pass over Meryl, giving her that, you better be right, look.

"Follow me." I motion to the rest as I move for the door. "I'm trusting you, Nuhm De'Ara and if anything goes wrong, I'll find you."

"You won't have to." She grins.

Meryl grabs a low powered sniper rifle and a bandoleer, strapping it across her chest; she pockets a modest looking forty-five caliber pistol. "Come on."

Upon opening the door, we're immediately greeted by a familiar smell of rotten eggs. My eyes burn and my nose twitches.

"God damn." Putting my left arm to my face and aiming up and down the hallway, "Ungghh, it's clear." I gasp. "Move to the fuckin' stairwell."

One step at a time, the room below reveals itself, the same as before yet completely different. The Metro seems older, decayed and rusted. Slimy black vines twitch and crawl in through the demolished entrance and from the outside, a hazed fog of red creeps in.

I look back and the expressions on everyone's faces reflect gut wrenching disgust.

"Just keep moving." Meryl says, grabbing me by the arm. "I'm sure it'll only get worse."

Nuhm De'Ara was correct, after all. The world around had begun to change. Everything stood exactly the way it had before, yet something corrupt was eating away at it.

I begin wondering just how long I'd been knocked out in the driver seat of that vehicle.

We push past shattered brick and hop down to street level.

"Alright, stop." Rob scans the area, suggesting we survey our surroundings for a moment.

Collapsed and dilapidated buildings decorate the horizon. Grey ash covers the pavement like a blanket of snow, which had stopped at some point between the crash and my waking up. Then brimstone pushed through the Earth.

"Damn!" Exclaims David.

"Yeah, yeah, she was right, I can't even tell which direction we need to go." I say as I slap my hands against my waist.

It's confirmed – Manhattan is no longer the towering and overpowering city it once was. You'd think we were living some sort of nightmare, but none of us are capable of waking up.

"We should head to the subway." Meryl suggests.

"You do realize that none of the trains are running, right?" Pointing out the obvious.

"Well duh, I'm saying we should walk the tunnels, probably safer than the streets."

A low and guttural growl emerges from around the corner of a few walls and what strangely looks like a few petrified trees. I blink, startled, aligning the sights of my weapon. "We got company, move!"

Shuffling feet, we head north quickly and quietly. Yet the further from the station we go, the darker it seems to become; Ground emanating orange glowing cracks, a hand bursts through and grabs me by the foot.

"What the shit!" Kicking it away, I stumble and fall backward to the ground, a puff of ash curling up around me.

"Hah, Dante, you look like a chimney sweep!" Meryl laughs, reaching out a hand to pull me up.

"What? You didn't see that?"

"See what?" She responds.

Strange, I think to myself.

Off to our left, a building loses its footing and collapses to the ground. The deafening sound of crumbling concrete and steel sends a shock wave across the plane.

The corner of my eye twitches with a nervous spasm.

David stands with his mouth gawking. "Christ, what caused that?!"

"Keep it quiet, we're attracting attention." Glowing eyes peer from dark corners as I swing around looking for a clear path.

Meryl grabs me by the hand. "Try not to let go this time."

I nod. "If you say so."

But before we can take another step forward, I feel something, another invisible tap on the shoulder and then a whisper, within my mind.

Go back...

Like a voice in the wind trailing away past my ear.

I don't know why I listened, but I could feel it – something was wrong.

"Turn around; we gotta get back to the station."

I pull Meryl around and walk fast, gun in the opposite hand and trudge through the ruins.

"But Dante..."

And before she's able to finish her sentence, before David and Rob even knew we'd turned around, a wave of heat blasts over us, followed by a gaping chasm of flame where the police station had recently stood. Brick and stone scatter into the air, the force throwing us back maybe twenty feet or so and my hand still grasps Meryl's.

8

Necrophagilia

I don't know how long I was there, on my back in the dust. I remember still feeling her hand, soft and frail, 'til I open my eyes.

Snow frozen to my eye lashes, smoke billowing out from the demolished train only a few yards away; I strain to wrench my eyes open. In my right hand lay Jack's badge, clenched tightly between my fingers, numb and nearly frost bitten. I bend my chest upward and immediately cough violently.

The cold feels unforgiving but the blizzard had come to a halt, now just slow falling flakes of white.

My arms sit dead and asleep as I dig my hands down into the snow against the concrete, struggling to push myself up. "Gah!" I snarl in pain as the bones in my legs crack, climbing, dizzy, to my feet.

I stand for a moment, shaking myself off. "Meryl." Saying aloud, "What happened to you guys…"

My fragmented memories were growing tiresome.

How in the hell did I even get away from this train?

Then a thousand needles pierce my brain, instantly pounding the inside of my forehead. Almost collapsing again, I hit the palms of my hands against my face. "Fuck!"

A cigarette, that's what I need.

Rifling around through my pockets for a mashed up pack of four smokes, I pull out one and fumble with it between my lips and the lighter that wouldn't strike until I'd successfully blistered my thumb.

Then I inhale; ecstasy in a stick.

Letting out a sigh of relief, I gather my thoughts and remember the threat that must have been growing, unless Ray and Paul had actually made it to their destination. A depressing afterthought echoes in the distance – hollow moaning and screams of terror suggesting otherwise.

My pistols only hold a few bullets, whatever remained from the recent firefight. Four or five in each, I guess, dragging myself across the untouched plains of ice and putting my back to the wall of a parking garage.

I had to have been out for at least an hour. Judging by the sound of it, there are at least twenty or more of 'em.

A rusted green sign on the side of the road reads Aberdeen Street, only a few clicks from Headquarters, but this is bad news.

Inching around the corner, I try to gather a head count, straining my eyes, still blurry from the rude awakening. A mass of bodies run in groups, a straggler here and there, probably civilians.

"They just don't listen." Leaning my weight toward empty air, shifting myself away from the wall and into the street. "We say go back to your homes…" My leg stops dead and with both hands I force it to move forward. "But no! You gotta see what that strange noise was, right?!"

Another familiar noise barely registers within my eardrums. I've heard it somewhere before, but it wasn't coming in quite clear.

I push myself into a jog, bobbing up and down, not fully recovered from my apparent nap. Pistols in front of me and fingers on the triggers, I aim only at what comes barreling toward me.

"Pop!" A single bullet shreds through the skull of a scraggly haired zombie, decayed grey matter spilling out from behind.

At this point I realize I'm moving in a zigzag motion, slamming against the red brick wall of a warehouse.

"Ah, no! Where'd it go!?" I search the ground for my smoke that had clumsily fallen out of my mouth. "Bastards!"

Flash, crack and bang, another three go down. Adrenaline pumping through my veins helps stabilize my motion, giving me a quick burst of energy.

"Get back to your goddamn home!" I scream at a frantic looking man, mouth gaping open and eyes just barely catching me as he runs by crying in a fit of horror.

With rage, I blast down the street.

One, the kneecaps of a fast mother fuck, blow out from underneath him.

Two, I graze the ear of an undead woman, standing around with a stupid look on her face.

Three, the intestines of an overweight man, spill out like spaghetti into the snow covered streets, confusing him enough to stop him dead in his tracks.

No pun intended.

And each magazine has been fully dispensed.

"Well." Holstering each weapon. "I didn't think I'd *actually* die tonight. Ya jinxed me, Jules."

That unregistered noise I heard earlier? A relic of past warfare buzzes from overhead and into the scene – a Blackhawk, mounted with gas powered Gatling guns – enough power to shred you into tiny little pieces.

"Who the fuck?!" I spew out words, unheard.

"Citizens of Harrisburg…" One of the pilot's men shouts through a megaphone. "You have thirty seconds to find shelter."

They plan on sweeping the area, obviously, but I've no idea who they are or how they could have been radioed in. Not to mention, who would've confirmed the usage of that much of our fuel reserves.

Waving my arms in the air, I yell. "No! Stop!"

Lead rains down like fire from the sky.

This time, I run as fast as I can, pumping my arms back and forth, toward a building across the street, also plastered in crumbling brick and a home of maybe fifty people.

A pair of arms pull me inward through the doorway and greet me with the smiling end of a hand cannon.

"On your feet." Watching me as I pick myself up, hands hung to my sides, instead of over my head. "You're going upstairs. We got a problem and we ain't waistin' no ammo or bodies to take care of it."

I push my hands back and forth. "Whoa, whoa, wait a minute. You wanna tell me what the hell your problem is?"

"My problem, is your problem." Lowering his weapon, slightly. "You come dashing over here with a damn hail of bullets following you, I save your ass an' now you do what I say."

He wears coke bottle glasses with a few strings of grey hair hanging down over his forehead, sweating in fear.

"Alright, fine, but I'll warn you," Lowering my eyebrows. "Don't point that damn gun at me ever again."

Gathering my surroundings, as he pushes me up to the stairs, I see the old, worn down entrance to an apartment building, a small hallway, a service desk and everything covered in dry-rotted wood – a heaven for termites.

There also seems to be a large group of people hiding in a small room to the back.

Stairs creaking and wobbling, I make my way up, noticing the man behind stopping and simply watching.

Gunfire blinks like strobe lights from a window at the end of the hall on the second floor and cracks in the wall breathe a chilling draft. The second door on my left, which must be what this guy had been talking about, glows red with mysterious fog.

"Fog?" Squinting my eyes and wrinkling my forehead.

"Mmhmm." I clear my throat. "Hey! If you're alive in there come on out with your hands in the air." Mind you, I'm not holding either gun in my hands, but I sort of hope he or she wouldn't notice upon coming out of the room.

Yet, the door lay still.

I make my way over, with melting bits of snow dripping off of me, hearing a rocking or a knocking sound, over a low hum.

I think about turning back and simply facing the gunfire, would be a little less nerve wracking.

Hands wet and shaky, I reach out to touch a rusty old knob.

You're gonna like this...

That voice – that whisper, again.

"Fuck off." I say, quietly.

I almost second guess my decision to turn this knob without holding a weapon.

It grinds as it twists, pushing it open slowly; I see tubs of dry ice lining the walls of a small room.

In my head, I wonder. "Where'd they get that sorta thing?"

Fed up with suspense, I swing open the door, slamming it against the wall, almost loosening it completely from its hinges.

"Alright asshole…"

I stop mid-sentence and stand wide-eyed.

The tops of the walls are lined with old swords, maces and knives. Torches set ablaze in each corner.

This person was obviously a fan of castle-age bullshit.

Black drapes cover the only window in the room, masking the flash of blasting gunfire on the outside.

Then, dead-center of the room, is an undead woman, laying strapped to the floor by chains. Patches of hair and flesh missing from her head, face torn up and mutilated – naked and quivering, hissing with anger through a torn piece of cloth she'd just barely chewed through. Her nipples stand on end, not the most noticeable thing in the room, but definitely something to take note of.

A man, looking as if in his late fifties, stands huddled over her with a slab of flesh hanging from his mouth, also naked, dick hanging down loose and penetrating the rotten vagina of a zombie.

He becomes more aroused, with every thrust, she makes in an attempt to break free or to catch a sliver of skin from his neck. Of course, he hums as if in some other state of mind, obviously insane.

If you've ever smelled rotten flesh, double dipped in diarrhea on a humid summer day – this smells worse.

I taste Julianna's spaghetti once more.

"Get your goddamn dick outta that corpse ya sick fuck!"

I had seen a lot of things, but this, this shit was one for the fuckin' books.

It takes him about twenty seconds to respond, moving his fingers over the top of her body, teasing her with the promise of "food."

"My Rose! My beautiful Rose! No one touches her!" Wiping saliva from his lips, he jumps up, snarling and yelling. "Get outta my chamber!" Reaching for a swinging mace, he lumbers toward me.

Last thing I need is a naked, sweaty, bald, boil encrusted and most likely infected man, running after me.

I quickly search around the room with my eyes, seeing nothing within close proximity that would do me any good, until, at last, I look up. Like an answer from whatever higher power exists, an old and extremely sharp looking samurai sword sits almost glowing in a heavenly essence, above the door.

With all of my strength, I leap directly upward, reaching and grabbing with one hand and the other pulling it out of its sheath, landing in a stance I'd seen in movies and holding it in front of me.

"Back!" I warn, yet still he comes.

"Heyaaahhhh!" He screams, arms in the air, preparing to smack me in the face.

I pull my arms back and with all of my weight, I swing the sword, twisting on a ninety degree angle, blade passing directly through his neck, sending his head flailing across the room and an incarnadine fountain shoots from his torso.

I jump back a bit to avoid splatter and infection.

"Hmm," I think to myself. "Not bad."

After the body finally falls to the ground – kicking it away – I drive the already blood-stained steel into the forehead of the poor dead woman that had been subjected to such a horrible atrocity – rape after death.

Judging by the sudden silence, you could tell the psychos outside had most likely finished their rampage.

"Good."

Making my way back down, I see him standing there, back to me, gun in-hand and talking to someone from behind a sheet of darkness that looms from the room in front of him.

Immediately upon turning around, he's got the gun in my direction again. I slap his right wrist hard and the shock releases his grip, causing the weapon to fall directly into my left hand.

"Alright, *now* who's got the gun?" Smirk on my face, I shove the barrel against his nose.

His hands go high as the ceiling.

"Ju…just wait a minute here, did you take care of our problem?" Teeth chattering as he questions me.

"Yeah, your zombie rapist is dead and gone, is that it? I got better things to do."

Before deciding whether or not to just shoot him and move along, a small, brown haired child comes from the doorway of the room the man's party had been hiding in.

"Please don't shoot Daddy." He sniffles and wipes an arm across his nose. "He's just trying to protect us."

This definitely hits a soft spot.

Sometimes you gotta remember who you are and what it is you are fighting for.

"I'm not gonna shoot him son, he just needs to watch where he points his gun."

Twisting the hand-grip around and clutching the barrel, I hand it back to him. "Name's Dante, Human Protection Unit number thirteen, PaxCorpus."

And a big, "I'm sorry!" look flashes over his face.

"Jesus!" He exclaims, holstering his face-hole maker. "I'm so sorry man, I didn't know, I was just…"

"Yeah, it's fine." I stand in clear view. "Remember this outfit, we all wear it."

He stands back for a moment and gazes at my black and white colored combat suit, fluffy large winter coat and a symbol across my chest that clearly shows, "HPU Thirteen."

You would think that these people would have seen me or another Pax unit by now.

"Daddy I wanna be Pax!" The little boy tugs at his Father's leg.

"Maybe someday, Johnny, maybe…"

"Now, if you people are alright, I've got business to take care of." I salute them with two fingers.

"Thanks again…" The man nods, pushing glasses up the bridge of his nose.

I make my way back outside, to the corpse littered streets, lying face down and torn apart in dark red stained snow. Looking onward into the night, you can see its large green and tan architecture standing out from everything else.

Headquarters was merely down the street from here, where I'd find the administrator, George. He doesn't entirely run the operation, but he makes sure things go smoothly.

For example, communications go down, he logs everyone that reports back to him, which you are required to do. If for some reason a unit or a single person fails to do this, they, he or she are presumed dead or missing, but only after a three hour grace period – plenty of time to get from wherever you are to the Capitol.

In this case, the people failing to show up are Ray and Paul. I'll be damned if I'm gonna lose two more fucking people.

The building, on the outside, seems like a mix between ancient castle-esque architecture with a hint of Roman inspiration. On the inside there's white painted stairs, leading up to both the right and the left and more floorboards reinforced by, you guessed it, wood – I grow so tired of seeing wood.

The walls reach upward in white and stone and all around the entrance stand medieval type lamps that burn furiously, piercing the darkness that pours in

In front of the stairway sits an old office desk, obviously pulled in after-the-fact, to accommodate our admin.

"Hello, Dante, you're a bit late, don't ya think?"

Five after one in the morning. Five minutes past the deadline.

"Yeah, well, I got a little hung up." Placing both my hands on his desk, leaning into his heavily unshaven and round face, eyes shadowed by a protruding brow. "Where're Ray and Paul? They haven't checked in, have they?"

He begins to speak, but I interrupt.

"And where the hell did that helicopter come from? You know how dangerous that was?!"

"If you'll give me a second to speak," He lights a smoke. "I'll tell you everything you want to know. Ray and Paul, as you've guessed, have not reported back to me…" Ashing on the floor. "And as far as your buddies in the sky, I haven't a fucking clue."

"You don't know?!" I shout, questioning in the demand of a real answer.

"Yeah, I don't know."

He looks as if maybe he's lying, scratching his ear and smoking. Everyone's got a tell, but you won't get shit outta George.

"Multiple teams have already been dispatched to the breach; they're taking care of it. What happened out there, Dante? You were supposed to stop this from happening." Sitting back, legs crossed, prepared to listen.

I light up a smoke for myself, pacing back and forth, rubbing my forehead recalling each consecutive event.

"We left my place, a blizzard came down, and I crashed our vehicle…" His eyes narrow toward me after hearing that. "We end up walking down to second, only to find some monstrous fuck wreaking havoc on the citizens, killing a woman in the process and I lose all of my ammunition, well, almost."

George puts his cigarette out on the desk, rubbing it next to about six or seven other butts. "So you were driving like an idiot, you let someone die and you put other peoples' lives at risk?"

"Let me finish." I point at him, blowing smoke in his direction. "We hustled on over to Amtrak, only to find… did I mention, this whole goddamn time, communications were out?" I say in a pissed off, sarcastic manner.

He sits, sipping at a glass of water, one large blue vein pulsing at the tip of his forehead.

"The train completely knocked out the tower; I sent Ray and Paul to take care of the breach. Maybe now, in retrospect, I should've just sent them here, but I figured the threat of infection en masse was more important."

A Pax unit comes down the left stairwell, talking amongst themselves as they walk through the lobby doors and head off in the direction of the crash.

"I took care of the train myself, you know, investigated it, only to find that it had been packed full of the walking dead, behind a damn welded door." Leaving out the part that involves my finding of Jack's badge. "And right up front, enough explosives to level the Harrisburg hospital."

His eyes widen. "A bomb?!" Almost knocking his glass of water off of the desk, as he shifts forward in his chair.

"Yeah, you didn't hear the fuckin' explosion?" Flicking my finished smoke against a wall.

"Of course I heard it, but I thought it had something to do with that chopper…"

"No, those crazy bastards just about shredded me to pieces, luckily though, some maniac with a pistol and a vendetta 'saved my life.'"

Now he's got a piece of paper, drawn from the drawer by his hip, writing down each detail.

"I won't entertain you with the retarded shit I experienced there, but that leads up to just before my arrival here, and now I need to know where the hell Ray and Paul are. I need to go outside that wall."

Drops of water drip down from the soaking wet strands of hair at the top of my head.

"If they haven't reported in by now, they're either dead or somewhere, anywhere out there." Pointing east in the direction of the breach.

Finishing whatever he'd been jotting down, he looks up at me, concentrates for a few seconds and begins to speak. "Alright," tapping his foot. "If this whole project, PaxCorpus, hadn't been mostly because of *you*, I'd suspend you right now, but, since you're a founder and all…" His eyes shift to the side, "I'm going to have to ask you to go home for the rest of the night. I'm sure Julianna's waiting for you anyway." Folding the sheet of paper and sliding it into an envelope, still watching me. "Once the wall is secure, I'll find out whether or not any of the teams were able to recover yours. If not…" He hesitates for a moment. "Then you can go out there and have a damned blast."

A woman in a white coat with long, curly blond hair comes from a door behind George and he hands her a manila envelope. "Now go, take the Jeep out front." Pulling a pair of keys from his pocket and two fully loaded magazines from another drawer, sliding them across the desk. "Get some rest and you can meet me at the New Cumberland airstrip, I'll be there all day."

Before leaving, I decide to clarify. "Now, you know I did my best out there, this isn't entirely my fault. Something bigger's going on here."

He immediately retorts. "And if that's true, we'll find out what, if anything is going on. Now go, get out of my sight."

As I'm walking through the doors, boots squeaking across the floor, he makes one final statement.

"Watch your back out there."

On the outside the weather is calm again, left with a chill and a choking atmosphere – the kind of cold that makes the hair on your arms stand on end.

A rusty grey Wrangler sits haphazardly parked and cockeyed against the curb, at least from what I can tell. The snow had buried most of the street and sidewalk. I've driven one of these before, long ago, maybe when I was a teenager, can't remember exactly.

But hey, that's my memory for ya.

On the interior are black fabric seats, covered in cigarette ash and windows smeared in yellow nicotine stains. Stacks of paper burst from the glove department and empty packs of Ace's smokes scatter random parts of the vehicle.

"Nice, George."

The beast runs like a tank, climbing over mountains of snow and shaking me around like a damn jumping bean in a barrel. At least he'd taken good care of its mechanics.

Although I didn't really know much about his pastime activities, other than the fact that he enjoys Tetris on an old Gameboy handheld system.

He is right though, the situation seems well under control, for now. Re-dead corpses still litter the ground in patches that seem almost perfectly arranged. Even in shitty situations, PaxCorpus excelled. That's what we train for.

The climb back to eighty-three south via Second Street takes what feels like twenty minutes at least, crawling a painful ten miles per hour, chugging on four cylinders. Sort of takes me back though, in the times from the past when I'd been a cop here in the 'Burg.

Every time we had bad weather, such as this, with more than an inch of snow, I'd always get called to go out and "rescue" people from ditches, banks and smashed telephone poles. As if it was safer for me to be driving around in this crap. Their cruisers were never exactly state of the art or top of the line.

Although we *are* talking about the state capitol that took over a hundred days to come up with a fuckin' budget back in two-thousand nine – pencil pushing bastards.

Thinking about the past and slowly driving over the bridge, brought me back to earlier times in my teens, when I was in high school.

My grades were never perfect but also never really that horrible. I fluctuated between B's and C's, most of the time, with the occasional A or an F. I loved English class though, which is what I originally wanted to do with my life – become a writer and sell art through words.

I wanted to write fiction. None of that boring columnist bullshit – I wanted to create worlds and people. I'd be in Math class listening to the teacher drone on and on about fractions and integers and I'd be writing about Jordan, the sadly misunderstood serial killer that stalked the streets, in the early morning, killing small animals – yeah, never really made that much sense, but I enjoyed it.

That sort of thing made me feel almost godlike, shaping and molding something from nothing, dictating and creating lives that would otherwise never exist.

But Ma and Pa had bigger plans for me. Writing hadn't been in their agenda, apparently, and to them, it didn't seem like a legitimate career choice.

I was, originally, supposed to join the Navy for training, but at the age of eighteen I ran out and moved in with a high school girlfriend of mine. We lived in a less than low class situation and before almost hitting bottom and getting kicked out into the streets, I became a cop.

Then I broke up with her, thoughtlessly and heartlessly, didn't matter to me though. I figured I could sit around in a squad car and continue my dream of writing, but the city of Harrisburg had bigger plans and distractions for me.

Snap out of it.

That damn voice again, of that unidentified woman or thing, whatever, broke my trance of past reminiscence.

I had begun to slide down into the Lemoyne exit, to the four-way traffic light, cornered by a gas station, an abandoned KFC and a Burger King. There she stands, middle of the road, just staring.

"Alright, it's time for answers, I'm tired of this little voice in the back of my head."

Standing on the brakes and veering sideways, I kick open the driver side door, slamming a clip into a single pistol and aiming it in her direction.

"Who, the fuck, are you!?"

She doesn't move, doesn't do a thing.

"Answer me, bitch!"

Don't talk to me like that!

The closer I get, the faster my heart beats, pounding against my chest. Then as she turns her head up to face me, my vision blurs and blinks like then lens of an old shutter projector film until I see absolutely nothing at all.

9

SubHorror

It wasn't making any sense. I felt as if I'd slipped into a memory wide awake, fully conscious and aware – as if I somehow managed to jump directly into myself, within the past.

But dreams sometimes have a tendency to feel real.

Am I dreaming?

Time had passed. I couldn't quite tell how much but as my vision returns, I see Meryl, David and Rob, all looking down into the dark and empty bowels of a New York subway.

"You sure we wanna go down there?" Rob faces me, seeming nervous, checking back and then down, evaluating both of our options. "Well?"

"Uh, um…" Unable to remember what had happened between the explosion and now. "Yeah, as Meryl suggested, it'll be safer than the streets, right?"

Meryl kneels down on one knee and looks through the scope of her rifle.

"It's pitch black, I don't see any light sources." Flipping on a mounted flashlight attached to the stock of her weapon as it responds with nothing but a click, "And our batteries are dead?"

David and Rob both test their own, to no avail.

"Shit man, I don't like darkness, I really don't like it." Dave whines, crossing his arms and looking back to see a crowd of the undead in the distance running toward us.

"Ah fuck! We ain't exactly in a position to argue!" Rob shouts, pointing his shotgun in their direction as he backpedals down the stairwell.

"Down, down, go!" I check the magazine in my rifle and find that half of it's been dispensed, aiming forward as we shuffle down.

Meryl grabs an empty belt loop on my back and uses my movement as a guide into the shadows.

My eyes search for even the tiniest shred of light, but not even a speck shines through.

Turn around and fucking shoot her Dante, put her out of her misery, now.

We all stop at once as I flip open my lighter and strike a flame, only illuminating the area directly in front of me for half a second before it quickly dies out, catching a glimpse of bodies scattering the floor and an empty, whispering railway.

"Damnit," I struggle to strike up a flame, as a metal gate at the bottom of the stairs creaks and clangs shut. "The hell?"

"Alright, everybody stay calm for a moment." I hear Meryl's voice but I don't see a thing.

"At least the zombies can't get past that gate," Rob speaks from a position that sounds further away than Meryl's.

"You sure about that?" David questions, even further away, with a chattering chill in his voice.

We all stay silent for an abrupt moment and my nose catches a large whiff of the air that surrounds us, smelling dank, with rotting flesh and that moth-ball smell.

Don't be so selfish.

I ignore the voice and its suggestions, not even beginning to want to understand why it had commanded a bullet for Meryl's flesh.

Then a sound from down what I could only guess was the tunnel came a screeching, rumbling and grinding.

Change the future, Dante, save her from the pain and the suffering – the loneliness, the anguish and the desperation. You wanna be a hero? Put a bullet between her eyes.

"Looks like we'll have some light here in a few seconds." At least that's what I hope, wondering what exactly was heading toward us, considering the trains are all down and unoperational.

A hand touches my shoulder. "You hear that?" She asks. "We evacuated the city, who the hell's controlling that thing?"

She proposes an obvious, yet interesting question.

Then the growling and moaning of the dead burst into the silence of the darkness, reaching hands and arms through the twisting shafts of the gate, desperate and hungry for our flesh.

"Wonder how long that'll hold…" Still fumbling with my lighter and a cigarette I'd placed between my lips, finally igniting a flame. "There we go."

Another hand smacks me against the back of the head. "Hey, cancer man, put out that smoke. The rest of us aren't tryin' to inhale that crap." Rob complains.

"Gah!" I wince. "Fine." Flicking a small, orange cherry in the darkness off to my side, which lands on something soft and begins to burn a small flame.

"Well I'll be damned." Exclaims David.

The flame grows and circles the small concrete room, blazing yellow and red, with a hint of blue, revealing broken benches, ripped apart pay phones and the numerous corpses of people who'd apparently been stuck below the streets.

"Nice to see you guys again." I turn to them, their faces all looking upset and disgruntled.

"Look, I've said it before, we did what we could. Many, many more have died."

Meryl's eyes stare at one group of the dead in particular – a mother and a father, clutching the hands of a skeletal child. The blazing flames reflect the shimmer of a tear down the edges of her face.

"It's just not fair." She whimpers, turning away. "Whoever's responsible for this, I'll have their lives."

"That's the spirit." Placing a hand on her shoulder.

Her eyes gleam amidst the crackling flames, her soul pours outward with an inner warmth that emanates from her trembling body.

"I try to be strong, but some things…" She squeezes her eyes shut.

Fine, don't do it, we'll play along with this charade.

Rob steps between us. "You guys going kiss or something? Shit."

Averting her eyes from mine. "Piss off Rob."

I look over to David, standing there among shadows with arms crossed and dazed.

The sound of the train grows closer.

My pistol stirs anxiously in its holster, my feet leading me to the edge of the ground by the tracks. I lean out to the side over the rails and get a glimpse of a hell-bound hunk of metal on wheels, shooting sparks and careening right for us.

"Get your backs to the walls, now!" I command, jolting for the parallel concrete where David had already positioned himself.

Don't board that train.

Meryl and Rob leap and skid across the floor to the crease that meets the mold covered walls; I grab Meryl and shield her with my head down from shrapnel that sprays into the open.

It screeches like a banshee howling at the night, coming to an abrupt stop. A metal shard rips into my left arm and sears the flesh. In pain, I watch David roll over, wiping pieces of glass out of himself. Rob seeming mostly unscathed, slides over to me and immediately puts pressure on my arm.

"Hey, Dave, help us out here!"

I release my grasp from Meryl and allow my head to fall back against the wall, "Auuggh!"

Pulling the machete off of his back, Rob slices away at the fabric of my suit and rips the arm away.

"Dammit!" I position myself upward, arm across my chest. "Anyone got a pair of pliers!?"

Meryl recovers; ripping a strand of cloth from the bottom of her shirt, twirling it around in the shape of a bandage and with both hands pulls hard on the bent shrapnel lodged in my arm.

Imagine a splinter, only made of metal, being yanked out of you slowly and horribly painfully. This is worse than a gunshot wound.

I grumble and growl. "Fuckin' shit, get that thing outta me now!" It finally slides, with its last, thinner, triangular shaped end, out of my skin.

"I can't tell if you've damaged any muscle tissue…" She wraps the bandage tight around the wound. "But at least it isn't your 'shooting' arm."

"Where're my goddamn smokes!?" The pain leaves me, for the most part, like a reseeding wave off from a shore. I cough. "I guess that's one way of lookin' at it."

Rifling through my pockets, she pulls out a pack and shoves another stick in my mouth.

I bend my head over slightly and inhale with a dying flame just inches from my side.

"Alright." I sigh. "I'll be fine. Get me up."

Two hands reach down and pull me upward as I struggle to my feet. "Thanks Dave."

But before he can speak a word, the four of us are interrupted by the sound of an announcer type of voice.

"Welcome ladies and gentlemen!"

"The hell?" I approach the subway car, twisting my arm around and pulling the smoke from my mouth with two fingers.

Now, given the chance to speak, David chimes in. "Careful there, we don't know what's inside."

"Please." It says again. "Board with caution and have your ticket stubs ready."

I reach for my rifle, which had recently fallen to the ground around the time this thing had arrived and strapped it, again, across my body.

"Stay close guys, I'm gonna take a chance here." Noticing, by the gate, as I look back, the undead stand there, staring and ogling with hungry drool dripping from their mouths.

Stepping inside, the lights flicker and buzz, I check left and right, no sign of anyone or anything.

"You sure about this?" Meryl hesitates, "I mean, it did just come out of nowhere."

Following me anyway, regardless, the three of them stand behind me.

"I don't exactly see any other options, unless you wanna go down onto the tracks with this thing rumbling around." Extinguishing my smoke on the bottom of my boot.

"Right." Rob pushes by, grabbing a ceiling hook, rifle in hand. "Wonder where it's headed?"

"Please ensure that all hands and feet are secure inside of the car as we begin our departure."

The door snaps and latches itself shut.

"Nice." David pats a hand against the glass of the doors window. "We're locked in."

I turn, forgetting for a moment, that I'd just severely injured myself and roughly brush my arm against a tall standing seat. "FUCK!"

"Careful there, buddy." Rob snickers.

David then looks around nervously. "I sure hope this ain't some kind of crazy trap." Eyes watching as the area we'd just left begins to drift away.

Back before all of this, I'd take this subway almost every day. It was a habit, just like the one o'clock lunch at McDonalds.

Ghosts from the past emerge within my subconscious – someone on their cellphone, jabbering away. A woman tends to her child, wailing and crying and a handful of disdainful, wrinkled foreheads.

Or maybe the loss of blood was starting to get to me, losing my balance, head swimming with dizziness – Meryl puts an arm around my back and stops my collapse.

"Whoa, take it easy." Propping me up. "No intensive thought for a while, okay?"

Her recent attentiveness to me had risen to be questionable. She wasn't really like this before, as a cop, but I suppose there are stranger things amidst.

The car begins to move faster and faster, a blur of nothing on the outside passes by.

"Hey, announcer guy!" Rob shouts. "Where we going?!"

And of course, it doesn't answer.

The car shakes back and forth as we move through the bowels of Manhattan, unaware of where we're headed or even why. I close my eyes for a minute or two and in my head, I say, 'I don't know what you're doing. I don't know who you are, but just stop with the whispering shit, you're drivin' me nuts.'

Here I am, talking to myself.

Driving you crazy is the least of my or your concerns. I told you not to board that train.

Still talking with my own little voice in my head, 'Why? You're connected to that thing from the bank, aren't you?'

Maybe.

I open my eyes and see the three of them staring at me as the thoughts in my mind grow silent.

Meryl raises an eyebrow. "What'd I just tell you?"

Squinting and leaning back against the train's inner wall, I grind the inside of my thumb against the area below the index finger of my right hand, bone meeting bone and creating a callous rough edge that wears away at the skin.

"You nervous or something?" She asks.

"No."

Yes.

"We will soon reach our destination, ladies and gentlemen, please ensure that all baggage is secure as you prepare for departure."

We're suddenly in what looks like a clearing, a forest of fog, no longer underground; Maybe Central Park, maybe nowhere at all.

"This don't look like Brooklyn." Rob states the obvious, rubbing the back of his neck. "We're stuck here forever, aren't we?"

We come to a complete stop and the doors shoot open.

"You have exactly sixty minutes before we leave for our next destination. Enjoy your stay."

"I'm not going out there." Meryl backs up and seems intent on staying inside, while biting the bottom of her lip.

The fog from the outside begins to envelope the inside and before I can tell what exactly is going on, my feet stand in soaking wet grass and I lose sight of the other three.

"Meryl?" I call out.

No answer.

"Rob, David?"

Again, not a whisper, not a sound.

A jolt of prickly needle pain climbs through my arm. "This keeps gettin' better and better." Drawing my pistol and holding it in front of me, I move forward.

Grass turns to blacktop and the fog withers away. An odd looking Jeep sits parked by a sidewalk, in front of a house covered in brick and green vine.

Something feels familiar like nostalgia or deja vu but I can't quite place my finger on it.

The sign toward the end of the street reads Fourth, intersected by another named Bridge.

"What kind of illusion is this?" I ask myself, looking around for signs of anyone or anything else.

The lights at the second floor windows of the building gleam yellow and a soft crying or whining echoes through.

"Hey!" Aiming my gun at the house. "Anyone in there!?"

I feel something poking and prodding at the back of my brain and I almost stumble over for a moment, blinking and shaking my neck. "The hell?"

The little voice in my head questions reality; Nothing seems real.

My feet begin to move without my command, up and over a stone stairway, passing a window on the side of the house to my left. Engraved on a wooden door is a symbol, in a circular pattern. The shape resembles a crooked smiley face, with jagged teeth and triangular eyes. This, I'm not quite sure I'd seen it before, but again, with the familiarity of things, I felt as if I had.

The door invites me in, swinging open with rotten floorboards underneath its sweep.

The walls, the floor, the ceiling – everything has a dead, grey looking tint to it. Kind of like a bad dream, but it feels real; More real than riding a train from underneath the streets that somehow emerges atop, in a park.

"Dante." A woman speaks my name, coughing and whimpering. "What are you doing?!"

I can barely hear the voice, but whoever she is, she uses my name.

"This doesn't make any fuckin' sense." I say to myself, moving through the living room, to a dining room all decorated in old silverware and pottery, pictures on the wall of things from another period of time; Bands from the eighties, pictures of men with microphones and smack dab in the middle, a table, set for lunch or dinner.

You don't recognize this?

"How could I?"

Keep moving.

"Get down on your knees!" My own voice says from beyond a stairwell at the end of a hallway, which I climb with every bit of caution.

Study your surroundings carefully and remember, Dante, remember.

"The hell am I supposed to remember?"

I pass a bathroom, door hanging wide open, through the window by the toilet. I see the streets, filled with undead observers.

Before reaching a bedroom at the very back of the hallway, I hear a loud thump and the "click-clack" sound of a pump action shotgun. Do I really wanna open this door?

"Stop it, Dante, you don't know what the fuck you're doing!" She yells out in desperation.

"I know goddamn well what I'm doing, you two-faced fuckin' bitch!"

I feel a raging ball of anger building inside of me, not quite knowing why, but five of my knuckles burst through the doorway, only to see an older copy of myself, with a blurred face and wishy-washy as if I were drunk.

With a shotgun pressed hard against her chin, my copy sits there, finger on the trigger, ready to blow this woman's head clean off.

"This is impossible." I say, eyes definitely not believing.

Really? Is it impossible that you're hearing my voice?

"I don't even know who or what you are."

These two people, me or not, hadn't noticed me entering the room, yet they both still sit here – tears streaking down the woman's face and a man filled with anger and pain in eyes I couldn't possibly make out. He holds this person's life in his hands, but why? For what reason?

Alright, I'm going to make this simpler, since you've got quite the memory problem.

"Make what simple?"

Somebody close to you is going to die, somebody very close to you.

"What? Who?" I think for a moment. "Meryl?"

The whispering voice chuckles and speaks, *No, most definitely not Meryl.*

"Then who the hell is this?!" Looking around. "Who the fuck are you anyway?!"

That doesn't matter right now. What does matter is that you remember, so we can stop this charade already and move on with the future.

"The future?"

"Dante, I don't deserve this shit." Words sneak out of the woman's lips, "abusing me and threatening me, you don't even have a goddamn motive." She grabs the barrel of the shotgun, holding it even tighter against her chin. "Pull the trigger, and see what happens."

"I can't watch this crazy shit."

Tell me, how do you feel about Meryl?

"Meryl?" I furrow my eyebrows, "she's a good woman, why?"

A good woman, you say? That's all?

"I don't understand, why are you asking me this?"

Nevermind.

I look around, the door behind me no longer exists. Only a window stands between me, these two visions and my way, hopefully, back to the other three.

Not having any interest in seeing this person's head turned inside-out, I fire a single bullet at the glass, push through what I think will be solid material and I pass directly though, like a ghost.

I shield my fall with my arms as I land down again on the grass, wet with mud caking up around me as I slide to a stop.

"AHHHH!" I roll over and grab my bad arm, grumbling. "Dammit!"

I seem to do a lot of falling down.

In front of me, about two-hundred yards away, crouches Meryl, firing sniper rounds off into what I can only imagine are the undead.

"Meryl!" I shout outward toward her, pulling myself up through the returning fog and rusted metal grating that the ground becomes.

Down below, beneath my feet, fire plumes and erupts with screams like a tidal wave of desolation.

This, also, is similar to something else – I know I've seen this before. In my head I see a gargantuan monster, the one I had put down with a single bullet between the eyes, reappearing for a moment, charging with furious might.

"Harrisburg?" I wonder, but nothing really resembles anything that I can remember from my hometown.

"Dante!" She suddenly notices me stumbling back and forth, staring in awe at the lake of ember, running to my side, still aiming at whatever she'd been firing at.

"Where'd you come from?!" Looking up at me with innocent eyes and frantic, trying to keep focus on two different things.

"What do you mean?" I point behind to where I thought would still be the house I'd come from. "Through the window of that building."

"What?" A confused look paints itself across her face. "There's no building there."

I shake my head again. "What. The. Fuck."

"We don't have time for this D, we're gonna be brain food here!"

She pulls me over to where she'd originally been standing and points in the direction of a looming horde with the scope of her rifle.

"Holy hell." I aim with the assault rifle, unslung from my back.

"They're moving slowly, but this is our only path."

"Our only path?" I say, noticing large and barbed wire fences, broken down concrete and pieces of buildings scattered all over that had a striking resemblance to things you'd see on Wall Street; Big electric scrolling signs and visions of important looking business men in penguin outfits – all completely blocking our way, aside from the bridge that led forward, into the undead.

The scenery began to change rapidly, parts of Harrisburg become Manhattan, and the sky melts downward, in red and black and the eyes of the dead beyond gleam with an angry yellow.

When all of this began, we had come to the conclusion that there were two types of zombie – the runners and the shufflers. In other words, people who'd recently turned and had not hit that rigor window and the others that had.

But even after seventy two hours, upon hitting said window, they'd, strangely, return to full agility. The science of it is mind boggling.

"So we gotta blow all our ammunition, huh?" I grit my teeth, pacing backward and letting an eye shift over to Meryl as she reaches into a larger pocket toward the knee of her pant leg. "What do ya got there?" I ask inquisitively.

"A surprise for our little bastard friends up ahead, probably stock brokers, too." She pulls the pin of a hand grenade. "Stand back and keep your weapon ready."

She means business.

I count to three in my head, her arm swiveling back and lobbing north.

The gore and all the madness, it was starting to bother me less and less. I'd learned to turn off the emotions – to almost completely desensitize myself to it. I pretend they aren't even human, pretend they're rabid animals ripe for the slaughter.

Yet, it isn't really much different than picking teeth and skull fragments off the side of a freeway or pulling a steering wheel out of someone's forehead.

"Keep moving." She slings the rifle over her shoulder and pulls a revolving six shooter from a holster on her left hip. "Blow right through whatever remains." Her feet peddle on forward as I follow.

Their faces glare through a hole in the fog, reaching arms out and growling, groaning, stiffly marching – Then, in a cloud of red, limbs and other random body parts flail into the air as a path clears directly through the center of them.

Passing swiftly, I feel arms and fingernails groping at my sides, but I don't look – I keep moving. Bullet after bullet, I discharge ammunition into anything standing in my way. You can hear the rotating chamber of Meryl's weapon going off to my left, running out of shots as we come to the opposite side, or at least, a clearing.

And there it is, doors hanging wide open; the train. It welcomes us to uncertain safety.

My legs burn, my knees feel as if they'll give out any moment. Pushing and pushing as the ground behind us shakes violently, giving way to the recent explosion and spilling downward into the sea of the dead – but we'd made it. Skidding into the compartment of the subway car and collapsing against the wall.

Together we let out a sigh of relief and gasp for air.

"Shit, I'm not doin' that again." Looking over. "You're not bitten, right?"

Shaking her head, unable to speak, she quickly looks over her own body and finds nothing alarming or immediately threatening.

I cough hysterically in a fit of nicotine rage.

"You," Catching her breath. "Should really quit smoking."

With a chuckle, I wheeze, "Nah." Pulling one from my pocket and lighting up.

"You know, if you're stressed, I know a way…"

But before she can finish her sentence, Rob comes hurdling through the sliding doorway.

"Goddammit!" Turning and firing into the fog, saliva shooting out of his mouth. "This dude's trying to kill us!"

"No shit." I say. "We aren't exactly dealing with friendly, non-homicidal people here."

I hesitate for a moment.

"Or 'things' for that matter."

He eyes Meryl and I. "Where's Dave?"

The doors slam shut and, once again, latch.

"Ah for cryin' out loud!" I jump up, peering through a circular window. "I don't fuckin' see him!" And I don't see any sign of anything at all, nothing, no one. "We've lost him."

I hadn't come into this thinking everyone would make it out alive. It's the state of mind you gotta have for this line of work, but dammit, I've got luck like a homeless guy has teeth.

"Were you two chased by some kind of winged demon things?" Rob asks, shaking his hands in front of us.

We rattle our heads and I say. "No, not exactly."

"More of those undead things." Meryl doing her best zombie impression, arms out in front of her, eyes all crossed.

"You're not the slightest bit concerned here, are you?" He accuses.

The glass behind Rob cracks and a pair of bloodied hands slide away.

"Help!" Screaming in terror as he's ripped limb from limb, David can be seen being dragged away into the night.

"Bastards!" Rob shouts angrily, smashing out the glass and finishing off the magazine of his weapon. "Well, now it's just the three of us; you two aren't gonna do anything?!"

"I'll tell ya what I'm going to do…" The train starts again with blinding speed, moving forward to wherever our next destination would be, passing streets and alley ways of what once was Manhattan. Erect, in the place of skyscrapers and corporate buildings, stand brimstone like structures and ivy-woven husks, riddled with strange looking bits of technology and markings.

In the sky, with a blur, clouds of smoke billow from each of the tallest monoliths.

"I'm stopping this fucking train."

"All passengers please brace yourselves, for we will be arriving at our final destination in t-minus sixty seconds."

Taking hold of a passenger seat on both my right and left, to keep from falling down, I begin moving toward the front of the train, to the controls.

"Dante, what are you going to do?" Meryl stands against the tin-can wall of the cabin, looking at me like I'm nuts.

"I just told you." Turning my head back for a second. "Hold onto something."

The conductor's cabin's only another car up. I have to pass through the link that connects each, but once through, it'd be smooth sailing.

With one foot after the other, I move with all of my strength. We seem to be going increasingly faster with each step that I make. Passing through the link, behind me, the doors jut shut, locking me away from Meryl and Rob, but I'd be there in less than a minute.

"Thirty seconds. We hope that you've enjoyed your tour of the city."

If you look through the windows, all you see are flashing lights and a haze of brown and red. It has to be moving hundreds and hundreds of miles per hour.

As I make my way into the cabin, I immediately notice that no one stands at the controls. No one "steering" or whatever you do in these things. It was navigating all by itself.

But who the hell was talking?

"What are you doing?" The phantom voice questions.

"I'm shutting you down." Pulling my pistol from its holster.

"Fifteen seconds."

The panels blink red and green and they spark from what seem like a few short circuits. The emergency brake won't budge, and this was expected, letting go of my grasp on the steel handle as I aim in no particular direction.

I squeeze the trigger and let a few bullets fly, metal and wires spill out and an electrical current shoots me back about five feet.

"Gggrraaahhh!" I jitter and jolt for a moment as my vision skews from the shock and the lights overhead shut down.

"I've done it," I gasp.

"Five se…c…"

The voice distorts, fading away, the train not slowing down or giving me much of any kind of control, even though I'd have no idea how to control it in the first place.

Maybe I just doomed Rob, Meryl, and myself.

Ahead, maybe one hundred feet or so sits a wall, tall and red brick. We'd obviously passed the supposed final destination, but now we were speeding toward a head-on collision.

Rob pounds on the door behind. "What the hell did you do?! We're going to crash!"

I look back for a moment as I dive to the floor. "Get down and grab hold of your ass!"

The subway train shakes and rattles, the whining sound of the wheels and the electric motors failing deafen as we all brace for impact – or at least I hope the others had followed suit.

We burst through and my ears ring from the sound of metal compacting and brick crumbling against one another. Too low to the ground to see what's going on or where we're headed, feeling almost weightless, as we glide through the air.

Then it tosses us around like laundry in a dryer, the tin can rolling, throwing me up, then down, to the left and back again, until it finally stops and all goes silent.

Through squinting eyes and fading consciousness, I see that strange symbol again, painted across a wall through a broken window, random fires in the distance and an approaching mob of real, live people that look as though they've come straight outta some post-apocalyptic movie – dressed in leather and metal, choker collars and strange silver jewelry.

"Get him by the legs and tie 'im up." One of them mutter.

"What about the woman and the other guy?" Another asks.

"The same, take 'em to the pit, the bosses are gonna wanna see this shit."

Before blacking out, I hear a voice and the feeling of hot breath approaching my right ear. "You hear that cop? We gonna have some fun wit ya…"

10

The Morning and the Mourning

A hand brushes my forehead, soft fingertips trailing down the bridge of my nose and a pair of lips touch mine. A cool breeze brushes over my exposed body and shivers run like a wave down my spine.

"So many scars Dante…"

Julianna's voice breaks the silence.

My eyes burst open. "MERYL!!"

Obviously perturbed by my words, she looks at me in angered confusion. "And who's Meryl?"

"Ah, no, nobody, I was, "Hesitating, searching around the room with my eyes for my smokes. "I was dreaming of another memory."

"Oh, of the evacuation, I assume?" She bends down to the floor from her sitting position next to me on the bed, picking up my pack and sliding a single cigarette out. "So what'd you do? Have a wild ride during the apocalypse?"

She places it into my mouth as I struggle to bring myself out of my grogginess. Mumbling, I say, "No, at least I don't think so, if you mean what I think you mean. We were on a train, a strange, strange subway ride."

In her other hand, my rusty lighter flips open and sparks into flame, holding it there in front of my face just long enough to get a quick puff.

"A subway ride, huh?" Tossing my lighter to the bed stand. "You happen to traverse Brooklyn? I was born there, if you even remember that."

With another blissful inhale of smoke, I reply, "No, we ended up somewhere through a brick wall, lying face down in the dirt."

"Really? And then?" Placing each of her hands on my knees.

"I don't know, we were apprehended." Cigarette dangling from my hand, almost ashing on the floor. "But we were riding through the streets on this thing and the guy who captured me taunted me, all like…" And in my best impression of his voice. "We gonna have fun wit ya cop."

Reaching for an ashtray and placing it below my smoke before it dirties her old, brown colored carpet. "How the hell was a subway train going through the streets of Manhattan?"

"Hey, what's with all the questions? It's not like I was just there a few seconds ago, I don't remember every single exact fucking detail." Taking another few puffs.

"Uhm, you know what, never mind, I don't want to know." Having a slight change of heart.

"I'm going downstairs to make some coffee, turn on my music, will you?" She asks, feeling most likely frustrated with my callous attitude.

"Sure thing, babe."

It was the same almost every morning – crank on that same, tired old rock from the eighties and go on with her ritual.

But this morning, it's different. I hadn't the faintest idea of how I'd even gotten home, although it's not like I have the greatest memory in the world, still…

Standing up, I shuffle to the wall mounted stereo and with a thumb, I depress the "on" button and blasting through the speakers comes one of her favorite damn songs. Something about women and train in downtown Manhattan.

I hadn't been expecting that, my head beating like a million tiny explosions were going off within.

The bathroom seems miles away. Walking down the hall to empty a bladder that sits painfully filled to its brim and ready to friggin' burst. I always have this problem.

She shouts from beyond the stairwell, barely audible over the loud sound of piss hitting toilet water and her music. "You want sugar, cream?!"

"Black's fine!" Zipping up a pair of jeans, I toss the cigarette into the toilet and scuffle down the stairs. "You know, it's funny we both lived in the area of New York, but never met until the war."

There she sits at a small wooden table in the kitchen, blocking a door that leads to the backyard, singing along to the lyrics of her song.

I sit down at an empty chair where an old tan and porcelain coffee cup greets me.

"You know, Dante, maybe we did meet and you just don't remember." She stops singing and takes a sip out of her cup.

Bittersweet magma trickles down the back of my throat, thinking for a moment. "Nah, I doubt it." Then I focus on her eyes. "But there's something that bothers me. How'd I get home? Last night."

"What do you mean?" She wrinkles her eyebrows. "You drove here. You came inside, made passionate love to me and then we fell asleep in each other's arms."

"Really?"

"What, you don't believe me? That's a little upsetting and disappointing, although I can't really understand how you wouldn't remember." Placing her cup down. "You do trust me, right?"

For a moment I see the strange vision from my memory, of a woman much like Julianna, down on her knees atop a bed, with a shotgun against her chin.

"Of course I do."

She sits back and grins. "Good. Wouldn't want to think you're considering marrying someone you don't trust."

An uncomfortable silence settles in.

"So, tell me more about this Meryl person." Picking up her coffee cup again and drinking slowly, like a judge in a courtroom.

A subject switch; I'll play along, I think.

"Just a sec, have you checked the generator fuel levels?" Taking another sip, I raise an eyebrow.

"Yea, they're fine, now answer my question." She persists.

"Look, I really don't see the importance, I doubt she's even still alive." Sort of hoping for the opposite.

"What makes you think she's not alive, I mean, you're here, aren't you?" Resting her cup against her chest, she sits back in a reclined position. "Maybe that's how you survived all of it to begin with, the strength of a woman, you know?"

She may be right, she may be wrong, but something tells me she's simply grasping for the sake of grasping.

"I really have no idea."

Lighting another cigarette, I blow smoke off to the side, away from her face.

"Chain smoker…" With disdain, chugging the rest of her coffee, she says again. "Now I want you to tell me, what happened between you two? Stop dodging the question."

I could tell she was preparing for an argument and when that happens, nothing stops her.

"As far as I can remember, so far, nothing. Not a damn thing happened between us." I puff, grinding away at the side of my hand again, like before. "Maybe we flirted, maybe I cared about whether or not she lived or died. I mean, come on, you cling to those sorts of things in a crisis situation."

"Sorta like Stockholm syndrome." She ignorantly shoots back.

"No, nothing like that, I wasn't being held hostage or anything." Then I think for a moment. "Not by her, at least."

"You know what, I'll ask again in the future when you *do* remember." Sitting upward and resting a hand on the table.

"I don't understand why it's so important…"

My eyes move off to the side, a little angry.

"Where're Ray and Paul, by the way?" She triggers a slight jump in the rhythm of my heart as I snap into present events and the realization that I'd almost completely forgotten about the current state of things here in the 'burg.

"Oh shit, that's right!" Putting my smoke out in the puddle of coffee left in the bottom of my cup. "They're fuckin' gone. Went missing last night after we received a breach in the wall; You didn't hear any explosions or gunfire?"

Her eyes go wide. "I felt a little bit of a quake, but didn't think much of it." Going from annoyed to worried. "How in the world did you lose them?"

"It was a mess, without going through all of the nasty little details – We split up, due to our loss of communications, to deal with the undead that'd begun rampaging through the streets of inner Harrisburg." Giving her the shorter version as I stand up, going through the refrigerator, finding nothing of snack-value.

"Those god forsaken demons were in *this* city, last night?!" She stands as well, with her face and body an inch away from mine, as I turn from an empty refrigerator. "I was here alone and could've been eaten by one of those things and you were out doing what?!"

"I was doing my job!" Lowering my eyebrows toward her and placing my hands on her forearms. "We're standing here, right now, having this conversation, because I did my job. And those things, as you referred to them, are not demons. They were people, like us. You haven't seen half the shit that's out there." I grunt. "Besides, it's not like you don't have any combat experience."

I probably shouldn't be patronizing her, but this was beginning to get old, with the argument and what-not.

"Don't talk to me like I don't know what's going on out there!" Pushing me back a bit. "Remember, I pulled you outta that fucking city, we've all experienced the horror!"

Releasing her from my grip. "You're right, you're right. I'm sorry. Look, they could still be alive; I'm meeting the administrator George at the airstrip today. I'm taking a chopper outside to see if I can find any sign of 'em."

She lowers her head. "So you're going to put your life on the line, again? You've got a death wish, don't you?"

She may have been annoyed and angry with me, but it was obvious that she also cared.

A woman's mind works in mysterious ways.

"Jules, I've said this before. I put my life on the line every single day, so maybe someday we can all live in peace, once more. If those guys are out there, I'm not only going after them, just because they're my friends, but because they're my team and we can't spare any extra bodies to fill the gap, not anymore."

Placing my hand on her chin and raising her face up toward mine, seeing her almost ready to break into tears. "Everything'll be fine. Don't give up on me, I…" Choking for a moment, I always have trouble with these words. "Love you. That's why I asked *you* to marry me. Regardless of the past and whomever I may have come in contact with."

There, I said it.

"I love you too, Dante." She sniffles a bit and shows a half-smile. "I don't mean to get so upset, it just gets so uncontrollably stressful sometimes, you know?"

"I know."

I know that better than most.

"If they're out there, I'll find them." In a last ditch effort to lighten the mood. "Why don't you cook up something good for dinner tonight?"

"What? I don't *usually* make something good?" She lets out a chuckle. "And don't say that, you're only setting me up for disappointment."

She seemed more of a pessimist today than any other.

"Don't say that." Embracing her with both arms, pressing her body against mine. "I'll bring 'em back."

"How about you just make sure you come back alive and that'll be good enough." Pecking me on the lips. "And try to avoid the injuries and the scarring." Glancing at my chest and arms as she backs away to remove my cup from the table.

"Hey, each one of these has some kind of story behind it, something to tell our kids about someday when all of this is over."

Moving a finger up and down one of my newest scars, which hadn't been there previously – the one on my left arm where that piece of shrapnel had opened me up. Which is weird, 'cause that could mean so many different things – a whole can of worms I didn't want to bother opening.

All according to the plan, lover-boy.

Not again.

"Children you say? You want *me* to have your children?" She stops dead in the middle of the kitchen.

"No, I'm just marrying you because I enjoy the companionship." I put my hands on my waist. "Of course I want to."

She simply shoots me a smile and continues placing random things into the sink.

Children, I can't even imagine having to raise children in this kind of world.

"By the way, since you don't remember anything anymore, your suit is in the living room, along with your coat, as always." Scrubbing at a cup. "You better get going so you can be back here faster. I'll think about that children thing."

And that's it, I'd found a way to distract her chaotic mind.

While moving to the living room, I catch a glimpse of two shadows sitting at the dining room table, Ray and Paul, glaring in anger – I shake my head and continue, stripping myself of my jeans and suiting up.

Then it hit me like a bullet to the face, tucked away in the pocket of my jacket, Jack's badge.

"How'd this get here?" I think to myself, pulling pants over my legs, strapping holsters and putting each arm through the sleeves of an under-armor type of garment.

I place it on the wooden entertainment center, which holds an unusable television, checking each of my pistols, locking and loading, sliding them snuggly behind my back.

She must've found it and thought it was mine or something.

Who really knows anything anymore, right?

After fully dressing myself, I make my way back to the kitchen.

"See ya tonight babe, keep the doors locked, bolts latched and windows tightly closed." With a kiss accented by tongue. "Stay safe."

"Love ya, D."

People love using the first letter of my name.

Not many get away with it either.

Out the door I stroll, to the Jeep, which sits exactly in the same spot it had in my memory.

"Well then…" I say to myself. "I guess she's tellin' the truth."

The morning, yellow and orange sun, had done part of its job with the initial first layer of snow that covers the ground. Pieces of the sidewalk could be seen, along with maybe a patch here and there of the road.

A cool breeze shoots through me; that kind of cold that makes it *too* cold to snow, where the roads turn to ice and the trees turn a sparkly white.

The inside of the Jeep feels worse, fumbling around with the thermostat and cranking it up all the way as I hit the clutch and the engine turns over.

In the rearview, down the street at Bridge, a Pax unit walks by, nonchalantly dangling their weapons around and chatting about something inaudible. I imagine them conspiring about the next attack and where it may be.

What happened last night was, technically, an attack. Considering the fact I'd found Jack's badge on the scene, regardless of what that may mean, it could possibly be considered an attack by ZeroFactor.

If that's true though, I'd count on another attack as much as I'd count on the undead being flesh hungry mongrels even ten years from now.

Regardless, things seem under control for the moment.

It'd only take about ten minutes or less to get to the airstrip. It wasn't exactly typical though. In the past it'd been used for smaller aircraft and private jets. Directly beside it sits an old Giant grocery store and behind that, an apartment complex of some kind I'd never even bothered visiting.

Across the street sits a sprawling trailer park that completely lines the edge of the road, where I remember an old man, with no legs, would sit and wave at motorists as they pass by. That was until he'd suspiciously vanished, out of the blue. One day he just stopped coming outside, I'd always wondered what had happened to him.

Maybe he passed on, or maybe it just got old, sitting there, being acknowledged by someone maybe once every blue damn moon.

But anyway, the aforementioned airfield is now used as one of the two areas that we land our cargo planes, the other being Harrisburg International Airport. Of course, we also have a few helicopters in reserve, for situations just like this one.

More or less like the situation I'd witnessed last night.

"Morning, Dante!" George, all bright and chipper, walks away from the conversation he'd been holding and greets me as I pull into the entrance.

Arm hanging out of the window, I grasp and shake his hand, asking, "Any of our guy's manage to smuggle in anymore smokes? I'm about out."

"Yeah, yeah." Pulling a fresh and sealed pack from his pocket. "I saved this just for you."

As fresh as they could be, I guess. Most of them came from ravaged convenience stores and gas stations. I know this, because I used to be one of the units that went on these scavenge runs. That was years ago; raiding liquor stores, getting piss drunk and pulling mannequins into the streets from clothing stores, shooting at them like stationary targets.

But gunfire would always give away our position, although we never really worried about that – Never lost anyone under my command.

Before tucking the pack away into my front pocket, I tear it open and light up, pulling hard on the emergency brake, shutting the vehicle off and stepping out.

"So what're you gonna do, Dante?" Itching his scalp, a mop of half-groomed hair.

"You get one of our guys to fly me up and out of the city, we circle the wall and hopefully find something." I explain, watching another unit prepare for takeoff to bring in some more scavenged items.

"And if you don't?" He speaks over the sound of jet engines, seeming a little less optimistic than usual.

"I haven't exactly considered not finding anything yet and what I'll do if that happens." Pointing at him and talking louder as the aircraft, maybe a hundred feet away, begins to race down the strip. "Just make sure we've got a full tank; I'm not coming back empty handed."

"Whatever you say, they're your unit!" He shouts, "Follow me!"

Through a small building, lined with plaster and dirty-white tiling, to the other side, where the main strip lays, a handful of helicopters wait.

"What are these again?" Examining the one with a pilot standing to its side. "Lifeline choppers?"

"Yeah!" He says enthusiastically. "You guys used to use these for high-speed chases and critically ill or injured people!"

"Of course, I remember those days." Giving him a grin as we approach the man who'll be flying me out.

"This is Kenneth." A hand on his back. "He'll be your tour guide for the day."

A skinny little guy, much like Steve, covered in flight gear, with a helmet – only his beady, brown eyes are visible.

"Hey!" He reaches out for my hand. "Nice to meet ya!"

I shake reluctantly. "Yeah, yeah, we ready to go?"

"As ready as she'll ever be, sir!"

"And at that, I leave you two to your mission, good luck!"

George wanders off back to the building where a few men in suits seem to be waiting for him.

Opening the side opposite the pilot seat, he stops me. "Put that cigarette out, please, no smoking."

"So this is gonna be one of *those* days, huh?" I toss it to the side. "Let's go then."

Sitting next to him, in the cockpit, I feel a bit awkward. Mostly because he seems a little too overjoyed about the whole situation.

As the blades begin to spin and we lift off of the ground, I brace myself for incoming small-talk.

Leaning his head to the side as the ground and the people below turn to ants, he says, "So how long you been here, man?"

"Six years." I reply abruptly, as I rest my chin in my hand. "Just take us over the wall and we'll circle around."

"I know, I know…" He assures me. "So you kill a lot of people huh?"

Ahead you can see the edge of the road and the grass where an extremely tall, chain-link fence stands topped with layers and layers of barbed wire. With scraps of metal and rust welded to not only keep it together, but to keep the extra violent dead from breaking through.

Or even things like what my unit and I had killed the night before.

I keep my eyes toward the window with a hand holding a pair of headphones over my head and respond in a slightly perturbed manner. "I've done things you wouldn't even be able to imagine. I fought a war we were sure to lose, I assisted in erecting this wall and I serve in the name of the people to protect what lives we have left – don't ask me if I kill a lot of people."

An awkward silence and a grunt follow his retort. "That's not what I meant, Christ, you're a little damn sensitive."

I always have trouble with new people; My personality isn't exactly easy to take. But you'd be this way too, if people that were apparently close to you vanished and you couldn't even remember why or how or even the reason behind your own survival.

"And how long have you been with Pax?" I decide to prod.

We pass over the wall and leave all remnants of the living behind, replaced by a scorched Earth and a battleground of death.

"A coupla years." He says, staring down at a blanket of dead grass and white-petrified forests of trees. "Been scavenging for a while, looking at getting myself a nice little home down there around Strawberry Square maybe."

Floating above the destruction, you almost feel safe, as if nothing can harm you.

"It's not like you gotta buy a place or make rent payments, what're you waiting for?" I reach for my fresh pack of smokes in my front pocket.

"Hey!" He jolts right. "No smoking."

"Humph." Sliding it back inside. "How about you just watch where we're going."

We'd passed over Newberry and began to make our way over the Susquehanna where the water is split by a make-shift damn, a mile or two before Three Mile Island.

"What're we looking for anyway? Aside from rotten corpses, bones and dirt?" He asks, diverting from my original question, tilting the chopper to the left as we pass over inactive steam towers.

Their concrete hulls are much more gigantic and foreboding in person – nothing but darkness reaches out from within.

"Keep an eye out for two men, hopefully alive and well." Thinking for a moment. "We'll most likely see them dug up in a foxhole somewhere along the wall."

Below, as we approach the shore of the opposite side of the river, you can see fallen piles of wood and structure, towns that used to stand years ago, the dead shambling around just outside of our safe-haven.

"You think we'll ever find a cure?" He asks me, eyeing a pair of undead pounding against welded steel.

"To tell you the truth, even if any scientist, that may still be alive, finds one, we'd have two more considerably large threats to deal with, regardless." My eyes bouncing around seeing nothing but repeats of a scene from just before.

"Yeah, that's right." Straightening out the helicopter as we begin to approach the area close to the breach. "Where do those monsters come from, anyway? They're goddamn frightening, maybe more than the walking dead."

I think back to a memory I'd recently recovered; I remember what Nuhm De'Ara had said to me, the non-believability of it and all. "They're coming through an extremely small wormhole in Manhattan, from an unstable point in the Universe." Looking at him with all seriousness.

He chuckles and coughs on his own saliva, probably forgetting to swallow in his own hysterical laughter. "Oh yeah?" He grins wide, keeping eyes on what lies ahead. "And who the fuck told you that? That's the most retarded thing I've ever heard." Shrugging me off as if he thinks, of all things, a time and space rip would be impossible.

From above, it appears that a few units were easily able to patch the hole over night, but aside lays a giant pile of bodies, hopefully mostly just the re-dead, than the recently living.

Kenneth aims the helicopter downward.

"Hey, hey!" I reach for the controls. "Don't take us down lower!"

"Bah, just a pile of bodies." Realigning and pulling it back up.

"Shit, where'd you learn to fly again?" Eyes still searching, finding no sign, no trace of anything.

Go East.

"What?" I think to myself.

You want answers; Go East.

I didn't really wanna listen, in fact, I probably shouldn't, but I was beginning to get desperate.

"Alright, Kenny, before we call it a day and give up, we're going East." Pointing toward a highway that leads to the old Interstate seventy-eight."

"Why?" He asks, a confused look on his face – wrinkled forehead and squinty eyes.

I've…" Deciding to lie. "Got a hunch. Just follow the highway."

"Alright." Scratching his scalp, doubting my hunch. "If you say so."

The Blacktop Catacomb is what we call this road now. In the past it'd be littered with traffic in and out of New York and New Jersey; as the apocalypse began, this was a road of panicked civilians, all packed together in grid-lock.

If one should ever venture out of the walls, on foot, stupid as it may sound, this highway would be the last place you'd wanna go. Steel coffin after steel coffin holds shelter to whomever or whatever lingers around.

Which makes me wonder, the hell would Ray and Paul be doing trekking down this road for?

Maybe they've been captured.

We move at a high rate of speed, swooping down over the horizon at a slight angle, nose down. Our faces pointed at the ground, toward decayed bodies, rust, dead grass and an eerie silence, aside from our chopper's blades.

"Keep a close eye, gonna be hard as fuck to spot 'em if they're out here."

He nods in acknowledgement, seeming almost nervous or uneasy.

"This is pretty creepy, man." I'd been right in assuming so. "We're getting further and further away from Harrisburg, who the hell knows what's out here. I mean, I go on scavenging runs and all, but that's different."

"Give it five minutes; if we don't see anything…" Fingers to my chin, tapping one after the other. "We'll turn back."

"Yeah, alright." Lowering his head a little and squinting toward each scrap of twisted metal and unturned Earth. "You know I guess there ain't much to be afraid of, not like a zombie can shoot down a helicopter, right?"

I couldn't say it to him, I couldn't heighten his anxiousness, but the fact that the road had been this calm so far was, in fact, a bad thing.

There should at least be crowds of undead or something.

Out of my left eye, to the very corner of what I can see, something dark and blotted sits beneath a pile of rubble and brush, with a round-like object pointing to the sky – at us.

"Fuck! Kenneth!" I reach for his arms before he even notices what's going on.

With a blow that knocks our heads against the glass of the large circular window in front of us, a rocket-propelled grenade strikes the tail of the helicopter, followed by a piercing ringing tone that deafens my ears and sends my vision swirling around like a whirlpool – Kenneth upside down, arms dancing around and out of his seat beside me, squeezing his eyelids together and screaming in silence as we sail toward muddy dirt and bloodstained pavement.

11

ZeroFactor

Down on my knees, the Earth feels cold and wet; Thick and frayed rope cuts away at my wrists like sandpaper and black cloth covers my eyes, tightly wrapped around my head, pinching my ears.

"Welcome back to the show!" He pauses for a moment. "Officer Marcellus!"

A man's voice echoes from overhead as if he's standing maybe seven or eight feet above.

Hands wriggling behind me, I hear a voice. "Where…" Meryl's voice. "Where am I?"

The sound of overjoyed cheering erupts from all around and then he speaks again. "Ladies and Gents, what we have here are three absolute genuine survivors. Three people that thought they'd actually make it outta here alive!"

You can hear in his voice that he finds this quite amusing and laughter comes trailing behind his words from the same crowd.

I manage to find a bit of strength and speak. "Who the hell do you think you are?"

"Who am I?" Laughing in a psychotic tone. "Why, sir, I am but a pawn in the destruction of a world you most likely wish to protect."

Something wet pours down over my head, leaking around my scalp and into my eyes, burning, like highly potent alcohol.

"Drink up!"

Glass shatters somewhere off to my right.

"It'll surely be your last…"

Then a second, more familiar voice joins the conversation – a woman's.

"That's enough!"

The ground shakes as a pair of feet clomp down beside me and a hand grabs me by the head, pulling away at the handkerchief that blinds me.

I can't believe my eyes, blood boiling, infuriated with trembling anger, "Nuhm De'Ara, you fucking bitch."

She chuckles, hand to her mouth. "What? Surprised?" Taking me by the chin. "Jack sends his regards."

Breathing through clenched teeth, saliva dripping from my lips. "You leave him alone."

"Me? Leave *him* alone? This was *his* idea, dear Dante. Stupid, stupid man."

Taking her muddy boot, she slams it against my head and forces me down sideways into the dirt.

"And you probably thought we were both dead, huh?"

Looking up and analyzing my surroundings, I see that Rob, Meryl and I are bound and imprisoned within, at least, a ten foot hole. On the brim, at the top, men and women wearing leather and animal hide, with nails pointing sharp from their shoulders, they circle around like vultures.

Remembering the explosion at the police station. "Why *are* you alive?"

"That was supposed to be a distraction, was supposed to maybe even kill the four of you, although, I guess we only nabbed the one."

"But why?" I ask, angry and confused.

"Why?" She looks up. "Hey, he wants to know why!"

Another bout of laughter ensues.

"I want you to listen very, very closely." Kneeling down, her hair dangling in my face like a spider's web. "It's obvious that you think you're some kind of damn hero but I bet you never would've guessed that your own flesh and blood shares the ideals of hundreds and hundreds of men and women that actually *want* to see this God forsaken society torn apart."

Pulling me by the ear, up against the dirt wall, as I grunt in wrenching pain, she continues. "Yet the only reason you and your little unit are still alive, is because of him. He's having some trouble letting go, but he realizes that death is for your own good – humanities own good, and that's why we, ZeroFactor, exist."

She shoves a cigarette from my own pack into my mouth and lights me up. "Enjoy your last smoke."

"You can't do this! You can't just murder millions of people!" Inhaling forced nicotine.

Laughing again, she grins wide. "How many people you really think are left?"

Pulling the blind folds from Rob and Meryl, she looks over. "If you haven't noticed, there aren't any planes in the sky, no military coming to back you up, at least not yet."

Both Rob and Meryl sit dazed as if they've been drugged.

"By this time tomorrow, more than half of the world's population will have withered away, joining the ranks of the undead. Serving their purpose in Mother Nature's will and this 'other' world that converges with ours will begin to take control. You've witnessed it; You *did* ride a subway train here, quite dumbfounded by that, aren't ya?"

Spitting the cigarette out of my mouth, I retort. "And when exactly did Jack make this decision? Before, or after you brainwashed him?!"

Now standing directly in front of me. "He made this decision on his own, just like the rest of these people. Something buried deep within that only lives within a few of us, which is what allows ZeroFactor to exist."

"You're fucking insane." From the look on her face, you can tell I hit a nerve.

"Don't you pass judgment on me, Dante, you're no better."

Untying me and removing the rope from my wrists, she says, "It's true that there are certain groups of people left that are trying desperately to form some kind of alliance to save whatever they have left, but it is our plan to stop that, before it even has the chance to grow."

"Not if I stop you." Grinding my teeth, I stare right through her.

"That isn't going to happen." Pulling me forward. "Now, we're gonna play a little game. Here in New Brooklyn, there's a peculiar building. It behaves much like the subway train you recently experienced, reflecting yourself and your memories; Your visions, in physical form."

With a clenched fist, I swing at her face, but she grabs me by the arm and dodges with almost inhuman reflex. "Nuh uh, I don't think so." With a smile. "You'd hit a woman, wouldn't you?"

"Go to Hell, I'm not playing your game!"

"Go to Hell he says." Looking up toward the onlookers. "This *is* Hell." A tethered ladder unravels and falls over the ledge. "Now, join your friends and climb out of the pit, we've no time to waste."

"When this is all over, it'll be me who puts a bullet between your eyes. You wanna die, I can make that happen." I say in disgust as she shoves me over to Meryl and Rob, standing and slowly coming out of their trance-like state.

"The fuck's goin' on, Dante?" Rob whispers.

"We're getting' outta here."

I lead the two of them to the ladder, not anticipating or even capable of imagining what it is that I'll see upon emerging from the hole.

You're going to go inside of that building and you're going to see, not your own selves, but something else.

She, the ever mysterious voice, begins to ramble once more.

I'm going to show you something that you need to see, the other two will be excluded, if possible. She believes that this place will trap you; will kill you, but she has no control over it. None.

One rung after the other, we pull ourselves up; Meryl and Rob almost shaking uncontrollably in nervousness.

Is all of this a result of the apparent mistake I'd made? Was it really I who had unleashed some unstable piece of the Universe?

Upon reaching the top, the ground, I see a society of maniacs – Something that looks as though it'd been building and forming over the course of a few weeks, not mere hours. Then it becomes apparent that our ticket out of this city, the remaining law enforcement stationed at the Verrazano, were most likely captured or killed by these people, or simply evacuated without waiting for us to return.

But maybe there's still a chance.

Beyond burning buildings, torches, cages filled with the undead and endless walls of graffiti, sits Manhattan Island, where we'd originally come from. From where I stand, the city looks like the barbed teeth of an enormous monster, ready to swallow us and the rest of the island whole.

Countless groups of people stand by rusted barrels of fire, conversing amongst themselves and looking, pointing at the three of us as we come up to the street. Beneath what could only be the Brooklyn-Queens Expressway, which means that we are only a stone's throw from our destination – a few miles, maybe closer.

Upon further inspection, every single one of these people have a weapon of some kind. Making a run for it, now, would surely end our lives right here, right now. I'd rather not be that guy.

Nuhm De'Ara, still dressed in her all black uniform, skin tight, seeming even more-so than before, hops up and follows from behind.

"Right this way." She says as she passes by and commands that we follow, every so often one of the crazies lashing out at one of us.

Bringing us to a large building, which stands taller than most in the Brooklyn area. Above the entrance, painted in red, is a sign that reads, "The Tower" – An apartment building, or a condo, something along those lines. Windows and porches with sliding doors all jut outward in exactly the same style all over its red-brick face.

"You'll enter." Nuhm says. "And *maybe* you'll survive."

It's gotta be at least thirty stories high.

"I don't wanna do this." Meryl grabs me by the arm.

You can hear the bastards we left back by the pit, chanting, "Die! Die! Die!"

"What'd you do with our weapons?" I ask, realizing the three of us are completely defenseless.

I find myself wondering why she doesn't just put a bullet into each of our heads now.

"You'll find them inside, but don't even think of using those tiny little brains of yours." Pointing off randomly into the distance beyond the building. "We've got sharpshooters all over watching every nook and every single cranny."

So she's giving our weapons back, but she knows we'll most likely end up dead – this is the plan after all.

The door creaks as she pulls on it and she states, "Welcome to The Tower, have fun and if for some reason you *do* survive, well, that'll be a pleasant surprise."

Not another word is muttered; Only the chanting can be heard as we're pushed inside by men with axes and bayonets, stabbing at our backs.

The entrance is dimly lit with blinking panels on the ceiling, like a malfunctioning strobe light. I grab a familiar looking handgun as the door slams shut behind us and about six or seven locks are heard clanking and latching.

"I don't wanna fucking do this!" Meryl begins hysterically screaming, pounding on the door.

"Shh, shh." I pull her away and in close to myself. "It obviously doesn't matter if any of us wanna do this or not. Just get a weapon and stay close to me."

I think to myself. 'So when you gonna fix this situation?'

Another door separates us from our fate, with lettering painted in green, reading "The end."

"Hey man, it's old Betty!" Rob shouts in surprise, taking his shotgun and a few shells from an old plastic and peeling table.

"Keep it down." I cock back the barrel of my pistol and hold it in a downward position. "Grab one of those knives too." Which hang from the wall, along with assorted six-shooters and submachine guns.

Meryl cowers in the corner while we stand arming ourselves.

"This is like, a damn smorgasbord!"

I reach for one of the submachine guns, curiously eyeing Rob. "You're just a little too enthusiastic."

He shrugs, averting his eyes from mine, probably feeling a little embarrassed over himself.

Walking over to a nerve-wracked and shaking Meryl, not remembering a time I'd ever seen her like this, I offer my hand. "Take this, a rifle isn't gonna do you any good inside of a building."

Focusing on the corner of the room as she lifts herself up, she says, "Dante, I need to tell you something." Still shaking. "I'm claustrophobic as hell."

"Ah, come on, Meryl, it's not like the building's gonna collapse while we're inside of it or something." Rob taunts.

"Hey! Come on!" I shout, pushing him back toward the opposite doorway.

"Well sor-ry!" He scowls.

Putting both hands on her shoulders in an attempt to comfort her. "Listen, once we get outta here, we're gonna find that psycho and put an end to this. Then we leave and never look back. You don't have anything to be afraid of, alright?"

She questions me in a skittish tone, body standing stiff as a board. "And if we don't make it out of here?"

"No one, and I mean no one else is gonna die by my watch, we'll make it out, I promise you."

Looking up at me with gleaming eyes, she says something I hadn't even considered. "And what about Jack?"

"If what that woman says is true…" Hesitating for a moment. "Jack's gone. He's long gone and he won't be coming back."

"And this is something you're able to come to terms with?" Rob, in a bit more of a serious tone, asks from behind.

Without an answer for him, I push by, heading for the door; Making one final statement. "Whoever's left out there, they need hope. We've made it this far and we'll make it out of the city. You two, the three of us, we'll call ourselves PaxCorpus, Human Protection Unit."

A pep talk sure to bolster their morale.

Pressing against the locking mechanism of a metallic push-bar. "No zombies, no terrorists, no monstrous alien fucks are going to stop us, got that?"

The two of them nod and follow as I step forward into darkness.

"This is where it begins."

Well, you're right about that, at least.

My arms fall limp, insects crawl behind my eyelids and white flashes against black – I can feel my eyes jittering back and forth.

"Wha…" I try to speak. "What's happening?"

You need to see something, not to understand but to know. To know exactly what you're dealing with.

I'm no longer standing in a hallway beside Meryl and Rob. The air feels different, something like humidity, something wet lingers. My hands look different, my body feels strange. The clothing I wear isn't like anything I've seen before, adorned with bold white lettering. "Z.F."

There's a woman with pony-tailed hair sitting beside me, with the glow of a monitor reflecting her profile.

This monitor speaks in a deep tone and she listens carefully.

"The building you're sitting a few yards away from is one of their facilities."

She lifts her leather-gloved hand, stretches her fingers outward and then back into a clenched fist.

"All you have to do is break in, eliminate all research personnel and destroy the underground lab on the second floor basement level."

"And that's it, huh?"

I've heard this voice before.

And now I can see that I'm sitting in the back of some kind of vehicle; Leather black material lines the sides, the roof and the seats we sit in – I'm sitting next to her with a large assault type rifle across my lap.

"You got it." The screen flashes something I can't quite see. "We'll be in touch."

With her left hand she slaps down the laptop's lid and turns to face me, with the same initials across the front of her vest, "Z.F."

Holy shit.

"Nuhm De'Ara?!" I speak, surprised with a jolt of anger, in a voice that is not my own.

"What?" Looking at me for a moment, dumbfounded. "You alright, Jesse?"

My name isn't Jesse.

"Excuse me?" I put a hand to my face and feel unfamiliar skin.

This strange woman chuckles and speaks again. "Stop fuckin' around! Come on, this'll be a short one, then you can buy me that beer you owe me."

Fastening a military cap to her head and cocking back on her rifle, she kicks the vehicle's door open wide. "Little ol' Stephanie's gonna need your help here, J-J." Jokingly poking at my chest. "Get up, let's go!"

I shake my head a few times and think to myself. 'What in the hell's going on?!'

Play along, if not for her sake, your own.

Play along, with this genocidal bitch.

Alright, sounds logical.

Stepping outward into green grass that lines the side of a perfectly clean black-top, two lane road, I smell the air and it reminds me of spring; That wet asphalt aroma, just before a drizzling. Over the top of a mountain in the distance, the sun sets orange and spills red across the sky into grey clouds of a looming storm.

Three hundred clicks ahead of us sits a small facility of some type, unmarked and lined with shaded windows.

"The Intel says they've got pretty heavy security, so we'll need to give the side entrance a shot." Turning to speak for a moment and then hunching over and sprinting for the side of the building that shows a single doorway, flat as the wall it sits between.

I follow reluctantly, holding my newly acquired weapon in front, staring down its steel sight. 'Shoot her, shoot her, shoot her', I think over and over but the finger on the trigger of the gun in my hands won't allow me.

The booming roar of a commercial plane passes overhead as we place our backs to the wall of the building, just next to the, aforementioned, peculiar looking door. "You sure this is a door?" Deciding to humor whatever joke of a dream this is. "I mean it's fuckin' flat as hell, no knobs, nothin'."

She pulls a Velcro strap from her hip and slips an electronic device out of a small pocket, placing it against the door as it magnetically attaches itself.

"What's that?" I ask, curious, looking at her, still, in disbelief. Everything about her looked the same, aside from the impossibly blue eyes.

"You know what this is." She whispers. "It locates the locking mechanism of any door and by using powerful magnets within, detaches them from their grasp and opens whatever we're trying to break into."

Not a piece of technology I'd ever heard of.

The device whirs and beeps with a slight hum and on its single liquid-crystal display, numbers appear, counting down from twenty to zero, followed by a click.

"And we're in." She states, sounding satisfied, without a care in the world. "You got this right? I mean you don't seem all too well all of a sudden."

"Yeah, absolutely." I wave a hand. "I'm great. You take point."

Her eyes look into mine for a few seconds before she places a boot against the concrete.

"On my mark." Preparing to count down. "Three," the sun completes its departure from the skies. "Two." The clouds light up with a rumble. "One." She bursts through the door as it slides inward, effortlessly, as I follow right behind into a brightly lit hallway, narrow, with shutters on each side.

At the other end of the corridor is another door with a security panel hanging from the wall, just to its left.

"What're these shutters for?" I ask, running a hand down their rigged texture.

"Probably an extra security measure." She says, analyzing the touch-screen keypad, seeming to type random numbers in an attempt to get it open. "This is gonna be interesting."

The door we'd entered through slams shut and two red bulbs flash on the ceiling, without a sound, as if signaling an emergency.

"You wanna get that door open? This doesn't look good." I say, eyes bouncing back and forth, from wall to wall, as four shutters begin to slide open.

Though a small slit, I peer at what lies behind each of them; A few inches of space between one wall and another, brightly lit with red and black circular tubes, all pointing directly at us.

I look back at the woman who'd called herself "Stephanie", grabbing for another interesting looking tool from the back pocket of her pants.

"Seriously, hurry up." I try to stay calm, keep my nerves at ease, wondering if this is even real.

"Five seconds." She states, nonchalantly, working away as the shutters completely draw upward.

I feel an imminent problem, like that tap on the shoulder you get when you know something fucked is about to happen.

"Move toward me, quickly." Glancing back at me, the mysterious man, for a moment.

Just inches from my shoulder blade, something red and blinding shoots outward from one side of the hallway to the other, leaving a crackling burning sound in its wake. A piece of cloth from my back falls to the ground in a smoldering flame.

"Oh, shit!" I dodge forward right next to her as she continues – barely paying any attention. "Open the goddamn door!"

"Patience…"

In the passing of two, maybe three seconds, the space where I'd been moments ago fills with these red beams that threaten both of our lives with a painful death. I watch, terrified, fixated – I don't ever remember being this terrified of anything, not in my entire career.

Someone else's thoughts, not mine; I didn't think that, the voice inside of my head didn't say that.

A hand grabs me by the arm, just as the room begins to completely fill with this "extra security measure" and pulls me though a doorway I hadn't noticed opening. Slamming shut again just as my feet pass the crease on the ground where a silver steel floor meets another.

"J, you really gotta stay on your toes." She says, releasing me from her grip and pulling a knife from a cushy sheath within her boot.

A man in a long, white lab coat jolts around the corner and before either of us get a good look at him, that same knife sails swiftly into his chest, causing him to fall like rocks to the ground.

She looks me in the eyes again. "Stand up straight, weapon in front and move as I do."

Her gaze dazes me for a moment, so beautiful, so maniacal, and so deadly.

"Alright." Regaining posture. "I'm good, I'm good."

From what I can see, it looks like hallway after hallway, with almost no lighting and glass windows that all look into labs full of empty chairs and tables. Syringes and knifes scattered around and your stereotypical microscopes, animal cages and a few dozen computer monitors.

I look back and Stephanie's already moving. "Guh." I grunt, pulling my weapon up and move fast enough to catch her.

"Left." She directs, checking a wrist mounted electronic map, and we veer in that direction, stepping over the body of a man that seems like a harmless scientist.

Another leans out from a corner ten feet in front of us, weapon in hand, spraying lead blindly – We duck and she literally taps a single bullet into a glass plated forehead.

"You can use that gun anytime, you know." Taunting me as if this is some kind of game and she's winning.

Everything came so fast. I barely had a chance to gather my surroundings, the situation. I remembered what the man in the monitor back in the vehicle had said, but what exactly are we eliminating, why am I being forced into this?

I turn, almost without having to tell myself to do so, punching a few bullets down behind as a group of men scatter before us.

"There you go." She exclaims, in an excited, relieved tone. "The elevator to the first floor basement is just ahead. Then we make our way to the second floor stairwell." Talking, blazing barrels and peddling feet in a sort of power-walk fashion.

"And then?" Concentrating as I walk backward, using her movement as a guide, squeezing the trigger as our opposing force grows in intensity, scattering like shadows in the distance.

"And then, the lab." She stops at a call button. "You know, why we're here?"

A muscle in my left arm spasms, causing me to miss a few shots, a bullet or two shattering a large glass window to our right. Placing a hand on my chest, signaling me to hold fire, she removes a pistol from her hip and in four, well placed shots, finishes off the rest of the black-suited men that were just recently heading our way.

As fast as she'd drawn the gun, she replaces it within a holster and presses her thumb against an innocent looking, solid-white call button.

"Got the jitters, again?" Looking at me from her side.

"It happens, sort of a twitch." I say, before I can think of a response.

It seems like a well fabricated dream, it just doesn't seem real enough to be, just that – real.

Pounding like a drum, the elevator ticks upward, Stephanie angling her electronic, wrist-mounted map toward me, pointing at a silhouetted elevator as it moves, on her screen, in junction with the actual lift.

That screen also displays three dark red heat signatures.

In my mind, I speak, 'Stop this! For just a goddamn second, what the hell is this?!'

I think you know what it is.

Frustrating, to say the least.

My hand automatically reaches for a knife hanging from a small strap at the bottom section of my leg, pulls on its rubber grip and quickly jams it between the rubber that separates the opening of the elevator door.

"Good idea," Steph nods, prying fingers between the opening and pulling with grunting might.

Just before the rectangular box reaches its destination, we manage to pry it open completely, hopping down onto the elevator's metal-grated surface, staring at three heavily armored men dressed in bulky black uniforms.

My hand, again, reaches for a pack on my belt I hadn't even known about, pulling out a putty-like object and four cylindrical trigger detonators – A plastic explosive – Breaking this ball of mass into four tiny pieces, just large enough for their detonator mates.

My lips move. "Start climbing." Pulling a dangling cord in her direction, I hand it to her. "Going down?"

She smirks. "As always."

To finish off whatever plan I'd been formulating, I attach each piece of the sticky substance to the base of the elevator's top, right where each cord of the pulley system holds it in place. From my back pocket, I pull a metallic device that flips open to a small button, climbing up to where Stephanie hangs – my thumb depresses the switch.

Four small sparks smoke and let out a miniature boom that detaches the elevator from its support wires and sends it down, screeching. The men staring up, startled and shouting, as their faces grow smaller, sliding and crashing to the ground maybe a hundred feet or more.

Dangling here in the air, the two of us strap the cords and wires to our legs. Fastening them tightly, I turn with a wink. "You ready?"

She nods again, aiming her weapon down as the doors below open; You can only guess what's about to come through.

With a jolt, we glide upside down as if diving into a pool.

"Yeehaww!" My voice exclaims in an enthused tone, firing through the metal shaft at a confused looking man leaning in to see what all the crazy commotion is.

What my mind doesn't know is how the hell we're going to stop ourselves.

Hair blowing in her face, she exuberantly states. "I would've suggested just shootin' those guys, but hell! Fuck it!"

Just when I think our heads are going to smack bottom, like the elevator, we stop abruptly, cords yanking at my feet, slipping only by the slightest degree. Upside down, we hang looking into a very different type of corridor.

Together we swing, carefully unfastening ourselves and leap directly into the first floor of the basement.

"I gotta say, J, I wasn't exactly expecting that." Pushing a few strands of hair from her almost glowing gaze.

"Why waste the ammunition?" I say, with a grin stretching across my face.

Obviously I was trying to impress this woman, for some reason or another. I, being whoever the hell this "consciousness" belongs to, this memory or dream.

If she really is Nuhm De'Ara, though, I don't understand the bipolar difference in attitude. If this is the past, what changed her?

Stop talking to yourself.

I blink; Jesse blinks; Whatever.

The walls stand tall, covered in green moss and black slime, almost as if we stand in a dank sewer. The air is humid, yet cool and vents overhead blow with a quiet hum.

"If this is the first floor…" She walks, gun slightly aiming downward. "I'm anxious to see what the hell lies beneath us."

"Well…" I come to a door that looks like the front of a locker. "How about door number one?" I swing it outward to reveal a room much like the ones on the ground floor, computers and chalk boards and a large table in the center, covered with sheets of graphed paper.

Steph moves through and approaches the table, lifting one of the sheets in her hand and examining it with a wrinkled forehead. "This…" She runs a finger across a line as I approach for a better look. "Looks like a ship."

My head just over her shoulder. "Huh?"

"Not like a boat or an airplane, I mean, this looks like a ship, something you would take out of the atmosphere."

Now that's strange, I think to myself.

It's got that sci-fi futuristic look to it, curved long and cylindrical, with another, smaller diagram of an engine that's labeled, "Scope Drive."

"Come on." Tossing the paper to the ground. "There's nothing here, let's move on."

Before exiting the room, she removes a small charge from her belt and places it at the base of the wall.

"That's one down." Taking a look back into the hallway. "And we're still clear, shouldn't be this way, shouldn't feel like this."

Suspicion creeps up my spine and I hear what she says. To me, it doesn't make any sense at all, but at the same time, something at the back of my mind suggests we're in for a twist.

We walk further into the bowels of the basement, coming to a fork – One end leading to what I can only guess is the stairwell and the other leading to a single room, door hanging open, inviting us.

"After you?" She places a hand out, motioning that I go first.

Gun sights in front of me, I move slowly, as the contents of the next room reveal themselves – Shelves with vials full of a blue colored liquid, tiled black and white floor covered and stained in blood and six or seven slabs, littered with rotten and decayed bodies.

I feel whatever Jesse had eaten hours before tickle at the back of my throat, the smell of death, like rotten meat, wafting into my nostrils.

"The fuck is this?" Walking forward an inch or two more, my left arm against my nose and mouth, staring down at a dead man, or at least appearing to be that way from afar, his mouth moves slowly as if gasping for air. "Jesus Christ!"

"Jesse, I don't wanna be in here." She puts a hand on my shoulder. "I don't know what they were doing but the dead are not supposed to move!"

With my gun at my hip, I fire, splattering its skull across the room, eying the other five slabs as each of the corpses begin to slide their legs and arms away from their cold steel resting spot.

He doesn't know what they are, but I do. Whoever these people are, whoever had been conducting these experiments, manufacturing blueprints, they've gotta be responsible for the future. Then I look down, again, at my chest, where I'd seen the lettering earlier.

Z.F.

How can I be so stubbornly blind, Z.F., I about slap myself in the forehead, "ZeroFactor?" I say out loud. "I don't get it."

Even though I'd spoken those words, Stephanie acts as if she hadn't heard me, pacing back, terrified, to the door we'd entered through.

"Let's just get to the second floor and finish this." The whimper of a cry trails behind her words. "I mean now, Jesse."

Backing away, eyes narrow and angry, I fire burst after burst as we make our way back to the hall. "RUN!"

Our feet lead us right to the stairwell, long and covered in a veil of darkness.

Someone else's fear begins to overcome my own rational thought. "Dammit!"

"Move!" She plunges forward and begins to pound feet down small, metallic steps.

I shuffle behind, looking back every few seconds at a square of light, just waiting for one of the undead to reveal themselves, like a ghostly phantom you think'll come outta nowhere, lying there in bed as you try to sleep.

Further away it shifts as we continue down what seems a million miles of steps.

When we reach the bottom we smack dead against something; Something rough and flat.

I can hear Stephanie searching for a knob or a latch. "Tell me that's the door to the second floor!"

Almost wanting to just wake the hell up already and get on with whatever's happening in reality – Reality, the word that should be more of an answer, than a question.

Yet another damned hallway spills its light into the darkness, as a sliding door bursts open at the fingertips of Stephanie's trembling muscles. "Alright!" She yells, eyes wide.

This hall has nothing but two extremely large doors at its end and a single man standing there with his back to us.

"Wait!" He shouts in a deep, bellowing voice, accented with, maybe, Russian. "Don't shoot!"

I sling my gun around my back, thinking I'll probably have no use for it at the moment, as Steph swiftly approaches with her weapon ready to press against his forehead. "Gimme one good goddamn reason!" She demands. "Why shouldn't I lobotomize you!?"

Calmly, he states. "Because ve vork for ze same people."

Shaking the end of the barrel at him, still terrified and full of adrenaline. "What'd you just say?"

"ZeroFactor." He slowly mouths the four-syllable word. "I'm guessing zhey sent you hear to wipe out evidence of zheir own atrocities?"

"I don't believe you." She says.

"Wait." I reach for her shooting arm. "He's right."

My mouth actually allows me to say it.

My hand pulls away at his white jacket and shows the same initials, in red lettering, across the right side of his chest.

"What?" Lowering her gun toward his abdomen. "They set me up, didn't they?" Firing a single bullet into his frail body. "Mother fuckers set me up."

Her foot slams against the double doors, bursting open with ferocity and we both walk in at the same time, to see those initials again, plastered against the wall to the back, surrounded by small encasings of glass – Inside, something that you can only make out upon closer inspection.

Mouth gaping open, I press a hand against one of the bubbles closest to me, Steph tossing her gun as it slides across the floor.

I see something you'd only expect to see in a third world, dehumanized country. Something only the sickest of the sickest would even think of imagining, yet it was still just as unimaginable.

She falls to her knees, cheeks soaked in tears of desperation and sorrow – Speechless.

These people, this organization; What lies within are children. They've been experimenting on children – Mutilating them, changing them, using them for whatever sick, disgusting shit they were trying to create.

"No fucking way." I say. "No goddamn fucking way, these heartless, gutless…"

I turn back toward the door, Stephanie's eyes looking up to mine, tears pouring, mouth open in a silent cry, she watches as my chest opens up in craters of gunfire, sending me sailing to the ground.

Flames erupt from where the bullets had come, spewing like fountains into the room, Steph oblivious and Jesse dying.

I can feel my lungs losing their capacity but I feel no pain, like a balloon losing its air. Everything begins to fade, her eyes on me as men in large hazard suits approach, grabbing her by both arms, dragging her away through the doors as the others continue their spray of fire. She kicks and screams in terror, legs flailing around and then she's gone.

A woman I'd probably never see again, at least not through my own perception – not in my lifetime.

The last thing I see is a final gunshot, right between my eyes.

It all fades away and suddenly I feel as if I might have better understanding, but I still wouldn't look at this as an excuse for genocide.

In limbo, I ask. "*This* is what you needed me to see?"

This is only the half of it.

"And what about Meryl and Rob? They're alright, aren't they?"

Oh, they're fine. Close your eyes, Dante.

All senses plundered, I breathe heavily, dry heaving and shaking. A hand grabs me by the chin, fingernails digging into my skin and another grabs an eyelid, forcing them open.

12

The Blacktop Catacomb

"Now you're a weird one, aren't ya?" Another finger pokes at a small patch of torn tissue, right around the armpit-shoulder area. "Dante Marcellus, PaxCorpus, Human Protection Unit, number thirteen, is it?"

"FUCK!" Shouting in pain. "Not this shit again!"

He chuckles, stabbing a small syringe into my arm, depressing the needle and speaking once more. "You know, you should be dead." Pulling back on my head, forcing me to focus on the blinding lights coming from the ceiling. "Your pilot is, at least. But this is good news, we need you."

I try to move my hands but rope tears and grinds at the fragile flesh of my wrists.

"Who the hell are you?" I cough on my own blood, gurgling up a wad of thick saliva.

"Well, I'm the reason you ain't flyin' no more, son!" He spits in mid speech, spattering my nostrils with mucus laced saliva.

"Christ…" Moving my head to the upward position as his face comes into view.

A tiny wooden room – A shack – Orange colored sun peeling through the cracks and cone shaped lights hang from the ceiling, bearing down, gripping at my eye sockets.

This man wears a white overcoat, looks like he hasn't bathed in months, has a few scars across his face and squints with large coke-bottle glasses.

I sit strapped to a wooden classroom chair, almost completely naked – exposed, wearing nothing but a pair of black and white striped boxers.

My eyes pass over him a second time, his coat not so white, more blood spattered with a hint of beige.

A surgeon, maybe?

"Here." He pulls a cigarette out of his jacket pocket. "Have a smoke."

A part of me wonders why my captors are always quick to offer me a nicotine fix.

Gently placing it in my mouth, he strikes a match, lights the tobacco and holds the smoldering sulfur below my nose before putting it out.

"You like how that feels?" He asks, sadistically, flicking it across the room. "Burns the eyes and gives you just the slightest high."

Pushing me backward in the chair, he places an ashtray on my chest and lights a smoke for himself.

"But that's irrelevant." Inhaling and biting his lip, looking at a sheet of paper hanging from a wire a few inches from the two of us. "I've some information here that I need a bit of clarification on." He thumbs the butt of his cigarette over my chest, ash falling down and crumbling, speaking again. "This has got to be some sort of coincidence or a miracle."

I take a large puff, inhale deep and exhale through my teeth. "What're you talkin' about?"

"We've got a bit of a problem and, well…" He points at me with the burning end of his smoke. "You're going to solve it."

"I ain't doin' shit." Spitting the half-smoked cigarette down into the ash tray. "You're ZeroFactor, right? Same fuckin' bastards from Manhattan." My mind rumbles for a moment and then a piece of the double-past hits me. "Child murderers."

He looks around as if searching for the approval of an invisible crowd. "Tell him what he's won!"

Déjà vu, these guys don't have unique personalities, it seems.

"You've a lot to learn; we are the ZeroFactor movement, much different from the corporation that once was." Scratching his head with a pinky. "Although, I wouldn't call anything we do murder, whether it be a man, woman or child – it's more…" Snapping his fingers in thought, "Righteous purification."

"I got somethin' righteous for ya, you ego-maniacal, demigod fuck."

With a cold and clammy hand he grabs my right hand side shin, pulls the butt out of his mouth and hovers it just over my skin, the heat slowly growing in intensity, like a magnifying glass in the sun.

Don't tell him anything.

"I'm going to give you a chance." Still firmly grasping my leg. "You give me the information I want and we'll give you a running start."

Yea, right, these guys aren't that courteous.

"Blow me." I mutter.

"Insulting me not once, but twice, before we even begin? Bad move." Clenching tighter. "But I guess I'll let that pass."

"Now." Looking me directly in the eyes. "I'm going to make this as clear as can be; Where's Meryl SinGarda?"

Of course he'd ask me something I can't even answer anyway.

"I…" Gritting my teeth. "Don't got a damn clue, actually."

"Wrong answer."

Holding tight, he plunges the cigarette into my leg and the skin sizzles as he holds it there for what feels like a century. I grip the arms of the chair in pain and a single droplet of sweat trickles down the edge of my forehead.

Trying hard to suppress all signs of pain, I let out a single gasp for air.

Not a word comes out of my mouth.

"This little cunt isn't going to cause any more problems for us, because *you* are going to give me the answers I seek." Tossing the cigarette to the floor, stamping his foot down on the cherry and reaching, with his other hand, for a scalpel. "Tell me where she is." He demands once more, holding the shining blade close to my face.

"I didn't even know she was alive, goddammit!" I plead, moving my head back as far as it'll go.

"Look asshole, I have a knife to your face." He pushes the flat side against the skin of my cheek. "Don't play fucking games with me."

My eyes on the blade, I consider just giving him false information.

"You were there, with her, with…" He looks away for a moment. "With Robert, was it?"

It's obvious that neither of us know the full story of what happened and why I'd even lost my memory. It's at least blatant that he has no idea I'd done so.

He sits back for a moment and withdraws the knife from my face, tearing the sheet of paper down from its perch. "Maybe this'll help."

Beginning to read, with fingers against his glasses. "We've lost an important figure within the Z.F. hierarchy. We can only assume that this is the work of one, Meryl SinGarda, the assassin attempting to tear us apart from the inside, out. Yet not one of these people seem to realize that *dying* is inevitable – this is our goal. Nonetheless, we need to maintain order, less we reach absolute chaos. Though, word is, she's going for our leader. At this point in time, we would not be able to handle such a loss. It would mean completely reorganizing and relocating – Something we cannot afford to do – We'd be scattered and vulnerable."

Crumpling the paper and tossing it into a small waste bin off to his side, he slides the knife against my cheek. "Now you're going to tell me where she is."

"I told you, I don't know shit." Teeth grinding. "I thought she was dead!" Shouting with utter sincerity.

The end of the blade pricks my skin.

"You mean to tell me that, being one of the central leaders of your stupid little organization, you've had no idea one of your top agents were even alive, let alone out here taking us down, one by one?" Shifting his hand into a curled position with the scalpel ready to tear downward into my flesh. "I don't believe you."

With a swift and clean swipe he opens up a small section of my cheek, blood seeping out, I groan in almost horrifying pain.

"You fuckin' piece of shit!" Squinting my eyes and lifting the chair with my hands, pounding its legs against the floorboards. "Fuck you, fuck you, fuck YOU!" A small draft sneaks in through a tiny pin-prick of a hole, on the inside of my mouth. "You're dead, you hear me, you bastard, you're fuckin' dead!" Tonguing the wound, mid-speech, as blood forms a pool in the back of my throat.

He chuckles, cleaning his blade and placing a damp cloth against my mouth. "I somehow doubt that."

My eyes roll back and my head begins to swim back and forth, dizzying pain clouds my thoughts and then a second needle strikes the side of my neck.

"Alright, enough of that."

The searing pain slowly drifts away.

I wheeze, breathing erratically. "I've got nothing to say to you."

"But that's not exactly what you *should* be saying to me." Angling the knife at the bottom of my chin. "This next one won't be so cleancut." Staring into me. "Where is she?"

"I…" Just before I give him another piece of disappointing information, a hand pounds against the wooden door at the opposite side of the shack.

"Thompson!" A voice shouts. "We need you out here for a minute!"

Sighing and obviously irritated, he pulls the knife away and places it down onto a metal pan. "You're lucky, but I'll be back." Standing up and pulling a large, silver, winterized coat over himself. "Don't go anywhere!"

As soon as he leaves the room and slips outside into surroundings unknown, my eyes search franticly, looking for a plan of escape. To the left, by the door, hangs a pair of pants, a shirt and my coat. On the adjacent side, my nineteen-elevens and a combat knife.

That leaves me naked and strapped to a chair.

You should get out of those restraints.

"No shit." I respond, out loud, rocking back and forth until the chair tips over. The mumbling that can be heard from the outside stops for a moment and I freeze.

Their conversation begins once more, as I let out a 'whew,' almost screwing myself over.

Rolling my head around, I notice a large splinter of wood just by my hands. Mustering as much strength as I can, I inch myself toward the sharp end and cut away vigorously at the rope between my arms. Once finally free, I undo the knot around my feet and painfully pull myself up, still dizzy from before.

Stop squabbling already.

"Easy for you to say." My words sounding garbled with my tongue pushing around between my teeth.

Before anything else, I grab a roll of medical tape from the surgeon's table and wrap the wound on my face as best I can, blood still trickling from the flapping tissue.

"Now I *do* need a smoke." Looking toward the door as I make my way for the clothing, sliding into the pants, the shirt and wrapping my coat around a shaking body. "What, no shoes?"

Searching for the floor. "Ah, that would've been a bitch." Noticing them off by the corner, I pound my feet down into their sweaty, cloth soles.

Dante... She nags.

"I'm on it." Stumbling over to my saving grace, I strap the double-holster around like a belt and place each pistol firmly within – Locked and loaded – Taking the knife in my right hand, I head for the door, just by the crack of the opening.

Faint voices travel through as I slide it open just far enough to see the two of them standing together, nearly inches from the building.

"The rest of the teams have already dispatched for Harrisburg." A professional looking military man says.

"Harrisburg? Dammit, I fuckin' knew it!" Yelling at myself within my mind, as if I should've somehow seen this coming.

That's right, you better hurry.

"They're in their most vulnerable state. We strike and we strike hard."

I stand against the wall next to the entrance, arm bent, elbow jutting out with the knife in a close quarters cutting position.

"I'll see you in a few." His hand pushes against the door and it swings open. My blood-thirsty friend stands confused, seeing an empty chair, turning his head to the side, only to see the sharp end of a serrated knife heading for his throat.

The impact hits the jugular, spraying like a fountain and then across, through the windpipe. Choking and gagging, he grabs the hole in his neck, attempting to keep it from separating head from shoulders. Falling down, back to the floor, in his last dying breath he manages to mutter. "You're too late." Blood spurting out and bouncing off of his tongue, like a sprinkler watering dead flora.

This garners the attention of the man outside, not hesitating to enter; He squeezes the trigger of an automatic rifle and sprays wildly into the side of the wooden walls.

Pulling a single pistol from my back, I dive to the ground, firing shot-for-shot through the doorway into his kneecaps, shattering bone and crumbling to the hardened, mud-covered ground.

The last bullet splits the cerebrum, leaving a carcass, gasping in terror.

"I dunno what you bastards have against humanity…" Standing up, looking into the fog covered landscape. "But fucking with me, a second time, oh…" Walking into the center of their encampment. "You will die. Swiftly. Without mercy."

On the ground lay the smoking remains of a fire from, most likely, earlier in the day and pieces of a man, a limb here, half a torso there; Is this my pilot?

"Sick sons' a'bitches."

I can only guess that this area lies somewhere between Harrisburg and Allentown – A camp surrounded by tents and small wooden buildings that look as if they're supposed to serve as barracks, recently constructed, as well. All of them are void of light, except for one, emanating from its cracks – The remaining team that had been mentioned shortly before and their heavily armored vehicle with its engine running near the edges of the road.

Among all strange things about this little area, it remains untouched by the dead or anything else you'd expect to be incredibly rampant out here, but maybe there's something else going on; A larger distraction. Not exactly something I'd normally be in a hurry to find out about.

Or maybe this is just another dream and I'm being torn limb from limb in reality.

Unlikely.

An AK-Forty-Seven and a gas operated, seven point sixty two millimeter assault rifle sit against a pile of firewood, with two magazines and a pineapple by its side. I pocket the ammunition, sling the AK over my shoulder and walk toward the occupied building, grenade in-hand.

Chatter and laughter echo through the double-doors – probably celebrating what they believe will be the successful taking of a preserved civilization. Two handles stick out from each door, perfect for a trap.

I reach down to one of my boots and remove a lace, strapping it tightly around the pin of the grenade. Its oval shape fits snuggly within the handle on the left, while the other end of the shoelace ties, easily to the other. Ducking below the windows, I make my way to the driver side door of the vehicle.

"Laugh it up." I sneer, inspecting its model and make; A burly, flannel-wearing man's truck, welded with aluminum siding, bullet-proof glass in the windows and to top it all off, a fifty-caliber mounted machine gun in the bed – That may come in handy.

The noxious fumes from the exhaust make my head spin. This thing's way more than a gas-guzzler. I'll make it there, to Harrisburg, if I'm lucky – If it's got at least a full tank.

I swing open the driver's door and lift myself up onto the step toward the seat, hovering over the oblivious pile of flab in front of me, snoring away and dripping with mucus from his nostrils. The end of my pistol fits perfectly between the cavity of his man-tits. It'd have to be quick; The explosion from the grenade might take them all out or leave a few to pursue. Firing a weapon would alert them earlier than I'd want.

My knife, still bloody from the action it'd seen moments ago, would do the job. Sliding it along his forehead, "You wanna die in your sleep?" I whisper.

Through the frost-covered windshield, the sun can be seen setting over the horizon of run-down buildings and dead trees, blurred by the fallen bodies of clouds over the landscape.

"Ah, screw it." Sheathing my knife and pressing my pistol, again, against his chest. A flash from the muzzle and a quick, slightly muffled pop sounds off as an empty shell casing passes by my left ear – Dead in seconds – I push him to the soil below, sit down and slam the door shut.

"This is gonna end up being a suicide mission, isn't it?" I say, attempting to speak to the whisperer within my mind.

They don't call it a catacomb for no reason and I'm sure someone will be waiting or watching for the last vehicle of the convoy.

"Right." Slamming the shifter into first as a group of men burst through an exploding and splintering doorway. "No time to waste, as you've said."

A part of me thinks of Julianna, pulling off onto the shoulder of the highway, wondering just how safe she is, sitting there at home, as if home were even really that safe from attack.

Another piece of me thinks of Meryl and Rob, wishing I could know what exactly their fate had turned out to be, considering Meryl just so happens to be alive.

Although, the question of my amnesia still remains, among other things.

Concentrate on your goal. You're not dealing with a bunch of random guys with weapons. Their leader is powerful, more than you know.

"What do you mean?" Talking to myself seems less and less disturbing, looking into the rear-view to see mangled bodies of shrapnel shredded soldiers, screaming in agony.

No answer.

"Damn you."

Everything I've been able to remember, thus far, seems so unreal. I mean, a ghost-train, which traveled across Manhattan? The further I delve, the more insane things become. Yet things don't seem all that crazy here in the present, you know, just the undead and blood-thirsty monsters. Oh and ZeroFactor, the annoying little flies that you could swat away if only they'd stop reproducing.

It's just that I've begun to notice certain similarities, certain things that mirror my past experiences.

But maybe I'm just going nuts.

The road, Dante, keep your eyes on it.

I snap out of my distracting thought process and almost plow directly into a pile of overturned vehicles. "Shit!" Veering off to the side and picking up the decayed and withered skeletons of those long dead and less fortunate, rolling over the hood and ricocheting off of the roof.

So far, there isn't a sign of anything. Only the silence and the sinking star in the distance. Static buzzes through a transmitter on the dashboard. I adjust its tuner, which reveals radio chatter, from what I can only assume belongs to the people maybe ten minutes ahead of me.

"Yo guys, any sign of our last team?" A random male voice asks.

"Not yet, bravo-alpha-lima-nine." A woman spouts a line of encryption, possibly a warning.

"Copy that, over." The first voice responds.

They sound pretty organized for a bunch of maniac bastards. Although, I don't really know *that* much about them.

Overhead and toward my destination, the clouds loom grey, meaning either rain or more damn snow is on its way. I'm already taking it slow, curving around wreckage, tall weeds and decayed bodies – Bad weather isn't something I really feel like dealing with, at the moment. Especially considering what's currently emerging from the brush around the highway's shoulders.

Not surprising.

The sides of the road begin to crowd with beast and Undead alike, slowly inching their way onto the blacktop. It would only be a matter of time before they hear the chugging of a beaten up and seriously weighed-down vehicle. I start to wonder just how well the extra plating would stand up against them.

I remember stories and myths of these death-trodden roads, all beginning on a scorching hot day, down in the markets of Harrisburg. A PaxCorpus scavenge team had just landed and with them they brought a disheveled and obviously out-of-his mind looking man. Carrying him by the arms through the crowds, his cries bellowed and shook everything within earshot, trickling down the alley-ways and bouncing back, striking me out of the gaze I'd fixated on some hot young chick's ass.

"They'll tear you apart!" He screams, disgruntled and hysterical. "I saw her, she was there! Among the dead!" Tossing his head around in a bobble. "My beloved Samantha, ripped flesh from bone, stalking me every step, around every turn, whispering things of evil and deception!" Tears flow from his eyes. "Monstrous aliens be the last of your worries!"

Passing by, he'd fix his gaze on me. "You, I've seen you. Be best you stay away from those roads, hell, travel the sky, forests or even underground, but stay offa the roads."

It didn't make much sense – shit – it still doesn't. Among terrorism, the undead and monstrous bastards seeping out of a wormhole, I imagined to still be wide open, apparently someone or something had found time to haunt a highway.

Our teams never travel by road though, always by air and, so far, that was the first we'd ever heard of it.

Then more and more refugees began to pour in, either gone insane from walking the desolate roads or just about "gone" enough to be considered dead.

We eventually sent out a team to investigate all of the claims, just for shits and giggles.

They never returned.

Could be coincidence, who knows, I can't see myself going insane out here. Maybe just being alone with the undead is what did it to people?

But maybe I've already gone insane. Only time will tell, I guess.

A light drizzle begins to descend from the clouds as I slowly draw closer to my destination, splattering the windshield in a smudged blur, with wipers streaking dirty glass.

The radio chatter had gone completely dead. Either they've made it to Harrisburg or they know something's wrong.

A few clicks ahead, through the darkness of the night, headlights shine in my direction, watching like a creeping monster.

The ground begins to shake, splitting gravel from Earth – figures pass by in front of me, palming the driver side window and staring in ghostly white despair. A highway of the dead comes alive, bustling with frantic civilians.

These lights ahead of me, they're no ZeroFactor transports, they're gridlocked escapees. Suddenly, I've no room to drive any further.

"Shit!" My foot slams down on the brake pedal.

A highway of ghosts – don't think your weapons'll do you much good here.

"I don't believe in ghosts." Staring blank into the crowd directly in front of me, huddling around and moaning manic depressive songs of lives lost.

Visions of a past I hadn't experienced flood my inner-vision. Families shelter their young, unarmed and running blind through an endless crowd of apathetic consumers, pushing others down and jumping from the hood of one car to another. Military aircraft passes overhead and sweeps the surrounding landscape in a cloud of explosive rain, throwing Undead and the innocent like ragdolls.

A woman cries in tears, mascara streaking down the sides of her face as flame disintegrates and melts the tissue from her face, then arms and body. From the sides of the road, undead charge and break through glass, clawing at those that survive the blast.

The pavement runs red with blood.

I watch this from the inside of my vehicle, with nothing that I can do.

A pickup truck on lifted suspension and large, redneck tires, rolls over smaller vehicles. These men howl like rabid dogs, hanging themselves and their shotguns from the windows, taking shots at anyone or anything as if they're enjoying themselves.

I grit my teeth in disgusted anger.

An impish looking fiend, pounding the ground and gripping each vehicle with its long and pointed claws follows close behind, gaining on the homicidal maniacs.

They aim their sites at family of five but before they've a chance to pull their triggers, the bed of the four-by-four lifts and spills over backward at the mercy of a demon. They scream in terror, blasting their weapons into the air is if it'll somehow save their pointless lives. It grabs one of them by the skull and crunches down, spilling grey matter from its drooling teeth. The others attempt to escape but suffer a similar fate.

"Serves 'em right, bastards." I think to myself.

A bush off to the left of the highway resonates with rifle fire, splitting the cranium of the monster and it topples over between the still frantic and fleeing survivors.

I try to tell myself that there couldn't have been any way for me to have an effect on this situation, if I'd been here, instead of Manhattan. I curse myself for ever relocating, but even then death would still come for millions.

You can't save them all.

Shaking my head, blinking, I yell. "Stop!"

Hands clasped against my ears. "Just stop it already!"

Hand on the rubber grip of my pistol, I aim toward the windshield, "I'm only human!" I tell myself this, over and over. Eyes bloodshot I feel like pulling the trigger; I feel as if I wanna blast away pain, but my arm goes limp and my head swims as if I'm waking up in a hung-over stupor, feeling heavy and sick from stale stomach acid.

Only human.

"I'm getting sick and tired of your psycho-babble." Gripping the steering wheel, knuckles white with sweat, I jam my foot down on the gas pedal. Tires squeal and rage, fiery eyes emerge in the rear-view, galloping behind and a handful of undead break into the scene.

Forging a path through the wreckage, I careen forward. A headlight goes out, a side-view mirror snaps off.

The ghosts of the past all stand to the sides of the road, gazing at a man of a shattered memory, an obscured collection of truths. I'm tired and weary-eyed – Can't take the anguish I've bottled up inside.

I see a vision of Meryl, holding an arm out in desperation, lips silently crying my name and I stumble over.

Another vision, Julianna, holding me tightly against her body, a mysterious glow emanating from glazed over pupils.

Then Jack, long ago, sitting together in a squad car watching criminals go in and out of a supposedly abandoned warehouse, somewhere between Poverty Avenue and Ghetto Boulevard.

"Fuck you!" I shout, shifting into overdrive, now holding my weapon over the steering wheel and balancing it with the edge of my wrist, firing wildly through the glass, till it finally cracks, at each undead as they attempt to crawl over the hood, splattering coagulated blood and cracking dry-rotten bone.

I jerk the steering wheel all the way to the left, spinning around, pushing open the door. Elbow a running corpse in the jaw, push another away with the palm of my hand; I climb into the bed of the truck and grip the mounted machinegun. Breathing heavily, sweat and rain soaking every inch of my body, I vibrate to the pumping of each shattering blast that lights the area around me in a yellow fury.

I keep firing, even though I can barely see anything at all, I don't stop. If anyone or anything that lives is anywhere near here, the only thing they'd hear is the sound of a man determined – The clanging chains, the sound barrier breaking every half second to a hailstorm of ammunition that punches through the darkness, dropping anything within a ten foot radius.

Each flash of recoil is a different vision – A different, undiscovered piece of the past.

I feel her breathing down my neck.

She, that voice in the back of my head, scratches at my brain, sliding front to back, pulling my eyes away and the air goes stale.

You wanna know what I am?

Rob and Meryl, sitting with arms on their knees, dirty and covered in blood – they look my way and she speaks. "Dante?"

You wanna know my purpose?

Over the edge of the scenery, the Verrazano and a few more clicks away, the Tower. Gunfire explodes from behind as we burst away from a screaming horde of the dead.

I am everywhere. I see everything that you see.

A pair of arms wrap around my chest and embrace, warm, then withering away. Eyes of a shadow and hair that flows like wind, black as night, over her blindingly white shoulders.

I am time – I see your past, present and future.

We run together, Meryl and I, bursting through the streets, weapons ablaze, taking her by force to our final destination.

I am space. That wormhole, ya'know, the one you opened. I wouldn't be here if it weren't for that.

The edge of the Milky Way Galaxy, blue and swirling like a tornado in the dark and an event horizon, staring deep – Terrifying and serene, all at once, sounds like muffled water in your ears.

Your future depends on me.

Half of the bridge gives way and crashes into the bubbling water – Dead-end. Meryl takes me by the arm and a crowd, led by Nuhm De'Ara and… "No." I speak. "Jack."

You see and feel the past, because of me. Without my presence, you'd never remember a thing.

"Then who, or what the fuck are you?" The belt winds down, ammunition spent and not a speck of life can be seen.

I do not know.

"What?!" I bark, in disbelief. "You know all of these things and you're going to tell me you don't even know what you are?!"

I haven't quite been able to figure it out, yet.

"Stop fucking with me."

I'm not fucking with you, but you definitely have not gone insane.

"Whatever." I hop back into the driver seat. "Just shut up!" Pounding fists on the steering wheel. "Shut up, shut up, SHUT UP!"

You don't know the whole story and neither do I.

"Drive." I think to myself. "Just drive."

Full speed ahead and I'm plowing through fresh and old corpse alike. In the rear-view a woman stalks, aura blazing with orange and red, faceless and casually strutting closer to the vehicle as if I'm not even moving.

Harrisburg – Five, a sign reads, bent and leaning off to the side of the road.

"Dammit." I groan, feeling around a velvet passenger seat for my pistol and firing a few rounds at the back windshield.

You're not stupid, stop wasting ammunition.

"GRRAAAH!" Leaning forward toward the broken glass, squinting through the rain that falls harder and harder with every foot I gain.

After all I've tried to do for you, you'd wish to shoot me?

The engine stalls, stutters and puts abruptly to a stop.

Well now, you're out of gasoline.

"That's it, I'm definitely nuts." Grabbing both guns, I holster, jump from my seat and run across the gravel through the down-pour.

What? You gonna run four, five miles?

She flings vehicles and debris like paper and ash. My lungs begin to feel riddled with holes, each breath drawing shorter. Coughing violently, I push onward.

You ungrateful bastard.

The gravel suddenly seems enticing, falling face first, knees bending and scraping against rock, flesh immediately tearing. I roll for about a second or two before stopping dead on my back. She stands with a glowing body and what looks like a barefoot against my ribcage.

Don't you get it? You wouldn't be alive right now if it weren't for me!

An apparition standing in a nude form above, looking down, face blank like the barrel of a gun.

I get a chance to reveal a piece of myself to you and you run like a god dammed coward.

"I…" Feeling exhausted, my body gives up – I give in. "I'm sorry?"

Without my guidance, my little nudge, you wouldn't be here. If you wouldn't have flown East, you'd be staring death in the face, right about now, actually.

"Fine, I'm done running." Feeling groggy, eyelids falling. "Just do whatever you're here to do to me."

Do to you? I have as many questions as you do and I'm finally getting a grasp on things. Only you can solve this mystery.

"Well, I don't know what to tell you." Attempting to sit up a bit, rain spattering into my eyes, hands waving around at a leg I can't touch, yet somehow it firmly holds me down. "I don't know who or what you are, why you're here and what the purpose of all of this is."

Then I want you to continue. There's a point in time where everything changes – A miniscule point in time that holds the answer to everything.

"Where do you even come from?" Everything begins to look wishy-washy.

A temporal rift, torn from the very fabric of space and time itself.

"And I'm guessing that wormhole has something to do with this?" I wipe my face with the unscratched and damaged hand.

Yes. Wormhole or black hole, these things tend to skew reality. The closer you are, the more the laws of physics and everything else become meaningless.

All rubber-bandy and bouncing back and forth, my eyes shake and rattle, her manifestation growing weaker.

Just get up and get going.

Fifteen feet away, the engine of the truck roars and headlights shine like rays of hope – normality returns and her voice goes silent, leaving a trail of ember in her wake.

I just wanna crawl in bed with Jules and sleep for, I don't know, a couple of days. A couple of miles seem like a couple of light years, especially through freezing rain. The increasing darkness and that little feeling you get, when you know no one's around but someone's watching you.

The cold numbs the scrapes and brush burns, the side of my face pulses with a small inkling of pain that will most likely increase as the recently injected morphine dissipates.

I'm out of smokes and out of my mind.

13

An Afterthought

"About time you get here." NYPD captain Jason Grimes says, looking like life shit him out into the clothes he wears, greasy, unkept face scowling and overly tight. Buttoned up striped shirt with cuffs that roll around pudgy wrists.

"Blow me. What's the situation, as of now?" Placing palms on his white marble desk behind glass and blinded windows.

"Humph." He crosses his arms. "Two years and you still don't have a bit of respect for me."

Revealing a remote control between the fingers of his left hand, he flicks on the television over his right shoulder; An old brown box that hangs in the top corner of the room.

Straightening up, I stand back and observe.

Grimes adds a few words before I can make sense of what's being broadcasted. "This keeps replaying over and over, ever since those dead things took out the president."

The broadcast shows a blink of a reporter standing in front of an abandoned hot dog stand and a deserted Starbucks, holding a microphone and jittery-nervous, to a short burst of white noise and a video that displays a symbol – A jagged toothed smiley face with arched, triangular eyes. And then a robotic voice begins to speak.

"We are ZeroFactor. Humanity has finally come to its end and now we have living proof."

An image of the White House fades in.

"Your President has forsaken you, withdrawing all troops from the middle-east and turning their weapons on you, the American people."

A blurred blob of a person appears, shadowed and pointing at the screen, "You have been apathetic, thoughtless and stupid for too long. Today, the things that I and my people fight for have finally come to pass. And today, the strong shall survive while the weak perish in flames. Today, we cleanse the world, starting, with you."

The transmission cuts out and begins to repeat itself once more.

"Bullshit, I've dealt with these guys before; They're nothing but ruthless, murdering terrorists." I look away, focusing on Grimes again.

"Afraid it's a little more complicated than that, regardless of your past." He shifts and reaches into his desk for a cigar. "It's damn chaos out there. We're lucky we've got the weaponry to hold 'em back."

He cuts away the end of the stogy, biting down and lighting up with the only match left in his book – He tosses a stack of papers in front of me. "These are also from the President, must've sent them out before the speech."

I take a sheet in hand and read out loud. "Blah blah blah, epidemic is classified, blah, we are dealing with is much more than a few terrorists, blah blah, this has encompassed the world. Safe zones are being setup, I address you, the law enforcement, you will stand alongside our military and host the evacuations." Tossing the paper into a waste bin. "That's it?"

"What'd you expect?" He puts out his barely smoked cigar, smoldering away, he stands. "The President was only an icon, and anyway, it's up to the people now."

"Enlightening." I strike open my lighter and burn a smoke. "This is totally fucked."

The rooms outside of his office begin to bustle with people screaming and crying, shouting. "There's no way out! We're gonna die! What are you people doing?!"

"God dammit." He stands with his back against the door. "I guess they made it inside after all." From his armpit, he pulls a revolver.

"Get a team together and head to the harbor. Jack's waiting for you in the armory."

"And what will be waiting for these people there?" Wrinkling my forehead in thought.

"A slew of choppers and boats are ready at the shore, we just gotta funnel 'em there." He says, aiming the sight of his weapon at the window.

"It's a deathtrap. There's no way we'll get them all out of here alive." Pulling open a blind. "Just look."

A couple of hours before, New York was a ghost-town, everyone sitting idly within their homes. Now, a tidal wave of panic and mayhem – looters, criminals and just plain old scared-out-of-their-mind people – all tending to whatever they believe is most important, in this situation.

Indistinguishable were the dead walkers, or runners, whatever you wanna call them.

"Dante, I have other teams already out there, but you're my best." Beginning to look serious, more-so than before. "I'm counting on you," Before showing me through the door and past the growing crowd of frantic bodies, he pulls and unfolds a paper from his shirt pocket. "This is a bit of Intel on your friends, the ZeroFactor." Handing it to me.

No name, no photo, but it tells of recent suspicious activity that involves a conspiracy – Military experiments with robotics and synthetics, diseases and viruses. Something the public hadn't even recently caught wind of.

"This doesn't tell me much, Grimes." I take a long drag from my cigarette and hand the slip of paper back.

"Keep it, it might help you identify the specific person it mentions." Opening the door.

14

You Don't Know Jack

Experiments.

"Military experiments," I ponder to myself.

Why this thought hadn't dawned on me before is completely beyond me. I guess it's just another something I forgot about, especially in the mess of all of the things that have happened in the past six years.

Nuhm De'Ara, supposed leader of ZeroFactor – this is who and what she is. Does this make everything she's done a personal vendetta against mankind?

Whatever, it's way too late for all of that.

Rain continues to fall, unrelenting and getting harder by the second. I shiver from my lower back to the base of my skull, holding onto the steering wheel, I once again begin my trek back to Harrisburg. It's probably already too late to stop them, but I've always got a job to do and this ain't any different.

This is why PaxCorpus exists. I won't abandon the people I've sworn to protect.

All hope is not yet gone, Dante. You still have time, very little, but enough, just stop talking to yourself and concentrate.

"Right." My left eye twitches.

The fact still remains that I'm the only one out here.

"Hey man." A voice to the right, not quite inside of my mind says. "How ya been?"

I continue focusing on the road and the rain that spritzes me through the bullet hole riddled glass.

"You gonna say somethin'?" The new voice asks.

My peripheral catches a familiar face – I glance for a second and turn back to the darkness.

"Jack." It couldn't be him, no way.

"Six years and you're speechless?" He leans in. "Well, given the circumstances, I guess I would be too."

Wreaking of booze and breathing heavily, he continues with his inquisition.

"So you goin' back to Harrisburg then?"

Glancing once more, I notice he's holding a Glock nine millimeter over his lap and pointing it toward me, with an evil looking sneer across his face.

"You're not Jack." I choose to respond.

"What makes you think that?" He shoots back, immediately.

"You just randomly appear in my passenger seat and nonchalantly begin a conversation."

Swallowing hard on a lump in the back of my throat. "You're just a figment of my imagination."

"You wanna test that theory?" He cocks his pistol with a metal clang and playfully waves it around at the side of my face.

The rubber of the steering wheel sticks to my hands like Velcro, sweating, soaking wet – The inside of my thumb rubs against the side of my finger and he begins to recite a memory.

Two miles to Harrisburg.

It was about nine o'clock in the evening, middle of a seedy spot on a street less visited in lower Manhattan. A group of terrorists had taken hostages in an underground strip and rave club – The exact location isn't clear anymore – but the terrorists, unbeknownst to myself and my team, were, obviously, ZeroFactor.

People gathered on the sidewalk, trying nosily to peer behind black tinted glass and cracks that scratched up and down the ruby double doorway. NYPD's finest stood around asking citizens to "Please get behind the yellow tape and stand back," since they and my team were the only ones that knew what was actually going on inside.

To the onlookers, it was touted as a little mishap involving drugs and some testosterone fueled douchebags duking it out within.

But, naïve as the public was, there's no way they'd know that we didn't use yellow tape and several teams just to cover a small area when all that's going on is a stupid little bar-fight.

The media huddled around vans and police cruisers, asking anyone that passed by what they had possibly seen. Suspicious as usual, that perhaps this wasn't exactly what the cops said it was.

For the most part, we did this simply to avoid panic. Attacks on Manhattan never went down well.

Although all of this, the pudgy donut wielding cops, crowds of concerned people and the obligatory media onslaught – This was all just the distraction.

Around the back, along an alleyway, overtop twisted and rusted gates and sloshing through puddle drenched dirt and gravel stood six of us – Six guns of the Emergency Response Unit.

Normally, our teams would only consist of five people, but that day we were charged with training a newbie – The perfect operation for training – This is what they thought, at least.

All knowledge of our actions were completely unknown to the people around front. Only the highest officials knew we were there; The people that would communicate with us throughout the rescue operation, keeping tabs and providing useful intel.

So, to be blunt, we were ghosts. Not entirely normal, but necessary.

We were supposed to slip in, eliminate the bad guys inside and shuffle the hostages out through the back door and home to whomever gave a shit about their lives. After that it was supposed to be pretty much golden and our cover would no longer matter.

If only that would've been even slightly true; If only it would've gone like the numerous takedowns we'd participated in dozens of times before.

I remember the air smelling like rotten diapers, steaming from the pipes of the roof, curling out and whisking on downward right to our crinkling nostrils. This was probably the result of half-assed, greasy bar food and the stench of twenty to thirty people constantly rubbing sweaty bodies together on a dance floor thick with smoke.

Or maybe I stuck my face in shit that day, I don't know.

The night was warm and sticky, your usual summer evening. Made me feel agitated and anxious, like I'd snap at a moment's notice if anyone dared give me even the tiniest bit of a problem. I was and still am a very angry person.

"You know, if it weren't for the ass-load of protection we wear…" Jericho wipes a drenched forehead. "I'd do this in a pair of jeans and a damn t-shirt."

"Yeah man, they tryin' to cook us out here?" Hugo coughs and rolls his shoulders. "When we gonna get this over with?"

Steve stands against the wall clicking the safety of his semi off and on, ignoring the random banter. His outfit hung loosely over his unusually skinny build, but even then, he was strong – Some people make the mistake of underestimating him, anyway.

Jack and I exchanged glances every so often, observing the rest of the team as they meander around as if they hadn't ever done anything like this before.

"Calm down, ya 'tards." I look over. "Sixty seconds."

I remember looking up at the night sky and only seeing a few stars visible, if that. Was a hard thing to get used to after living in a place like Harrisburg, where you could simply drive into a field and point out constellations.

"Star gazing, Dante?" Jack swiftly puts a hand to my shoulder blade. "You know we're the only ones in the Universe, right?" Letting it fall back to his side. "No use wondering about things that don't matter."

"Don't be so stupid." I flash a half-frown, a little aggravated at such a close-minded statement.

Barry, a stout looking man with hair that encompassed most of his face, gives his own two cents. "Yeah, Jack, you heard of Area fifty-one right?"

He scoffs, placing an arm against brick and bashing his head into the muscle. "Don't tell me you actually believe in that shit?"

"I do." He responds very seriously.

"Alright guys, synchronize, safeties off." My eyes pass around the small alley, watching each of them form up. "We've got about ten seconds."

Ballistic helmets flip down and laminated polycarbonate protects our faces, with the rest of our armor made up of mostly Kevlar and a type III body armor that protects against most seven point sixty two millimeter full metal jacket rounds – But not so much against explosive blasts.

"Five seconds." I hold up a fist, ready to signal. "Barry, I want you in the back, behind everyone else. You're still new to this, remember that."

"Aye-aye, Cap'n." He salutes with a swagger.

"We ain't pirates." Jack responds in a less than happy tone, almost offended for some reason.

My ear piece beeps and a voice comes over the fizzling static. "Execute, now."

A thin lining of explosive wire smokes and then snaps the lock off of the door, violently swinging open, we swoop in.

Jack, Steve and Barry head right, the rest of us hug the wall to the left, heels barely touching the ground. We make our way through a hallway blinking in florescent white light – A few doors leading to dirty and women's undergarment littered rooms, with more trash and crumpled paper than anything.

Bass pounds from the dance hall, rumbling chips of paint from the walls as we approach a slightly ajar passage.

A waft of grease and rotten meat swims through and a light brighter than in the hallway shines out through a battleship style door, with one of those circular windows.

I throw my fist into the air.

Two men can be heard speaking amongst themselves, but too inaudible to make out any of their words.

Curling each finger slowly, I signal a countdown.

My index finger twitches upward and a split second later the barrel of my suppressed automatic submachine gun points and clicks in the direction of the two men, standing casually, eating chicken bones and comparing rifle sizes. Jack follows through with a single tap and both of them end up on the floor, bathing in filthy blood.

"Hope ya enjoyed your last meal." Jericho mutters, stepping in from behind to get a quick view of the damage.

"Clear." Gritting teeth and grunting, pushing the group back through toward the main hall entrance.

I remember thinking to myself. "That's two of them, how many more of them could there be?" We only knew the civilian headcount, unfortunately.

The rest of the area behind the scenes was empty and unoccupied, meaning we were about to head into a shit-storm.

My ear piece beeps again. "Your covers been blown." The commander states in an angry tone.

A finger jolts to my ear, surprised. "What?! What do you mean?!"

"One of your hostages just updated their Mybook status, said 'there are dudes here in black suits and masks, maybe we won't die after all!'"

"You gotta be kidding me; We just cleared the entire back area!"

"Just get going."

"What's the problem?" Jericho comes up from behind.

"One of the hostages are out and about and he or she just so happens to have a smartphone." I swing my arm down, pacing back and forth.

"Oh that's awesome." Jack sighs. "Fuckin' morons." Stepping out of the shadows of another hallway with the rest of the team.

"They're just scared civilians; They don't know any better, cut 'em break." I wrinkle my forehead and turn to him. "What's with you?"

"Nothin' man, why don't we see what's behind door number two?" He jokes, approaching a shaking, wooden doorway, puffs of smoke escaping from beneath its frame and techno-trance beats pounding with furious, machine-gun anger.

Steve taps me on the shoulder. "Wait, I've been here before, I know the floor plan."

Hugo taunts with a laugh. "You? *Here*?"

"Alright then." Turning with my weapon across my chest. "Let's hear it, but make it quick, we don't know if these guys are monitoring the web or not."

He points to the left of the door. "Off to your left here you have the bar, some stripper polls, the DJ stand and a stairwell that leads to an overlook sorta lounge area." Lifting the shield that covers his face, he adjusts his glasses with a thumb. "In the center is the main area, where people mingle or pretend that they can dance or whatever…" Lowering eyebrows in thought. "And then to our right, you have this crazy lounge area with naked chicks and little kiosks selling glow sticks and stuff."

"Well, shit." Jericho interjects. "We're walking right into a deathtrap."

"I know I'm a rookie and all, but the majority of these bastards are probably up on the second floor, just waiting for someone to come through either of these doorways." Barry states, with trembling nervousness seeping from his eyes and shaking at his fingertips.

"That's correct." I kneel down. "But we have an advantage." Waving the smoke around, I point something out. "It looks like this place is basically the way it was before the attack, meaning we have the camouflage of noise and fog-machines." Standing up straight again, I reach over to Steve and flip down his protective shield. "If we stay low and move swiftly, we'll hit 'em no problem."

That's usually how it would go, after all.

"Wait, wait." Jack places a hand against my chest. "Won't they notice the door opening?"

"Most likely, but if we move as I described it shouldn't be much of a problem." Reassuring him and the rest of the team. "Once we're through we'll take point behind the bar and assess the situation from there." I reposition myself so that I'm facing the five of them. "Ya'll got that?"

They all nod at the same time, Barry still shaking nervously with flops of sweat leaking down all over himself.

"Hey." I walk over to him and place a hand on his shoulder. "I know this is your first real serious experience, but we'll make it through this; It's what we're trained for."

He stares deeply into my eyes, almost innocently. "Got it, Dante." Half-grin painted with doughy-circles beneath a sweaty brow.

"Alright, defensive positions everyone." I twirl an index finger in the air and walk to the door. "On the count of five, we go in and move fast as hell to our left." Coughing and clearing my throat. "Neutralize anything that gets in your way." Adding even more to the obvious, "Unless of course it's a hostage. Don't do that."

"I hope you're right Steve." Jericho looks in his direction, mumbling through his lips and under breath.

"Shh!" I point at him. "On one." I bend my knees and curve my back. "Five." You can feel tension in the air and the music punctuates that. "Four, three." I visualize taking down my targets, clearing my mind. "Two." Placing the hand not holding my weapon on the door. "One."

We went in, crouching and sprinting for the bar, cutting through synthetic fog and dancing lasers – Blue, green, orange and a few red. We were invisible to the opposition up top but that didn't stop them from firing randomly into the darkness upon seeing the door open – Bullets ricocheting off of the concrete dance floor, a few barely missing us.

I catch a glance, scattered on the floor – Neon colored hair nestled between sneakers and boots, a drug induced garden of hysteria.

Each of us slides, one by one, behind the marble and wooden bar and it's plethora of inebriation, catching a quick breath before the storm. The shrapnel and likely death from above comes to a halt and we were in the clear, for the moment.

I turn my head to Jack. "Take Hugo, Steve and Jericho, and secure those hostages."

Judging by what I'd seen, there were less people than we'd been told – Maybe ten or closer to fifteen.

Then, turning to Barry next, directing my voice to the rest of them still. "Barry and I got these assholes."

Yet we didn't really know if they all actually *were* up top, it was more of a hunch, a gut feeling.

"Yessir." Jack taps each of them and whispers something.

"Let's do this, Barry; See if your training was worth the time spent."

He nods, still oozing with fear.

"Go." I command, already in motion and heading for the stairs as Jack counts my steps, preparing to move.

The upward climb bends like a river, around and around until we make it to the top, kneeling slightly out of view, behind the very last step, seven or eight of them pace back and forth, watching the ground below. One of them points at another, stammering through his words, spitting orders and then moving toward our position.

I pull a flash grenade from the bandoleer around my chest, designed to stun and disorient. Removing the pin, turning my head just to notice Barry a centimeter away from the side of my face, I slide it across the floor to the single terrorist's boot.

The strangely dressed man, in leather and bondage, looks down in confusion as I put a hand on the back of Barry's head and duck.

A loud pop and the room fills with white for half a second. We stand, aiming our weapons, single-shot firing and dropping one after the other as they flail around on the ground, pulling the triggers of their assault rifles, randomly. I grab Barry by the chest and force him forward – a few of them hadn't been blinded, standing behind pillars deeper within the lounge area.

"Shit." Barely able to hear myself speak over the music. "We got a standoff, Jack, status?" Putting a finger to my ear as I push Barry behind a pillar and take cover behind another.

"Situation's under control, but it's lookin' pretty grim, how 'bout you?"

"We got some stragglers fuckin' around up here, but they ain't really fighting that hard." I respond as the pounding bass pauses for a few seconds – Shouting resonating within the large room and bouncing back – gibberish sounding rage.

This is where it got exciting.

Pulse pounding drums slam through speakers in the ceiling and around the building, gunfire recoil flashing from below and around the corner, centimeters from my shoulders. I turn and reach out with one arm, weapon in hand, firing a burst of rounds and only managing to chip away at another concrete column.

"Give it up, ya fucks!" I shout through partially clenched teeth, Barry standing with his back pressed tightly against his personal cover, frozen and scared.

"What do we do?" He says, frantically. "We can't flush them out!"

"We flank them." Pointing to the area off to our left, revealing a table and two pieces of furniture – A couch littered with cum stains and a circular chair, riddled with cigarette holes.

Another round or two ricochets, nearly hitting Barry in the leg.

"Fuck." Looking down, he moves aside and takes a glance over the edge of the balcony.

"What do you see?" I ask, impatiently.

He presses a clammy finger against his helmet. "Jack, watch out, three tangos moving in on you."

"They'll take care of that." I motion toward him. "I want you to blind-fire before we move. It'll give us a few seconds of a grace period."

Nodding, he readies his weapon and I position myself to the side of the pillar that faces the aforementioned fornicated furniture, preparing to sprint.

"Do it." Pointing two fingers in the terrorists' direction.

Blasting a slew of rounds off, he follows behind as I take a dive for the chair. Moving toward the couch, I notice a thin piece of wire set to trap my feet, hardly missing as I rebound against the wall and fall backward to the floor.

"Hell!" Watching Barry head right for it. "WAIT!"

I still don't know what the hell that was made of, but I certainly hope I never see it again.

I inch myself back as far as I can as he trips the wire, slicing cleanly through his ankles; It sends him sailing to the ground in screaming terror. His head, falling directly toward another piece of identical wire, bounces like an empty barrel off of the solid floorboard and instantly splits in two, brain matter spewing out.

"Goddammit!" I slam my fist against the wall five or six times. "Fuck, FUCK!"

"What the fuck just happened!?" Jack shouts into his ear piece.

I stand, gun aiming forward and finger squeezing the trigger, I dash.

"Go to HELLLL!" Shouting in visceral anger, I kick one foot against a column and send myself backward, dropping both of them before they'd even realized I'd come from absolutely nowhere. Picking myself up, I grab one of the half-dead bastards by the collar, pull him up, demanding he answer me, before I push him over the edge of the balcony. "What are you?!"

"Eat shit." He spits back.

Grinding my teeth, breathing heavily. "Who the fuck do you work for!?"

"ZeroFactor." He lets out one word; One I hadn't understood at the time, as I let go, watching him fall limp to the ground.

"Motherfuckers."

"Dante, you wanna answer me, dammit!?" Jack shouts, again.

I breathe slowly for a few seconds, attempting to calm myself, not looking at the carnage only a few feet away, I respond. "It's Barry, they setup some kind of tripwire all over the place." I look down, seeing Jack staring back up at me in confusion. "And of course, he tripped it. Shit sliced clean right through him." I remember thinking I'd never have to utter these words. "We got a man down."

"I offer my condolences, but we got bigger problems down here." He walks out of view.

"Oh, really?!" Raging even more-so after such a blatant, apathetic disregard for another man's life.

"It's the hostages." He pauses. "They're strapped with enough C-Four to topple the entire building, but shit, they probably planned on tearing this place down anyway, right?"

"I'm gonna come down there and kick you in the face if you don't show me a little goddamn compassion for these people!" I grab hold of the railing and send my feet over the edge to the ground below, spinning around to face the rest of the group. A handful of the captives look up at me with tears in their eyes, looking very, very helpless.

Jack turns to me, standing among the fallen bodies of the remaining terrorists.

"They're proximity and timed." Tossing his weapon to the ground. "We can't save them."

"The hell you mean we can't save them?!" Grabbing him by the cloth of his suit. "Call the fucking bomb squad in."

"I understand that you're angry." He points at the first visible man, chest strapped with explosives and wires, sitting there on the floor. "But we only got ninety seconds left."

One of them begins to scream. "Get us out of HEERREEE!!"

"He's right, Dante, there's nothing we can do." Jericho adds. "These guys intended to kill everyone in the building, including themselves.

"Shut the fuck up." I snap back, slinging my weapon out of my hands. "We can't just leave them here, I won't."

"Whyyyyy!" A woman from the group stands up, hands wet with tears, she begins to move.

"Sit the fuck back down!" Jack shouts at the poor, trembling woman. "You're gonna kill us all!"

"No, Jack, you're killing these people by leaving them here." Whipping my nineteen eleven from its holster and pointing it in his direction.

"We don't have time for this shit, D." Aiming his weapon back at me. "Either you stay here and die with these people or we get out. Now."

The rest of the group stands behind Jack, beginning to move for the door we'd come through, with fifty seconds left on the timer.

"These guys got the right idea." He lowers the barrel of his gun to my waist. "Shoot me if you want, but I've made my decision." Turning his back to me. "We're leaving."

I watch as they walk away, looking down, avoiding eye contact with the soon-to-be dead.

Thirty seconds.

I hesitate; I wanna crumble and blame a God for their pointless death. Then I bolt right for the front door, not looking back and pouring into the streets filled with cops and the media, bursting through, with hands in the air, I exclaim. "GET BACK! Get away from the building! Go, NOW!"

Dashing for the corner store two clicks ahead of me, a few people follow my lead, confused, with the NYPD demanding we "Get down on the ground!"

"No time!" I shout one final word of warning, diving through the doorway of the thrift store as the entire block lights up in a ball of flames and crumbling dust. The Earth shakes and rumbles as the nightclub comes toppling down, dragging the buildings adjacent to its location along with it. The dizzying rush of adrenaline causes my vision to blur, seeing what looked like a cop car flinging itself against the building next to the one I'd taken cover in, knocking over a reporter's van and filling the street with debris.

That day was a failure. One I'll probably never forget, no matter how fragmented and distorted my memory becomes. Why Jack slowly, but surely began to show me and the rest of the team such disregard for human life was beyond me then. Now, though, I think I see the connections – The psyche that led him to where he is now.

The only question – Does that sort of thing run in the family?

15

Julianna Moretti

"And so you see, Dante." Jack finishes the excruciatingly long reminiscence of a memory I'd not wanted to recall. "That situation just about defined who I am and who you are." Still pointing his little sidearm in my direction. "Why I'm in the position to bring on the new world order and why you're fighting a hopeless battle."

"Fuck you, Jack, fuck you." Sneering with a curled lip.

"What? You got a problem?" He laughs. "You do realize these people, all of them, you've only prolonged their lifespan by maybe a few years or so. You're just delaying the inevitable."

I reach across to the passenger side of the vehicle and attempt to slug him in the face, but his image dissolves into nothing and once again, I'm sitting here alone, nearing the on-ramp that leads to the heart of Harrisburg.

Shaking my head, I put my foot all the way down on the accelerator, hitting a clear zone of the highway, giving me just enough room to speed the rest of the way in.

Then I remember the fuel gauge.

Just before reaching eighty-miles per hour, the engine gives out once more and I come to a depressing and abrupt halt.

My forehead hits the steering wheel column and I sigh. "If anything, you could've given me a cigarette." Not quite sure of whom I'm talking to.

You're almost directly in front of the wall now, Dante.

The mysterious voice notes.

"Oh." I laugh at a high and then a deeper pitch. "What a coincidence!"

The door to the vehicle about falls right off, after enduring a swift kick and a slam.

Green signs overhead read, "Union Deposit Road – Half a mile" and maybe fifty or sixty feet ahead sits the barricaded wall that separates me from my own creation of salvation, ZeroFactor and things to come.

In order to get back within the walls, I'd have to head southeast to the site where the train had slammed through – where those ZF sons' a bitches had most likely already made their way.

The weather remains harsh, freezing and unforgiving – Mother Nature's a bitch.

I reach inside of the truck and retrieve one of my pistols, cock back the slide atop its steel surface and a bullet loads into the chamber. The other sits resting in its holster, breathing cold against my lower back.

"Alright." I whip back my head, flinging water out of my eyes and hair. "Let's get on with this."

They're inside of the city now and sadly, things aren't looking too good.

"Why ya say that?" I begin my trudge through the dead grass and the mud.

Someone knew they were on their way, someone on their side, from within.

"An insider." Wondering who this person could be, maybe George? My squad, Paul and Raymond? I'd never found their bodies, after all.

I'm sensing something, like a mental block or a field of some kind coming from the center of the city. I can't see anything, which means I can't help you. At least once you're inside.

"That's wonderful news." I spit and wipe the edge of my lip.

From behind a black mass – Overshadowed petrified trees and a cluster of rotten bushes – A figure emerges. I kneel down in the brush, watching as it closes in on me, closer, walking slowly, untouched by the rain. I reach around to my shoulder and pull a small flash light from a clip, clicking once and aiming simultaneously, my gun and the light.

"Julianna." I say quietly, the light bouncing off of her face, revealing a cold stare and sickly pale skin. "No."

Undead, ghost or some kind of mind-fuck – I can't tell. It seems real, but then, so did Jack.

Out of pure curiosity, I allow her to approach, lowering the deadly end of my gun to the ground.

"And what sorta shit is this?" I ask, watching her cautiously as she moves, arms at her sides, head tilted and mouth half-cocked.

Her hair hangs frazzled around her neck and twists like a vine, down and around her bare breasts, nipples almost triangular in shape.

"Jules, is that you?" I ask a different question, hoping for a response.

She draws closer and I reach out with my left hand, the skin of her face soft to the touch and as I pull my fingers away her teeth snap like a bear trap.

"Fuckin' hell." I raise my gun again, backpedaling as a knot forms within my stomach.

"Stop moving and say something goddammit!" Shouting into seemingly deaf ears.

The bastards, they'd gotten to her – This has to be real – My mind decides, as strange warmth pours into the corners of my eyes.

Her icy-blue lips move and my heart stops dead – she quivers erratically like an insect as she struggles to make words.

"Dante…" Left hand reaching for my forehead. "Embrace the infinite continuum." She mutters, eyes focused on the ground and arm stretching with her cold, wet palm against my face.

Light rains down like the shutter snap of a camera and the air turns to suffocating humidity – My knees covered in dirt, kneeling in a fox hole under a clouded sun, visible landscape appearing twenty different shades of grey.

"I remember this." I think to myself.

This was Harrisburg, in the middle of the war to take back the city. Twenty seven days after I'd woken from my coma.

Tracer bullets light up the sky just over my head and screams echo in their buzzing pass.

Death dealer against my chest, I lean upward and rest my chin in blades of blood-soaked grass. My arms stretch outward and I grasp the column of the rifle with one sweaty hand and the trigger with the other, right eye peering through its telescopic sight.

In concentration, I block out all distractions to the best of my ability and only focus on what lays ahead – ZF foot soldiers and a swarm of Undead pouring down over a hill.

Searching through the mass, I find my target, grinning, armed with a Gatling cannon, shoulders as large as mountains and spilling lead all around.

Inhaling, my lungs fill with cordite and the noxious fumes of burning buildings, out of view, only the stacks of smoke peeking over the horizon.

The target pauses.

My finger squeezes the trigger – A loud burst, the muzzle flashes and ears ring – An arrogant grin turns to a startled frown, falling dead to the ground as his skull splits in half leaving a gaping hole where his face used to be.

Not wasting another moment, I shoulder Double D and sprint up and for a tree off to my left toward the top of the hill where his body lies. Bullets buzz by, wind whips right through me and I throw my back to the bark, re-equipping the rifle and spinning to look down a decline in the grass toward a gas station that rests on a corner and a curb just off of Cameron Street.

The running dead bolt for a couple of strays fleeing desperately toward our troops.

I focus the scope and watch, whispering. "Just a few more feet..." Setting my sights on the, hopefully, full gasoline pumps.

My right index finger squeezes once more and – Crack – the first shot tears a hole in the aluminum, immediately afterward, another, in the exact same spot, causing the pumps to rupture and burst into flames.

A group of five or six undead fall to the ground, burning to dust and ash.

This kills two birds with one stone – The refugees make it to safety and I've got myself a tiny window of a distraction to make a sprint for Harrisburg Area Community College – This is where our emergency medical team had setup shop.

Bursting downhill, I leap onto the pavement with every bit of energy I've left, running a triathlon; Rifle bouncing against my spine.

Around a curb to the right, passing fields of green, I come up on a group of ambushers, waiting to pounce. Pulling both side arms from my brand new double-holster, I bring them up and in front, pounding shot after shot almost blindly as I pass freshly laid corpses, showered in unexpected confusion.

The final road leads directly into a large, metal fence, surrounded by barbed wire and five or six Pax Units keeping watch. I swing my hands at the gate, still holding each weapon. "Dante Marcellus, Unit Thirteen, let me the fuck in!"

The gate slides open. "Welcome, she's waiting for you in the courtyard."

"Yeah, yeah, got it." Zinging by, slipping the beauties back into their handcrafted, leather home.

The parking lot comes next, littered with military grade vehicles and other raggedy looking scraps of metal – I slow down to a speed-walk.

Through tall and untrimmed grass and between a few red-brick buildings, lies the courtyard; The central nervous system of our current operation. Within each wing of the college were different types of cases – The recovering, the men and women in critical condition, strategic planning and, of course, the dead – Restrained and strapped with belts and chains to brown-stained gurneys.

In the middle of the confusion, the crying and screaming, the scattered desks and stacks of paperwork, stood this woman.

She looks up, eyes dark and piercing, hair matted in sweat and someone else's blood; Yet beauty still shown through.

"Dante!" She shouts with as much enthusiasm as she can muster, taking someone dressed in similar clothing and pulling him into her place at the check-in desk. Walking fast and pushing through the black Friday reminiscent crowd, she says. "How're you doing?"

"Well, for a guy who's been lying in a fox hole for about twelve hours – I'm great." I respond with a bit of a smirk.

She stops at about two feet in front of me and crosses her arms, with a semi-forced smile.

"But hey, I never did have a chance to thank you." Rubbing the back of my neck. "You know, for pulling me out of that mess I'd gotten myself into."

Referring to Manhattan, of course.

"Not a problem, D, it was hell that morning, goddamn literally." Shaking her head and gazing a bit off to the side. "I remember finding you all beaten half to death, dozing in and out of consciousness and all. You were lucky."

"I was…" Grinning and moving in closer.

The clouded sky lights up for a millisecond and a deafening screech follows – The ground shakes and a mortar shell strikes not more than three clicks from our location.

I cover my head out of sheer instinct and pull her in closer, grinding my thumb against my index, noticing everyone else around us down on the ground with heads between their legs.

"Bastards." I say, letting go of her, I ask. "You alright?"

"Yes…" dusting herself off. "Never get used to that shit."

Without much hesitation, business resumes as it was.

"I never told you my name…" Taking me by the hand, running a finger around and over my knuckles. "Julianna Moretti."

"Good to…" I swallow, feeling a needle in the center of my chest. "Meet you, in full consciousness."

She blinks a couple of times and pulls her hands away from mine. "Now, if you've got a bit of time on your hands, I could use a little help."

"Sure, whaddya need?" Smiling and cracking a joke. "Think I've got my quota for the day."

"Good." Lifting a vial from her front pocket – A black and grey, digitized camouflage suit. "Take this to Lawrence in Whitaker Hall."

The wing for those that remain in critical condition.

I cautiously remove the vial from her grasp. "What is it?"

Wiping hair out of her eyes to get a clearer view of mine. "A sedative used to calm the restless, ease their pain and to regulate their heartbeat."

"Ah." I stare, for a moment, at the bluish liquid. "Not a problem."

"Come back to me once you've finished." She requests, turning hastily back to her work. "Alright, next!" Waving a hand in the air, signaling for some Pax soldier to step-up to her desk.

I must have been in a trance. The hysteria and tragedy around me suddenly bled back into motion, like time unraveling before your eyes. Then I realized how stupid I must have looked in front of Julianna, attempting to flirt and joke in the middle of the worst human crisis in history.

No matter – I made my way to and through the sliding doors of the Whitaker building, only fifteen feet or so from her desk.

People, injured and dying, sit on wooden benches in droves, all looking up at me at the same time, pleading. "Help me! Help us! Don't leave us here!" Their fingers brushing my legs as I pass by and come to an intersection in a hallway, hundreds of people in both directions.

"Dammit." I say to myself, wondering where this man could possibly be. "Lawrence, anyone know a Lawrence!?"

A skinny little guy with dirty blond hair and an ostrich-looking neck pokes his head out from within a doorway. "In here!"

Inside of this dimly lit room were those gurneys, with no straps but plenty of deathly looking people.

They all had large chunks of flesh missing.

I'm guessing this drug made the death and undeath process a little less painful.

He stands by the side of a man with grey hair and skin as wrinkly as a grape, hand on his head, the man frowns and looks over in my direction.

"The cure?" He barely manages to speak.

"Yes, Father…" Lawrence reveals the identity of the man. "We have here what you've been waiting for, the release from your suffering…"

I see something in him I sort of wish I were able to experience myself, although not a great experience or anything you really want to ever know – A closeness, a connection – For a moment I think of my own Father and of his disappearance.

Where'd you go? I constantly wonder to myself. What was so damn secretive that you couldn't even tell your own family; What made you abandon us?

Do you even care? Do you wonder of your Wife; Our mother and what happened to her? Cause I sure as hell will never know.

With a hand on the kid's shoulder, I turn around and whisper quietly. "This man's your Father?"

He nods with a hint of a tear at the corner of a pair of eyes that seem like a mirror or a reflection of a person in need of answers and hope.

"Cherish this moment, never let it go." My hand slides down the sandpaper skin of my face. "PaxCorpus is here for you."

With squinted eyes, trying hard to hold back the water works, he lifts his head upward and opens a palm. "Just please give me the sedative, I don't have time for chatter."

I offer a pat on the back and slip the vial into his hand, with a few last words before quickly leaving the room. "I give you my word, you will have justice; We all will."

Letting him to his work – Filling a syringe and puncturing the frail arm of his Father – I walk back toward the shadows of a catacomb. The last thing I catch a glimpse of, as I pass into the hallway, is a pair of heads held close together with a green line on a monitor that straightens out with a silent tone that no one ever really wants to hear or acknowledge.

I couldn't even remember what it was like to lose anyone close to me. Well, aside from Jack, but that's pretty much up in the air.

Returning to Julianna's desk, she looks up again. "Alright, thanks for that. He's a good guy. Kind of feel sorry for him…" Lifting a single sheet of paper. "But we've got bigger problems on our hands."

"Oh?" I tighten the strap of my rifle. "Need a delivery boy again?"

She chuckles and clears her throat. "Actually, no. I need you to escort me somewhere outside of the base." Moving beside me and fingering the paper she'd been holding. "We're almost out of water and it seems the local All-Mart, or what's left of it, is the only place with a plentiful amount still in reserve."

My eyes catch themselves wandering up and down; Undressing this beautiful woman from head to toe. "Wait, what, did you say All-Mart? You kidding me?"

"No. What's the problem?" She raises an eyebrow.

"Fuckin' shopping center hell is ten miles from here."

"What?" She laughs again. "We're not walking!" Pulling a pair of keys from her pocket. "I've got a rover around the corner in the parking lot." She adds. "With a deck, stock full of my favorite tunes."

"Whoo-boy." I wiggle my fingers in the air. "Let's go then, gonna be a bumpy ride."

There was something about her, something that rendered everything else almost meaningless, giving me the ability to act in ways I normally wouldn't. Regardless of the current and dire situation and the fact that we'd be heading directly into hostile occupied territory.

That'd be either ZeroFactor or better, the risen bastards.

16

Knee-Deep in the Dead

She'd insisted that I drive, while taking full control of the vehicles sound system. Fortunately for us, the glass had been reinforced and made completely bullet proof, so the guys behind us – Yep – More like annoying tailgaters that just won't take a goddamn hint.

Singing to the sound of a man singing a song, apparently all about Italian chicks, she kept her eyes closed and bounced to the beat as bullets pinged and popped off of glass and the steel siding.

To be honest, I found it a little weird, maybe even crazy. Sure, I'd make jokes but, well… Damn.

Takes all sorts of things to deal, I suppose.

Swerving down the on-ramp toward I-Eighty Three South, I roll down the window of the over-sized almost Humvee like fuel-burning, monster machine and reach a pistol out, pointing behind.

"Fuck off already!" I shout, looking into the side-view mirror and pulling the trigger as wind tugs at my eyelids.

A single projectile strikes a tire and the side of their vehicle crunches over as if it'd been side-swiped by an insane force and sends them sailing off onto the shoulder.

"Whoa!" Julianna interrupts her singing and abruptly smashes her finger against the pause button. "Not only do you have a mouth that would put Samuel L. Jackson to shame, God rest his soul, but you've got a hellish rage I've not seen in, well, anyone!"

Adjusting my head back toward the road and our destination exit, I press my middle finger against a plastic button that causes the window to automatically slide back into position.

"And you're point?" I ask, glancing for a moment to see a slightly startled and surprised look across her face.

"Not-for-nothin', but I think *you* need to relax and maybe, I don't know, enjoy the moment, 'cause that's what life is, right?" She leans in toward me. "No one's promising you tomorrow."

Either I'd met the most interesting woman in the world or I'd just taken in the company of a person that would most definitely get me or the two of us killed. Although, she *had* managed to save my life – the question of why was still beyond me and would remain so.

"Don't get me wrong…" I began a rebuttal. "But you seem curiously happy, or maybe almost bipolar. What the hell is so enthusing?"

"Stop the vehicle." She demands, toppling herself over my shoulder, causing me to swerve to the side of the road.

I ease my foot onto the brake and pull to a stop, just out of sight, behind a small collection of trees and I notice something; The world had gone completely silent. No gunshots, no explosions.

"You hear that?" Looking around with a twitch.

"No." She responds, placing her hand on my own, the one that had been white-knuckling the gear-shift.

"What, wait, what are you doing? This really isn't the time…"

Her body moves in closer to mine, soft lips silencing my persistent worry.

"We can't…" Speaking through her tongue. "I don't even…" Then I simply give in.

Hot breath and our sweat-covered skin grabs against leather seats, too tight of a space for two people to be making such awkward movements.

A flash of darkness streaks across the inside of the vehicle.

She does all of the work, bare breasts and erect nipples hanging and mostly smacking me in the eyes.

Rain pours in through broken glass, little prickly bumps lining every inch of my arms and legs.

Moving up, and then down, in perpetual motion, her lips swollen around an uncontrollable and eager, throbbing painful dick – teeth gently pinching the skin of my neck.

My heart rate increases and this image becomes blurry, blinking in and out. The sky then fills with complete darkness.

"Dante…" her voice sounds like an echo in a tunnel hundreds of miles long.

And I blink, open my eyes, focus, sitting passed out on the side of I-Eighty Three, inside of a long-ago, abandoned vehicle, quite like the one from the past.

"What…" I wipe sweat or rain away from my forehead. "The hell was all that about?"

Expecting to hear the voice give me a reasonable answer as to how I'd managed to slip in and out of a memory and simultaneously make my way into the, now, ZeroFactor occupied Harrisburg – I receive no such thing.

The bandage on the side of my face had peeled away at some point, to reveal, surprisingly, healed and scarred skin. I examine this with my right hand in the broken rear-view.

"Alright." Dismissing the fact that I'd somehow, once again, managed to heal at an inhuman rate.

I pour myself onto the pavement, bones crackling from a state of prolonged non-movement.

"Dammit." I say out loud. "I gotta move."

Remembering that the last real thing I'd seen of Jules was some undead, ghostly looking thing, which may or may not have been truth.

My mind finally pulls itself together.

"Julianna, Julianna…" I pat my backside for my guns and find them nearly dangling out of their holsters. "Shit, don't be fuckin' dead Jules, don't be dead goddammit!"

I do the only thing I can possibly think of; I start running south, toward New Cumberland.

But what I'm running into is a complete mystery, along with how long I'd been "out."

The Lemoyne exit that leads down to Bridge Street is only a skip or two in front of me. If you've ever driven that street, before the fall of ninety percent of mankind, you'd know how much of a horrible, twenty-five mile an hour stretch it is, or was.

Hauling ass down and around the cracked and slush covered pavement, my weapons are ready but my chest bursts with what feels like fire, building within and threatening to combust.

I cough with a hand balled up to my mouth, coming up to the traffic light, four way intersection that separates New Cumberland and Camp Hill.

Stopping for a moment, hands on my knees and gasping for air, I survey a large barrage of vehicles, mostly the size of dump-trucks, blocking both the route into Camp Hill and the road straight ahead that goes further down toward Mechanicsburg – Meaning ZF are definitely here and goddamn half running the place.

Continuing to the only unblocked road, I'm met face to face with an undead, stumbling out from behind a smaller vehicle I had also not seen in Harrisburg before now – Black and glossy, covered in mostly strange symbols, along with the one I've seen millions of times before – Obviously their "tag."

This walking corpse has familiar eyes, although missing most of his jaw, tongue hanging from muscle and tendon, nose bloody and clothes covered in mud – This man was the

Father of the child from that apartment building I'd been forced into liberating, at gunpoint.

"So I'm too late then?" He stands there, almost looking half conscious, struggling to understand, his head rolling around in a dizzying pattern.

Six years I fought to keep these people alive.

Six fucking years I devoted of my life to ensuring that at least a small fragment of humanity remains and now we're down to this; Shit-sucking slobber mouths all around and genocidal bastards here to burst my bubble.

I curl my lips and arch my eyebrows down in anger. "Sorry about this." Thinking of the child for a moment, wondering of his existence, then placing my hands on each side of his head, with a quick twist, then a snap. A not-so-fresh corpse tumbles to the ground. On his waist still hangs that little hand-cannon, gleaming in the rain, almost asking me to take it.

I do, fitting it snuggly between my pelvis and the belt of my pants.

Looking down on through the street brings back memories, always with the memories, things from the past I'd experienced – I'm getting that feeling again.

Buildings ablaze, twisted metal carnage and unseen gunfire echoing in the distance.

Day one all over again, except this time I'm going through, not out.

This isn't the road I've traveled hundreds of times.

This isn't the road home. This is a road littered with questions that will inevitably lead to an answer.

With the death of one, comes many. Like flies to a steaming pile of shit and fast as hell, they run.

My stomach literally turns upside down, causing the hair on my arms to lift and stand on end and bowels scream at my brain. "Evacuate!" You'd think, all I've been through, this wouldn't seem so bad.

But it feels real; Overwhelmingly real.

No longer a skewed memory of the past or some fucked vision that doesn't make any sense – I realize that this could be the end for me. I could die here and I could possibly never, ever figure out why. Another unfinished puzzle left to rot.

This is what goes through my head, pounding feet through slippery snow to the nearest pile of wreckage for cover.

A window on the second story of a house off to my right bursts out in shards, the screaming body of a woman sails to the ground and twists in agony, followed by the incessant laughter of one of these insane fanatics – The iron sight of my pistol aligned to his forehead and finger non-hesitantly squeezing the trigger.

He doesn't fall half as gracefully.

Before making my next move, before revealing myself to the oncoming horde, Julianna's voice echoes a conversation of the past within my mind.

"You know I love you, right D?" She asks.

"Of course." I respond reassuringly.

"You know I'd do anything for you?" Leading me into one of those obvious woman-questions.

"Yeah, what're you getting at?"

"You'd never abandon me, right?" Having doubts of my loyalty to her, for reasons that are beyond me.

"No, never." I confirm. "Everything I've ever said to you, even if those things seem far away or long ago; They all still stand true. I'd still give you the Universe if I could."

Again, I get a tickling hand up my spine and I feel the guilt – I've gotta get back to her, no matter what.

If I believed in a God, I'd probably pray.

Holstering one of my nineteen elevens, I hold the other in my right hand and the steel cannon in my left.

Whispering to myself one final thought before engaging almost certain death. "You can't be dead, I won't allow it."

A high wind rolls in and the rain shifts, stabbing at my skin with its icy chill – visibility plummets and for a moment I taste metal in my mouth, rolling my tongue around. A second passes and vertigo settles in, my head swimming, almost vomiting.

I crush my eyelids together and grit my teeth. "Come on, dammit!"

They're getting closer.

The nausea drifts away and again I can see and think almost clearly.

Turning, chamber slamming, magnum rounds rotating, the end of the barrels flashing yellow against my face, I search frantically for my next destination as gnarled teeth and jagged fingernails claw in my direction. Side-stepping forward, I pull myself into the bed of a truck and to its rusted and red rooftop.

The undead spread as far as the eye can see, at least, as far as the weather allows.

"Impossible." I think to myself, standing here atop a vehicle that seems like a boat in the sea, surrounded by circling sharks.

I need a diversion or I'll never make it on foot.

As my luck has it, from a run-down hair salon on the opposite side of the street, a man bursts out, arms flailing around and screaming. "Help!" Running directly into the bastards and desperately pushing through to my position.

A life for a life, I suppose, bad luck for him.

The undead focus their bobbing heads and gnawing teeth on the man as he runs. I jump down, sliding heels through wet snow and I bolt as fast as I can through an intersection and a second traffic light.

I feel almost bad, almost shameful, but it's far too late to think of these things.

"Gotta be getting close."

Firing wildly, veins hardening and bursting with a tightness at the very top layer of the skin on my arms – The undead fall, dropping to the ground like a tumbling forest of rotten trees – All people I'd sworn to fight for.

No matter how many times I repeat this to myself, it just won't sink in.

The hammer of the Magnum slams against a hollow chamber, punctuating with a loud clank.

A zed comes up close, preparing to bite with its slimy, yellow teeth as I whip it in the forehead with the butt of the empty handgun; Tossing it to the ground and reaching around to my back for the extra pistol.

Continuing on, my body begins to jitter and shake. The sleep deprivation clamps down and tears at my eyes, taking control of my nervous system

All I need is a quick breather, just a little break.

Up ahead, a small brown restaurant that stands almost sunken into the ground, on the corner of another intersection, welcomes me with open arms and an orange light gleaming from its windows.

My foot lands square on the center of the door to the lobby, swinging open to reveal five, very surprised ZF men; All dead and blood-spattered faster than you can say, "blistering bombardment of ballistics ya belligerent bastards."

Back slamming against the door, my lungs empty, fill, then empty again – Feeling as if a million razors grind at my chest.

I click the auto-release on both pistols and watch two empty magazines fall and clank against the ground, unsettling dust and dirt in a poof.

The area within is filled with vacant dining booths and a long, stretched out serving counter, still ready with rotten and decayed portions of food, waiting to be delivered.

I pull two fresh clips from my pockets and slam each one individually into its designated slide, just under the palm of my hand – Reloaded and still breathing heavily with a staggering huffing and puffing. For a moment, I almost doze off, but then the low humming sound of the building's generator slowly makes its way into the passages between my eardrums, causing me to blink a hundred times and snap back into reality.

"Enough." My consciousness states, loudly.

My legs bend forward and I twist around, open the door with guns in front of me and pace myself faster and faster toward Fourth Street – Home.

Now I'm not even shooting, I just wanna get back. My elbows do the work this time, holding them outward and slamming through slack-jawed zombie after zombie. Like a tunnel,

I can see the light, but it only seems to inch further away, the closer I come.

When I finally make it to the center of town, passing that large church that Julianna attends every Sunday, the undead simply disappear; Wandering away behind me and fading down separate streets and alleyways.

I turn right onto Fourth, panting, coughing violently – There it is – Home, all red brick with its sore-thumb of a white door, but something isn't right. An armored vehicle, like the one I had driven before. One of those ZeroFactor fucks had been or is still here, yet the lights to all of the rooms lay grey and dead.

Not wasting any time, I rush up the stairway and throw myself through the door and into my living room. Turning back and forth, ready to fire on anything that moves – But it's empty.

Into the dining room, nothing, just the same dinner table and entrance to the kitchen, as if no one had bothered cooking or eating.

Up the stairs, to the hallway, past the bathroom and at the end – I blink and see that vision from Manhattan – The door to our room barely closed, left open just slightly, I slam through.

"Jules!" I shout, putting my weapons away and embracing an unconscious body that lies on an unmade bed. "Wake up! Please!"

But she won't respond. Something had definitely happened here and we can't stay. I've gotta get her to the HQ building. If anything still stands with any semblance of a chance for survival, it'd be there.

Putting two fingers against the side of her neck, a faint pulse vibrates against my, most likely, ice cold skin. If that isn't going to wake her up, she needs something I don't have.

Carrying her in my arms, rushing down the stairs and out the front door again, I head for the vehicle – My fastest way there, regardless of who it may belong to. Laying her down gently on the passenger seat and fastening her safety belt, I circle around and jump in, ready for a bumpy-ass ride.

With a turn of the key, the engine roars with growling anger and I slam my foot down on the gas, almost forgetting to pull my door shut.

"Just hang in there, babe…" I put my right hand on her leg, clothed in a pair of blue jeans.

The rain comes down harder and little bits of snow can be seen within each tumultuous drop, as I push on through the opposite direction

I'd came, eventually leading back to a horde of mindless bastards. Much easier this time, as I plow right through them, knocking bodies over like bowling pins. And before we know it, blasting through rain and snow covered streets, we're here again, at the Camp Hill – New Cumberland intersection and that little slice of road that leads right to the highway.

I merge onto the onramp and glance at Julianna, her hair partly covering her eyes; She wrinkles her forehead and lets out the tiniest whimper.

"A few more miles." I say, hoping she can hear me. "I don't say this a lot but given the circumstances…" Here I am rambling. Looking back at the windshield as we come up to the eighty-three north bridge. "I *do* love you."

In the faint distance I can see the wreckage of the SUV I'd rolled just a day earlier, at least, it seems like a day earlier – Who knows if that's really how long it's been. But then the vehicle begins to shake and I start to think the engine's about to fail, at least, until I realize it's not the vehicle that's shaking.

Making it almost to the center of the bridge, the first thing I see is concrete shooting straight up, like a fountain, into the sky, followed by a cloud of choking smoke and a blaze of flame.

The windshield shatters and glass hits me dead in the face. With that, the bridge begins to cave in on itself, turning the road into a steep slope that carries on down into the Susquehanna.

Slamming on the brakes as hard as I can, pulling back on the emergency, doing everything I can think of to stop the vehicle. Rubber grinding and burning, we slowly slide right into the bubbling and frozen depths of the river.

"Fuckin' shit!" I yell, looking over again at Julianna as water begins to rush inside, wave after wave, like a shower of ice cubes. "Goddammit!" I unbuckle her belt and pull her out of the seat with both arms across her body. "Come on, wake up! WAKE UP!"

Fully submerged, too quickly to make any efficient attempt at escaping, I hold my breath and watch her face as the world slowly slips away into a wishy-washy cloud of nothing.

Right before losing my mind, like all the times before, just as my lungs fill with water and my brain decides that I'm really going to die this time – Her eyes open, with a wide and surprised look that would make you think that she's the one staring into the eyes of a ghost – Then black flows in.

17

The Answer that Lies Within

We'd somehow managed to travel through the void of space and time. How I know this isn't really explainable in a string of coherent words. Doing so was mostly infinitely improbable but it's more space travel than time travel – Although, the Universe is exactly that – An infinite number represented by a measurement that we refer to as time.

This building, this tower, is very much real. On the outside, yet within are all things mostly impossible, or more generally speaking, things that aren't likely to be experienced on the outside, regardless of the fact that some extra-dimensional rift had been opened, by yours truly; To some unstable part of the Universe, that slowly merges with our own.

What's even more mind boggling, is the fact that only I will come to remember what was just seen and heard. While Meryl and Rob remain completely oblivious, as if they're just now being pushed through the door to this Tower. I already know this, before it happens.

Right before I emerge from the abyss, I see a single vision that invokes a sense of nostalgia or a state of paramnesia. The Milky Way Galaxy and I'm outside of it, a dark void that spins with overpowering dominance across the black, glowing almost heavenly and I'm being pushed toward the chasm.

    Like black feathers in the wind, I drift back to a familiar setting, regaining myself within the chamber that separates us from the outside and the first floor of The Tower, once more.

18

Blatant Disregard

"I don't wanna do this." Meryl grabs me by the arm, same as before.

"Yeah." I look at her. "You're claustrophobic."

Rob interrupts. "These are our…"

"Guns, yeah." Seeing him from my peripheral. "Obvious."

I pull them around and stand them next to each other, preparing to make a statement. They look at me with confusion dripping down their faces, wondering, probably, how I'd guessed what they were going to say.

"Look." Taking the same weapons as before from the same peeling green table. "None of this is actually real."

"Whaddya mean?" Rob asks, with a stupefied look across his face.

"This building isn't what it seems, it's playing off of memories that are not our own." I respond, cocking back on my pistol's steel slide.

"Dante, you're confusing me." Meryl puts a few fingers to her forehead. "You act like we've been here before."

"That's because we have." Dragging a knife down the side of my leg and sliding it into a small sheath that hangs just below my knee. "It doesn't matter. The problem, is that of our escape."

In the back of my mind, I'm waiting for her whisper, but she doesn't come. The little voice inside of my head seems to have left.

"And again, how do you know this?" Rob insists I answer the question that the two of them have posed.

I can't tell the truth, they'll never believe me. "Because I've seen our future, I can't explain it, I just did."

"Ah, where's our Delorean then?" His eyes wander, seeming entirely unbelieving. "We have to get back in time, right?"

Meryl turns around and begins pushing against the button-locking door that leads back outside and fails at her attempt to open it.

"Dammit!" She yells with an aggravated and fearful tone.

"Calm down." My hand reaches for her shoulder. "I'll lead us through this."

"I hope you're not going insane or something, we can't have that right now." Pausing, then looking up at me. "I just hope you know what you're doing." Seeming a little unconfident.

"Through this door here, keep hold of your weapons." I approach the door once more, just like last time. "Do exactly as I say."

Upon opening it, an impossible light shines through, blazing blindingly into our eyes – This was different from before, not a dark hallway anymore.

"Great." I think, rolling pupils upward.

The light that scorches our eyes just so happens to be coming from the Sun and it peers over the horizon of Earth's northern hemisphere and a greyish pock-marked surface that our feet stand upon.

"Uh…" Rob stands behind with his mouth gaping. "Is this the fuckin' Moon!?" His voice cracks and scales up in volume as he, most likely, realizes that none of us should have the ability to breathe.

"Holy shit!" Meryl runs forward. "What is this?!"

"Keep your cool guys, like I said, none of this is real." I remind the two of them, angling my head to the side, seeing dust and larger mountain-like craters – Yet I find myself looking for the American flag, almost as if I expect it to be here, real or not.

I turn around and Rob shakes his head a bit, removing his hands from his neck and finding that he can, in fact, take in breaths normally.

"Weird." He says.

Meryl keeps walking, in a slow paced, low-gravity motion. "What's that off in the distance?" Seeming slightly un-phased by the insanity that is our situation.

"Looks like a structure of some kind." I move with bounds that feel like pushing through water.

This definitely makes less sense than the last experience I'd had in this tower.

Does this suggest a moon settlement?

"I don't get it, Dante, why would we be in some imaginary dream, on the Moon, of all places?" Rob expects me to know the answer, considering what I had just said, moments ago, as he follows behind.

The only answer that makes any sense, spills out of my mouth as if I had, in fact, said it once before. "Because this is someone else's nightmare." Holding my pistol downward, as I leap slowly toward the building that Meryl continuously heads toward, unflinchingly.

"Meryl!" I yell, struggling to catch up with her. "Wait!"

Her hair waves around in single strands as she looks back, catching her eyes glimpsing at mine and then again looking toward the building that grows larger and larger as we approach.

Its shadow is overbearing, more-so that than of the dark side of the Moon, looking down with its window-less concrete face. Single, large silvering lettering hangs above an electronic air-lock, reading, "USMAF" and directly beneath, in small writing, "United States Medical Advancement Facility."

She stops directly in front and Rob and I finally catch up.

"A medical facility…" Meryl's voice goes up in question. "On the moon?"

"Looks like the government's been hiding something." Rob adds.

"Not really a surprise." I say. "But we don't know if this place actually exists."

I then remember the blueprints in the ZeroFactor facility, the ones that depicted a vessel for likely space travel.

"You think this is where the undead came from?" Wiping his fingers along the electronic keypad inquisitively.

"I'm not sure how that'd be possible." Looking back at a giant blueberry in the sky. "Since we're about three days from Earth."

I feel a slice of my childhood shooting back, reading all of those space and solar system books and I wonder, not of Mars, but of Jupiter – The planet that scared me the most, with its giant spots and wiggling waves of clouds. Scientists called it bigger than any other planet in the solar system. To me, it was like a monster.

To me, it was the most terrifying and fascinating thing, at the time.

"That doesn't mean anything." Meryl interrupts, pointing at a large collection of survey vehicles and what seem to be oval-like pods, fifty meters or so from our position. "Bet you a million bucks they used those for transport to and from Earth."

"You know, Meryl…" Noticing that her attitude is the opposite of what it had been just before entering this supposed alternate realm. "You don't seem too worried about any of this, what's going on in that head of yours?"

"Nothing." She smirks. "I'm just not afraid of space!"

"Alright, damnit." Rob pushes between the two of us. "We have one option." Looking at the airlock. "Let's go inside of this here building and see if there's a way outta this crazy crap."

"Uhm…" I turn and notice the door we came through no longer exists. "Okay, sure, you know the code to open it or something?"

He laughs with a hand against his head. "The hell we need a code for?" Aiming a six-shooter at the pad, he fires a single shot, the recoil barely lifting his hand and the bullet striking metal that disperses like confetti underwater.

Of course that worked.

With that, electronic gears turn, latches unbolt and the door slides open to the left and to the right, separately, revealing a small dull and white looking room with words labeling it as "Decontamination."

"Well, I guess that makes sense, don't really need tight security in a place no one ever visits." Putting a hand out. "After you then."

We walk inside and the door snaps shut, beams of blue slip out of the cracks and corners of the walls – A sudden jolt of anxiety rips through me – They scan us up and down, back and forth. A soothing female voice announces, "Decontamination complete, no anomalies detected. Please report to the front desk immediately." A similar door opens directly in front of us, stuttering for a moment before it completes its process.

"And what do we have here!" Rob enthusiastically shouts, walking into a room filled with dust, flickering panels and sparks that bounce off of light fixtures on the ceiling.

The same voice, slightly stumbling over its words, greets us with more information. "Wel… ccom to the United States Medical Advancement Facility, a pre… premier organization striving hard to enhan… en… enhance quality of life." It pauses for about thirty seconds more and continues. "On behalf of the USMAF, we congratulate you on be… b… being hired to aide us in engineering the…" And that's it, as if it's missing the rest of its data.

"Interesting." My eyes scan around the area.

"You two smell that?" Meryl flares her nostrils, turning around a full three sixty degrees.

"Hmmmph." I take a deep breath. "Smells like absolutely nothing."

Waving his hands in the air. "Oooooh, watch out for the spooky space monsters!" He chuckles like an elementary school kid would.

"I wouldn't let your guard down." Readying my pistol. "We *are* still, technically, inside of that tower."

"He's right." Pumping the stock of a shotgun she'd picked up earlier. "We're obviously not really on the Moon, which means we're most likely going to run into something strange here in a moment."

On the opposite side of the corridor sits a triangular sized room and through broken shards of glass are faintly flashing terminals. An automatic door, that's been short-circuited, jitters back and forth, scraping against steel like fingernails on a chalkboard.

"Let's check this out." Waving for them to follow.

"Mmmm, K." Rob aims around as if searching for hostiles.

As we move forward the air becomes thicker with an odorless substance that makes your lungs pump harder and eyes feel dried out, red and itchy.

A piece of my brain pictures Ben Stein and a beach ball.

"Blah." Meryl slings her shotgun over her shoulder and wipes both hands down the sides of her face. "What's that?"

"Not sure." I say, picking a large broken steel pipe off of the ground and jamming it into the door, stopping its repetitive motion completely.

The flat monitor to the first terminal glares red, reading, "..//Outbreak Alert – Subject Thirteen Thirty One compromised."

"So…" Rob leans in from behind, just over my shoulder. "They were experimenting?"

"Maybe." I reply, turning to the second monitor.

This one reads, "..//Security breach – Sector Twenty Six."

I try tapping the Enter key a few times but the screen remains unresponsive.

"Check this out." He turns the rotating screen of the third monitor toward me.

"..//Viral outbreak not contained – initiate termination of Subject Thirteen Thirty One."

They all seem pretty cryptic, not really providing any specific information, but whatever had happened, or whatever this place had been trying to convince us of, must have been pretty damn nasty. Although, there aren't any bodies, no signs of anything other than trashed equipment and a broken electronics system that controls the doorways.

"Must've been an evacuation, if they were unable to contain whatever this outbreak was." Rob fiddles around with the keyboard of the first terminal. "Oh! Here, read this."

I slide over and find that he's discovered some sort of log system, which reads, "Intercepted logs, as follows." My eyes trail down the paragraphs of something that puts a little more sense to all of this.

They're all dated twenty-ten, reading:

This is a systems check.

I am posting to this log from a location that I cannot reveal.

This requires me to relay a number of signals from numerous satellites within the orbit of Earth, meaning that if you're viewing this upon the time of publication, two or three hours have already passed.

Keep checking back -- These bastards, whom I also cannot reveal at this time, will pay.

Scrolling down a bit more, a second transmission:

These walls that cage me are grey and sterile and the air smells like nothing, not even the sweat of my own body lingers.

I'm not sure what they've done to me, but I can't feel myself or my thoughts. There are no mirrors or windows in this room, although the tips of my fingers reveal wires and tubes that weave themselves in and out of the base my skull.

My hair used to flow long and black past my shoulders but now only half remains. One side shaved almost completely bald, the other trimmed haphazardly and frayed.

When I sleep I dream of nothing and when I wake I feel my eyes burning and blood-shot, like a hangover after an endless night of boozing; Pounding against the inside of my head, infernally beating.

They're coming now, I hear them, their feet gently tapping against steel, twisting and unlocking the bolts of the single, large blast door that keeps me here – Stop transmission.
 Then one final interception before the screen scrolls into a blank page of nothing:
 I'm losing track of day and night. I no longer know how many days have passed since I've been captured. I don't even remember how I came to be here. Here, being somewhere between nowhere and hell-if-I-know Avenue.

The pain in my head has stopped for now but it's been replaced with a loud, annoying screeching sound that blasts through my eardrums, like metal clanking.

Sometimes it stops for a while.

Other times it seems to last forever.

I don't understand.

Stop transmission.

Rob looks at me and I look back. "Well, I guess we know, partly, of what happened here."

Keeping the entire reason to myself, which would both be unbelievable to the two of them and take entirely too long to explain; I know who this is and I'm beginning to understand.

"That's fucked up man, sounds like they mutilated this chick." He isn't entirely putting two and two together, but he doesn't have all of the pieces to the puzzle, as I do.

"I guess so." Swinging around to see Meryl staring at something on the wall behind us. "Hey, what're you doin' over there?"

"It's that symbol." Running her fingers against roughly carved grooves. "Must've taken something strong as hell to put this here."

"ZeroFactor." I move in closer to her. "That stupid looking jagged-tooth face?" Raising my eyebrows. "The fuck is it supposed to represent anyway, aside from a buncha maniacs?"

No one's got an answer.

But I suspect that an inkling of a hint lingers in the back of their minds.

"S'pose we'll move on." Sort of wondering if they'd stockpiled smokes on a moon base.

"So when's the shit gonna hit the fan, eh?" Rob tosses the keyboard through the broken window to the lobby area and watches the wires snap and keys strike against the parallel wall.

"I fully expect something crazy to happen, just keep your guard up."

On the outside of the room lies another hallway and yet, another door, this one jammed crooked and half open. Seems as if someone had attempted to divert passage or even stop it.

"You first then." Pointing with the end of this pistol through the corridor.

Snapping on a shoulder-light, the passageway lights in a yellowish tint, light sources becoming scarcer as we venture forth.

The rays shine through the half-cocked door, illuminating a small circular area of white, speckled air – no sign of movement, as I lift my leg on through and pull the rest of myself in after it.

"Seems alright." I say and wave the two of them in, wondering what the whole point of our presence here is and why it's considerably less dangerous than my last encounter. "Come on in."

But maybe we simply haven't gone far enough within.

I watch Meryl pull her body through, clothing sticking to her skin – Tight and perfectly rounded with that ass that I just can't take my eyes off of. It makes my blood pump a hundred times harder – Then I notice her connecting eyes with mine.

"And what exactly are you staring at?" Walking right past, with a wiggle to her strut, crouching and aiming her pump-action around, listening.

"Uhm, heh…" I blink a few times and notice that Rob's got a sneer across his face. "Let's find a light switch or something."

"Listen." Rob puts a hand on my shoulder. "I know that love can bloom on the battlefield or whatever, but seriously, we don't need you thinkin' about sweaty, hot sex when we're both sorta depending on you to lead us through this shit."

"Damn, you doubting my leadership abilities now?" I shake him away. "You *can* mind your business, I won't lead us to death, I promise you."

"He's just mesmerized." Meryl stands, hand on her hip. "Probably hasn't been around a real woman in a long time."

Spotting a panel, frayed wires and a few switches, I move, looking back for a moment. "Both of you, just stop, we don't have time for idle stupidity."

Her hands in the air. "Sheesh, fine…" She follows behind and Rob remains stationary where he'd entered the room.

"You alright, D?" She moves into my shoulder. "I'm not entirely wrapping my head around you, as a whole; your personality and this current situation, like how you knew what would happen back in the entrance."

I squint and grab two matching wires, scowling and breathing angrily through my nostrils, I touch them together with sparks spilling like droplets of water onto my hands. "Look, I don't need either of you to understand what's going on, it's going to come together." Pinching and twisting the tethered copper. "Trust me."

The room blinks on with extraordinarily bright light.

"Oh, I trust you." She says. "I wouldn't have come this far if I didn't." Checking the cartridge of her gun. "Hell, I would've left your ass back at the station if I thought for a second you'd stab me in the back or something."

I spin around the room and catch Rob, arms crossed.

"Chu lookin' at?" Grilling me with his eyes.

A stinging sensation percolates within the frontal area of my brain, just beneath my forehead, like a lingering headache, all pounding against my skull – something feels as if it's trying to access my thoughts, I can feel it – My hands lose control of the metaphorical steering wheel.

19

Nuhm De'Ara

The room's colors turn negative then positive, spinning around and hazy, I slap a hand to my forehead and struggle to keep my balance. Meryl catches me by the arm and Rob walks over from his poised stance.

"Hey." He says in a concerned tone. "The hell you doin'?"

"When was the last time you ate something." She asks. "Or when was the last time any of us ate, for that matter."

Good question, but pretty much irrelevant.

"Forget it." I shake my head and blink, not able to figure out what just happened. "I'm good, I'm good, let's just keep moving."

The walls are lined with large, brown canisters with little rectangular windows on the upper-front side. A reflection beneath my feet looks back up at us, eyes seeming black with dark circles that meet the edge of a five o' clock shadow, long overdue.

Inside of one of these containers, looking through misty glass, seems to be a badly damaged body; Eyes closed and mouth gaping open, as if dead and kept in some sort of suspended animation state.

"You thinkin' what I'm thinkin'?" Rob presses his hands against the little window.

"We're not sure this is an undead." Rubbing a finger along my chin. "Could be some kind of experimental cryostasis pod or something, maybe failed?"

"Possibly." Meryl replies, like she's got a better idea.

A shadow creeps by, just out of sight.

"What was that?!" Rob swings around with his gun aiming at empty space.

A wave of cold-heat surges through me, from head to toe.

Then another, right out of the corner of my vision.

"Fuckin'…" Meryl jumps and slides her back to the wall between two containers.

"Shhhh," I put my left index finger to my lips and hold a pistol with my right hand. "Told you somethin' stupid was going to happen soon."

An elevator at the far end of the room dings three times and signals that it's about to hit our floor, numbers lighting up reading, "three."

"Not good." I wave two fingers. "Meryl get the left, Rob you're right."

"I'm always right." With a finger and a thumb he taps the side of his head and moves.

Racing from side to side, the dark figures pass by, never making their presence fully visible.

"Dammit!" Standing at the left side of the elevator. "What's going on!?"

"Ignore it." Standing right in front. "It's screwing with us," I say.

"What is?!" Rob shifts his eyes in my direction. "The building, or those ZeroFactor dudes?!"

Before I can think of any kind of an answer, the elevator dings again, shadows still increasing the intensity at which they blur by. Reaching our floor, it rings and slowly slides open. On the other side of the doors is a completely transparent compartment, looking out into the dot splotched blackness of space. Old and dry blood simply appearing smudged across the glass that separates space's vacuum and us.

Meryl's eyes bounce back and forth as she looks inside, carefully. "Erm, you think we should get inside?"

For a split second, Nuhm De'Ara's face appears directly in front of me, attached to a fast-walking body, too quickly to make out any real detail.

An invisible force pushes me against the spine, flinging me forward into the elevator. Eyes wide and hands scrambling, I grab at every flat surface, attempting to gain some sort of balance.

"I'm gonna be sick." Puffing my cheeks and feeling a burning dance upward into the back of my throat, slicing on its way back down.

Meryl and Rob stand outside still, looking in, as a large cloud of onyx dust forms behind them.

"Guys, get in here, now!" I yell, watching it leak like water around every crevice, every inch of the room we'd recently illuminated, now covered in darkness again, quickly enveloping the two of them.

Jumping to my feet, I pull both of them by the arm and drag their dazed bodies inside, just as the doors close.

"It's eating itself alive." My mind concludes.

"Snap out of it, you two." Snapping my fingers in front of their glassy looking eyes, "Come on!"

I catch a second glimpse of Earth, visible from our moving platform, vibrating and forming larger than life cracks all across its surface.

"Now approaching sector twenty six, research and development." A voice speaks, from above the door.

This is definitely the military research facility that conducted experiments on that Nuhm De'Ara woman, or should I say, Stephanie. As improbable as it sounds and as many questions as it poses, this has got to be the answer.

I imagine a voice whispering to me. "This is for better understanding, this is your enemy."

No.

This is a simply plain portrayal of madness.

I long to touch my feet to the gravel again, even if it's littered with the undead and maniacal terrorists.

"Mmmmph…" Meryl sighs and puts two hands on her thighs, sitting upward, "What just happened?"

"I…" I'm interrupted by a strange sound looming from above, most likely the floor we're traveling to. Like steel scraping steel, dragging hollow metallic sounds against chain grating and it almost sounds like screaming. An ominous thumping reverberates and shakes the elevator door, pounding every two or three seconds, then again, screaming steel and as we approach, the two sounds merge together as one.

"I think this is about to get ten times worse." Giving her a hand to stand, as Rob comes back to awareness as well.

Blood seeps through the cracks of the sliding door in front of us as the automated voice chimes in once again. "Destination reached, please proceed to nearest subject monitoring facility."

"The fuck." Staring in awe as Rob pulls himself up, backing away from the gallons of blood leaking into the lift, as the doors prepare to open.

"I don't like the looks of this." Pulling his weapon up toward the door.

"Right." I respond. "I haven't liked the looks of anything since I got back to this damn city."

The elevator whips open faster than the blink of an eye – Expecting to see insanity pouring from every crack – We don't.

"Well…" Rob cautiously walks through the opening. "That's a relief."

A hallway, lined in polished silver and black and an endless line of doors, sits completely empty.

"This can't be right." Meryl states, all surprised and gasping, probably wishing for reality to come back to us. "It's gotta be a trick or something."

I step out into the fresh hall, leaving prints of an unknown persons or creatures blood in my tracks.

"Come on." Aiming down my sights. "There's going to be an exit up here, somewhere, I know it."

Hoping, at least; Considering the fact that the building itself seems to be deteriorating.

I look over each shoulder as I pass the first set of doors, each numbered in sequence. This is all too familiar. On top of that, they're all locked, not even responding to the strike of a shoulder.

Meryl turns to me, gun across her chest. "Now what?"

"Walk with me." I say, counting each locked entrance. "We're looking for thirteen thirty one."

Both of them follow but I catch a look of uncertainty on Rob's face as my head switches left to right.

"Sup Rob?" Turning back for a moment as I walk.

"I dunno, man." He grinds his teeth together. "I like to think of myself as a somewhat optimistic person and all – I know what you're thinking – But, like, we've gotta be walking…"

Meryl interrupts and places a hand on my arm. "Into a trap."

Counting thirteen twenty two, twenty three. "I know just about as much as the two of you, but stick with me here," winking, "I guarantee there'll be an exit."

"If you say so." He sighs. "But what the hell do you think that noise was before? And that blood?"

Before I can come to an understandable or at least reasonable answer to his question, we arrive.

"Alright you two, same as before, weapons up." Placing my hand on the doorknob, knowing it'll be unlocked, looking up and down the hall, seeing absolutely nothing.

20

Thirteen Thirty One

What we're greeted by is an extremely small cubbyhole, a locking mechanism that twists and latches, plus one more door – A blast door.

"I guess they didn't want anyone getting out." I examine the edges. "Or at least no one's supposed to get out."

I reach a finger out to the door to begin opening it, but just as I touch the steel, it slides open gracefully.

"Alrighty." My lips move, dumbfounded.

In the middle of the room sits a cold and dusty looking, mechanical surgical slab. A large bungle of wires hanging down from the ceiling, all twisted together. The grey concrete walls extend far apart and there isn't a single window that shows any kind of view.

As the three of us walk through, brushing past cobwebs that hang down and sprawl into our faces, I realize that this building probably has handfuls more of rooms just like this one; Sort of makes you wonder.

"Spiders?" Meryl swats a thick coating of web out of her face. "On the moon?"

"Remember, Meryl?" I glance at her, almost condescendingly.

"Oh, right." With her fingers in quotation. "Not real."

A cold gust of air passes by just as a long burst of clicks go off, followed by a loud screech.

The blast-door from behind shuts and locks.

"I don't like the sound of that…" Rob says, twisting around to the section of wall adjacent to the door.

"Hey, I definitely smell something now." Meryl takes in a deep huff.

The air's different; Smells like embalming fluid, that stench that stings your nostrils like ammonia and tingles all the way down the back of your throat, impairing breathing and inducing vomit.

"Aauuuggh." Rob grabs his nose. "Fuckin' hell man."

"I'd say that this is strange…" Cupping my hand to my nose and mouth. "But this entire journey's been the epitome of just that."

"Check this out." Meryl approaches the surgical table in curiosity.

Meanwhile, I scan the area again and again; No exit, no sign of anything.

The slab she must've been bound to seems to have dark red and yellow stains all over it.

"Whoever was here…" Running a finger along the grooves where a body could have been laying. "Sure as hell wasn't treated with any kind of hospitality."

Again, like before in the elevator, that hollow metal sound and scraping like the desperate cries of a banshee echo from just outside of the room.

"Hey you two…" I point a finger toward the vibrating wall. "I think we may want to step back."

Not a moment later, two knife-like, long and slender fingers pierce the concrete and metal door, cutting through and disappearing again, just barely missing the flesh of Rob's head.

"Shit man!" He scrambles for the other side of the room with Meryl and I as we head backward.

Then a second set cut through again, four this time, grappling at the already open edges and peeling away at the walls like a sardine can, slowly opening.

"What do we do?!" Meryl shouts, gun in the air.

"Shoot!" I command, squeezing triggers and spraying the darkness with pounding gunfire. I kneel, dodging random bits of shrapnel as our attacker reveals its form. The large metallic arms reach down and dig into the floor, bending and pulling the attached body forward and away from the growing smoke.

"Yes…" A heavily distorted, scratchy sounding female voice says.

"Nuhm De'Ara." I cease fire, realizing they've no effect.

"You will die, the three of you."

"And this is what you *really* are?" I ask, raising an eyebrow as her arms shrink down to proportional size and her feet land gently upon the cracked stone floor.

"I am many, many things, but this…" Pointing at the slab. "Is where I lost the person that I used to be."

The ghost of the woman from my previous experience in the Tower, beautiful and lying out on the table, hair half shaved and wires connecting to her skull. Her eyes twitch behind closed lids, mouth moving softly. "Where am I?" It echoes with a depressing shift in tone.

"So what, you're an experiment?"

"Dante…" Rob interrupts. "You're speaking to some imaginary robot woman here…"

I put my hand up toward his face. "What'd they do, replace your body with machinery or something?"

"A type of cybernetic alloy, mostly." She says, running bladed fingers along her tongue.

"And what of the bodies encased on the bottom floor?"

"The undead, naturally." Running them, now, down along the side of her mangled and half metal face.

"Jesus…"

"Nope, Jesus Christ himself isn't going to save you, or anyone, for that matter." She says, "I leave this building and I bring my terror, my anguish and my anger to Earth." Placing each hand against my chest, "I," penetrating skin, "am," blood gushing, driving further and knocking wind from my lungs, "ZeroFactor."

21

The Last Remnant

"Alright." Waving my hands around and blinking, hyperventilating, "Nobody say a damn thing!"

We're back again, front door of the Tower.

Meryl stares in confusion and worry. "What is it?"

I gain my bearings once more, turn ninety degrees and grab both my pistol and a shotgun from that stupid green table.

"D, you O.K.?" Rob approaches with a quizzical look on his face.

"Stand back." Aiming the barrel of the shotgun at the locked door. "We're getting the fuck outta here!"

"No!" Pushing it to the side. "They'll just shoot us the second we go out there!"

Determined, I shake him away from the gun and say, "This is the third goddamn time we've been in this stupid ass hallway." Pulling back on the pump-action slide. "They're not out there anymore, trust me."

The two of them back away, picking up whatever's left of the weapons collection and watch in nervous anticipation.

"Third time my ass…" Rob grimaces.

With a burst of sparks and the swift clearing of gun-smoke, the door swings open wide to reveal a barren landscape spilling inward. Cold and stale air fills the night and the sky gleams down with speckled dominance. Not a single armed or otherwise unarmed ZF unit remains to be seen, not even glinting with the flash of a rifle scope through some window or behind a pile of rubble.

"Strange…" Meryl walks forward, scanning the area. "How'd you know?"

"Gut instinct." Reaching for a bandoleer full of shells and strapping it around my shoulder and chest. "Let's go."

The pit we'd been held captive in, a few clicks ahead of us, is now filled with fresh dirt. All that remains are the slowly dying fires filling a handful of metal canisters that line the broken sidewalks.

"And how long were we in there?" Rob asks, kicking over a barrel and watching its contents spill onto frozen mud covered pavement.

"Couldn't have been more than a few hours." Meryl says, ears twitching upward. "Wait, you guys hear that?"

My focus centers on a small plastic bag that lay half open on the ground just in front of my feet. I reach a hand down and barely notice myself clutching it between my fingers and shoving it into my front-right pant pocket.

An echo of buzzing, soaring wings and chopping blades washes in and consumes the dead silence of the night.

"That's right." I whisper, Meryl's eyes shifting to mine.

"No, they couldn't…"

"Both of you…" Pointing at each of them. "Listen up!"

Rob raises his hand and jokes. "Yessir!"

"When I volunteered for this recon mission, they'd mentioned a fleet that'd be flying in to finish off the devastation, whether we made it out or not."

"In other words, they're going to wipe out the city?"

"Exactly." I think for a moment. "But these guys could very possibly be prepared for this."

Meryl interjects. "A bunch of anarchist bums, parading through the streets with third-world type weapons? I don't think so."

"I do think so." My eyes trail back and forth for a moment. "We gotta move."

"Why not just flag 'em down?" Rob begins waving his hands in the air as a mass of silver dots fill the sky.

An overwhelming chill reverberates within my spine – The air fills with the smell of jet fuel and for a split second my vision jiggles like the flutter of a heartbeat.

I see a quick glimpse of two figures carrying my body, limb for limb.

Then Brooklyn shoots back, without a second passing.

"Hey D!" Rob waves from ahead. "You're laggin'!"

"It's a little more than lag." I say to myself, beginning to jog, arms swiping back and forth, shotgun in one hand, pistol in the other.

I knew our last hope would soon be here but I got that feeling – That gut-wrenching dread, again.

Meryl and Rob drop their pace as I catch up.

"What're you guys slowin' down for?" I point ahead, "to the Verrazano, move!"

It sits there gigantic and looks closer than it really is. My own judgment says about a mile, two miles, maybe even five. That doesn't really matter though; All we gotta do now is survive just a little longer.

The wind begins to blow furiously, pushing against us like a giant, icy hand from the sky.

"Guys!" I shout, dodging behind the wall of an alley just as I catch their attention, "Over here a sec!"

"Do either of ya have a smoke?" I ask.

They both stand there and stare at me gawking and dumbfounded.

"Neither of us smoke." Meryl hisses and raises both hands, "Now tell me this isn't the reason we stopped!"

"Shit." I peer out carefully past the wall. "Alright…alright, we got about a half mile of a death-trap coming up."

Silence falls for a short second; You can hear their moaning, nothing but howling cries of the dead.

"What?" Rob steps out, "Those zombies?" He asks. "They're, like, barricaded all the way down the street, behind steel flippin' gates."

I pull him back as a bullet just barely brushes by his hair.

"Oh fuck!" He pats his head, feeling around for a hole he might not have noticed exploding from his cranium.

"Right then." I push the two of them away from the open. "Now, I got a plan."

"Wait." Meryl raises a hand, reaching for her scoped rifle with the other, "How the hell did you know there was a sniper?"

"Snipers." I say. "And if you haven't realized by now, I tend to notice things."

Not as easily as I had been before, without that spooky little guiding voice.

Meryl allows herself to fall back against the wall, hand to her chin, clutching the trigger of a single-bolt action with twitching fingers.

Rob slaps his hands together erratically.

"So then, smart-guy…" Anxiously questioning, "What's the course of action?"

The mud beneath my feet comes up in gobs of brown and black, squishing between my fingers as I spread its filth like butter all over my skin, my face and my clothing.

"Uhm…" Meryl watches, puzzled. "D?"

I rip a leg from my pants, tear a gaping hole in the center of my shirt and finish off by rubbing both hands through the thin bristles of my not-so-fresh and clean-cut hair.

"You really are insane…" Rob's eyes go wide as he backs away, like he's seen directly into my mind, knowing what I'm about to ask of them.

"You two got knives, right?"

Meryl nods and Rob feels around the leather of his belt.

"I want both of you…" Looking most likely completely off of my rocker. "To do just as I did."

"Camouflage," Meryl says, "But they'll spot us like turds in a punch bowl."

"They won't," I wink.

"Ah, hell no!" Rob shouts, pointing his finger at my nose, "That's the stupidest idea…" Throwing himself a little temper tantrum, "You can't be goddamn serious!"

"Get on with it." I demand of them, as they stand frozen, probably trying to wrap their minds around my psyche.

"Meryl." I motion my eyes three clicks past the alley toward one of the locked gates. "You're going to blow that lock off and we're going to allow them to spill into the streets."

"Yeah." She shakes her head in acknowledgement. "I get it now, but it's freakin' insane, D, you've gotta realize that."

"I realize it." Clapping my hands together. "Now let me see some skin! I want the two of you to look as dead as you possibly can."

Slowly, both of them tear little pieces of clothing.

"You wanna be believable, a little more than that guys." Crossing my arms for a moment; I do feel almost a little crazy.

Rob completely removes his shirt, tearing gashes in the knees of his pants and kneels down, contemplating the mud and its slimy texture.

Meryl shreds the bottom half of the stale-with-sweat wife-beater she'd been wearing this entire time and uses her knife to take diagonal cuts out of her pants.

"You know, Meryl…" I begin, eyes fixated.

"Don't even say it." Looking up from her little work of art, "Notice things my ass…"

For once, I let out a chuckle.

When they finally finish, I stand back for a moment to observe the two of them, looking all raggedy and mud-soaked.

We, in fact, look like a handful of turds.

"Alright, Meryl." Giving her the go-ahead with two fingers. "Take off that lock and when I say go, you two keep those knives directly in front of you, aim for the brain, watch for gunshots, keep your eyes down and don't get snagged." Pulling my own serrated blade from my leg. "Just run; run like Wallyworld's on a fire-sale and you're fresh outta bread and milk."

Despite the humorous take on our situation, I seriously doubt their morale's even close to slightly high. In fact, I bet the two of them believe this is the end.

"Go!"

My feet burst into movement at the loud pop of the rifle, catching Meryl's shoulder blade in recoil and pushing her forward with me – Knives straight out.

Behind, Rob yells. "Wait!"

"We can't leave him!" Meryl screams, looking back just slightly as the stampede fills the street, bursts of what sound like fifty caliber rounds going off and blood already showering the close vicinity – Dark red and sticky black.

"He's gotta catch up!" I say, feeling a bit of remorse, subconsciously crossing my fingers, jamming my blade into the eye socket of an oncoming dead-runner and swiftly pulling it out again. "If we slow down or stop, we're dead!"

Sixty seconds later we're both completely covered in blood, among other things. Only reason I don't lose track of Meryl, is because I haven't let go – Left hand on her arm, right hand clutching a gore encrusted knife – Running through undead and stray bullets.

A part of my mind, amidst the frantic chaos, wonders what has and will become of Rob.

"Go for the eyes!" I shout through teeth, keeping my head slightly tilted downward to avoid ingestion of infected material, for lack of better words.

Above the mindless moaning, hungry clawing, huffing and puffing, the frequent gunshots are but a whisper.

"Dante!" Meryl yells out in terror as a half-rotten man grabs her by the leg – She'd missed the critical stab.

My knife instinctively moves back into its sheath, as I lift Meryl from her feet, huddling and hurdling through the masses; I carry her, running, muscles aching, and the fierce wind of too-close-for-comfort bullets passing by, as my mind scrambles to think of step two of this genius plan.

"Hey!" Peeking up from my shoulder. "Where to?!"

Merely shouldering the onslaught, my eyes dart left, then right – Empty vehicles, apartment buildings, the wreckage of other buildings, all crumbled and more damned locked gates.

I hadn't considered this problem. Sweat gushing from every pour, arms ready to give-way, I make a snap decision.

"You ready for this?" Looking down into her panicked eyes.

She nods, giving me that "You fuckin' stupid?" look.

We make it to a small clearing at the front of a small convenience store, swiftly lowering her to her feet, I swing the shotgun from my back and thrust it to her, pulling my pistol from its holster, I fire through glass and we dive to the ground behind an empty cigarette kiosk.

"Oh thank God." Gasping for air, I grab a full pack of, most likely, stale smokes, tear it open and shove a stick into my mouth. Fumbling with my lighter and striking flame to tobacco – Inhaling. "Catch your breath, this ain't over yet."

22

At A Loss

I try not to imagine Rob being torn limb from limb.

I try not to imagine the death of someone that it was my duty to protect, as usual and oddly, someone I'd become sort of comfortable with, regardless of the stupid bantering and lame jokes.

Both Rob and Meryl, in the middle of all of this, I feel as if they're becoming closer to me than my family ever really was.

Here I am, for the umpteen-billionth time pondering loss, failing, always failing.

What kind of man does that make me?

To my right, against my side, head momentarily resting against my arm, her chest moves up and down.

Nothing had followed us inside, amazingly enough, but that gives reason for suspicion.

"You alright?" I ask. "Not gonna go all zombie on me or anything?"

Shaking her head, "No." Struggling to utter words, "But don't EVER do that again."

I hadn't even realized if I'd been bitten or infected, though I feel relatively fine, for the most part, aside from being covered in mud and blood.

Tapping the end of my pistol against my forehead, I brainstorm the next plan of action, puffing away at a slowly smoldering cigarette, savoring every drop of nicotine.

"What're you thinking?" She asks.

"I'm thinking…"

Then the sound of footsteps echo from the back of the shop.

"You've got some balls…"

A shadow reflects from a tiled wall and it speaks.

Meryl struggles to her feet, slowly, shotgun in-hand, surveying the half-empty shelves and the little area that leads around to an unknown little hole of darkness.

"Ya'll blast your way through Manhattan and think you can just waltz right through our Brooklyn territory?"

He must be some random ZF soldier, I think to myself, standing, and pistol aiming at his shadow.

"But now, you ain't goin' nowhere."

Revealing himself, a mustached man in a green combat suit, holding a sawed off in each hand, one aimed for me and the other on Meryl.

"Name's Jackson." He introduces himself, "Tom Jackson."

"A name means nothing if you're a dead man." I reply.

"Is that so?" He snickers. "And you must be Dante, the bosses little ass-itch."

"You mean that psycho-bitch, Nuhm?" Aiming my weapon higher.

"Watch yer mouth, boy!" Clicking back on one of the hammers. "Now, who's this sweet piece o' ass?"

"You watch *your* tongue, asshole!" Taunting him, "You so much as touch her and I won't even give you the courtesy of a quick death."

She looks over, from the corner of her eyes and gives a slight grin, aiming the barrel of her shotgun from behind a snack shelf, directly at his head.

"Oh…" Pulling back on the other hammer. "You think you out-gun me or something?"

Unfortunately, he's right.

Won't matter who shoots first, we'll all likely end up with lead poisoning.

"Tick-tock." Moving closer, "Make your move. I don't think our hungry little friends outside are going to stay subdued for too much longer."

That's why they hadn't come in after us; Something's got hold of their minds.

Or someone.

The cigarette in my mouth burns down to its last puff, smoking to the butt, right into my eyes, burning, but I can't blink.

"You know, that's bad for your health…"

His eyes twitch, growing nervous; Not so confident after all.

A gamble – I'd always hated gambling – Which one of his hands would have a slower reaction time.

Thinking back, he walked into the room, aiming his right hand weapon first…

"Meryl?" I say out of the side of my mouth.

She's got the advantage.

"Enough chit-chat!" He commands viciously. "What's it gonna be? The explosive ends of Betty and Martha, or my best buds just outside the shop?"

Is she thinking what I'm thinking? Can she read my thoughts?

One can only hope.

His right finger begins to move.

I drop down, swiftly, to my knees.

Buckshot sparks and shatters from both sides of the store and the air fills with smoke.

I hadn't been hit, but neither Meryl nor Tommy-boy make a sound.

I see her face as visibility returns, down on the ground, her lips move in pain, "I got him."

But he'd grazed her shoulder by an inch – only a flesh wound, thankfully.

The bitter taste of adrenaline drips from my tongue as I slide across the dirty and trash covered floor, lifting her from underneath her arms and sitting our bodies upright.

"You'll be fine." I reassure, taking a piece of torn cloth from my pocket and wrapping it tight around her wound.

Looking back to where he'd been standing, now replaced by splattered blood and brain-matter against the wall.

"Nice shot."

The crowd outside begins to move again, bum-rushing our location.

"Come on." I lift her up, her eyes gazing into mine, "We gotta move."

I envision a ladder in the back of the shop where we could make it to the roof. What we'd do when we get there is beyond my imagination at this point in time, but it offers some form of temporary safety – If the snipers can't target us – The bastards and their limitless ammunition.

"Up!" I grab her by the arm and head for the back, undead bursting through already shattered glass.

Passing security cameras and consoles, the money safe and the cheap radio that only plays two stations – A ladder sits just as I'd imagined, chained up and bolted with a little key-lock, rusty and probably half stuck in place from neglect of usage.

"Now stand back!" Putting a hand to her chest and aiming with the other, firing a single round that sends shrapnel and steel bursting in two – The little gate swings outward and welcomes us to a possible escape.

"Hurry!" She yells directly into my ear, hands grasping at me as the undead begin to close in on us, and squeezing through the tiny slit of a niche that separates us from the rest of the store.

I slide the ladder downward and as they rush in, I push her up before myself, firing rounds as her feet climb, rung for rung. "Go, go, go!"

Twenty seconds later we're pushing through the hatch, about gasping for air as if emerging from a whirl pool in the middle of a sinking submarine.

"Shit!" Shouting as I slam my foot down on its lid.

Meryl rests against a collection of ventilation pipes and asks, through gasps of air, "What?!"

"I left my goddamn pack of smokes down there!"

"Hah!" She chuckles for a moment. "Serves ya right!"

I almost wanna snap back at her with some stupid retort but realize that it's the nicotine talking; Like a fuckin' doper needin' a fix.

"Here." Unwrapping the bandoleer from my chest, "Reload."

She takes the barrel of her gun in her hand. "Hey, good thing," snapping the shell hatch open, "I'm empty."

I had only hastily grabbed two magazines for my pistol from the Tower, without any further thoughts. I only hope that's all I'll need to make this final "jump" to the bridge.

After catching our breath for a moment, she asks yet another question, same one she keeps asking and I wonder how I'd even become the leader of this charade, to begin with. "Now what?"

The hatch to the roof rattles, from what I can only guess, a few dozen cold and dead hands, pushing and clawing at its metal interior.

Probably smelling the flesh, the sweat, the blood, eager to rip us apart.

But if someone is actually able to control these things, I wanna know who or better yet, how.

I spin around and notice that neither of us have literally lost our heads either.

"Guess we're out of line-of-sight."

"Guess so…" She says with a look of urgency and hungry lust pouring from her reflective, glossy eyes.

The aircraft in the sky, the military strike team I'd almost forgotten about, grows nearer.

We don't exactly have a whole lot of time, but I feel something; I feel exhilarated, anxious, nervous – my heart beats a million times a second and pounds against the walls of my chest and I can't even tell if it's the danger looming in the air or the fact that I could quite possibly be falling for this woman – Meryl.

The inside of my thumb rubs against my index finger.

"Nervous, again?" She asks.

Next to our little convenience store, here, is another building, only slightly shorter and has the rungs of a ladder dipping over its side.

"Shoulder your weapon, strap it tight." I look to her, buttoning the top of my holster around my sidearm.

"What?" She wonders. "Why? What crazy idea do you have now?"

"How're your legs feeling?" Remembering the "almost" tackle she'd experienced, only a few minutes earlier.

"Uhm…" Patting herself down and pulling back on both ankles in a stretch position. "I already know what you're going to ask…" Pointing at the ledge, "You go first, cause if I fall short, you're catching my ass."

We're going to jump it, seeing as it's only a few feet, but there are things like vertigo and the strong gusting wind to consider.

"You bet I will." Preparing myself, walking back to a safe distance, swinging arms back and forth. "Just watch me."

Feet in front of me, sprinting for the edge, I prepare for the leap and for a moment, I'm weightless, sailing over an empty alleyway and landing lopsided. Swiveling and regaining balance, I turn myself to Meryl again, just standing there and staring at me, then down at the ground, as she gains her bearings.

"Come on!" I shout with a hand out to her, waving, "It isn't that bad!"

I lean myself over the brick of the building, ready to catch, just in case.

Arms flailing around, she runs slanted downward and jumps but doesn't make enough of a leap.

"Shit!" I reach out, "Hold on!"

Grasping for her hand and catching the tips of her fingers with my right, tightening the hold as I grab with my left.

"Dammit, Meryl, what was that?!"

Pulling her up slowly, she says, "I don't know." Coming over the top to the roof, "I felt like something was holding me back, like a hand or something, just pushing against me."

Wrinkling my forehead in thought as I let go of my hold on her hands. "Hmm…"

"You know, this isn't the first time we've experienced something like that and considering…"

She stops me with a hand to my arm, "Just shut up for a moment, let's not contemplate too much here." Looking up to the sky with its swirly orange clouds, maybe the last wondrous dawn sky we'd ever see.

The chaos below disperses and reappears with absolutely random movement.

It seems as though we'd only just realized that the two of us are only human, we may not even live to see tomorrow and what, if anything, the future brings.

Funny, considering all the madness we'd managed to survive thus far; Luck only lasts so long.

"Just…" Her hand moves to my face and I look down into her eyes, always seeming captivating, breath taking and within there's a reflection of little roaring dots passing overhead, flashing and I can see just a hint of a quiver in her lips.

Pressing mine to hers, frozen in a short stint of silence and time, I overtake her tongue and for a moment, my vision is clear and I can see the sudden truth of it all and what lies ahead.

We aren't placed on this Earth, in this life, to make a shit-ton of money.

We aren't here to reproduce as much as possible, before we die, just so our children can repeat the same animalistic process of overpopulation without any relevant information or knowledge to pass on to the next generation.

We most certainly aren't here to see how much more shit we can own, compared to the next guy, whorishly consuming and attaining things we don't need; A billion things that won't matter when it all comes crashing down before us.

We're here for these little moments of clarity, to share just a split second with another human being and to pass on anything, something that actually matters, maybe what you've experienced, maybe something that'll actually change the world – But how many of us actually ever accomplish that?

I release my lips from hers and a warmth emanates from her pulsing body, enveloping the two of us, just for a moment – A little moment in time that'll be gone in five seconds and who knows, maybe we'll both be dead ten, twenty, thirty minutes from now, but at least we tried, at least we fought, tooth and nail, for what we believe in.

Then a giant blue flash erupts at the tip of the horizon and it sweeps the entire area in an electrical, vibrating boom that could interrupt, even, the moon's orbit.

23

The Fall

Five stinging fingers across my face, blurred vision and long hair pouring down into my eyes. "When ya gonna snap out of it, D?" A voice, too unintelligible to make out.

A sharp stab in the front of my skull pulses like a knife digging into my cerebral cortex and my eyelids flutter from the needling pain.

"Dante!" Meryl shouts, shaking me by the shoulder. "Get the fuck up!" Right into my ears, her voice throwing me back into the fray.

Down on my back, the sky raining steel winged objects, burning in flames and growing larger, in shape and size, by the second.

"What the hell's goin' on?" I ask, coughing on my own mucus and saliva.

Pulling me upward. "We have to go, we gotta get to the ground or we're fuckin' done for!"

I would beg to differ.

Stumbling around, she guides me to the ladder on the edge of the building and we slide like snakes down the rungs, slamming boots to the pavement.

I draw my weapon and she draws hers.

"We're not too far now." She says. "But this whole situation just went from bad to outright horribly insane."

Little pops and booms begin to sound-off from an unseen area, screeching and loud as hell, echoing like a screaming hawk.

Out in the streets, the dead have cleared, a straight shot right to our final destination – Maybe only a mile or two and then it occurs to me – What's falling from above.

"They set off some kind of crazy electro-magnetic pulse!" She yells, as we dive behind the wreckage of an old four-door vehicle and a military fighter comes down, humungous, slicing through the gravel and slamming into a million different shards of metal, part of its wing nearly halving our bodies.

Further past the bridge, maybe seven or eight clicks away, a helicopter swirls out of control and slams into the side of a large, tall standing building and erupts into an inferno that spills into windows and atop abandoned, parked vehicles on the sidewalks.

"You gotta be shitting me!" Brushing shards of debris off of myself. "What kind a fuckin' EMP is gonna bring down a fleet of military aircraft?! And how far does it stretch?!"

All around, every direction, not a single unit remains in the sky, now crashing into the streets and whatever else remains of Brooklyn.

"O.K., go, go!" Shoving Meryl forward, climbing past smoking wreckage, a pilot in the seat of the jet, ripped into a few different pieces of gore. "Fuck…"

A fissure forms directly in the center of the street, cutting down between us. The force of so much weight slamming into the ground had literally caused an Earthquake, right in the middle of New York.

No turning back.

This is it.

We've just lost all hope of salvation, my mind tells me.

We hustle down through the streets, dodging shrapnel, fire and collapsing structures of houses, apartments; Whatever these places used to be.

Ninety Second Street leads us right to the on-ramp, not long, not far.

Struggling to keep balance as the Earth finally stops shaking, the last aircraft falls off in the distance, directly into Upper New York Bay, creating a wave that crashes into the shore of a park and flooding into the streets with a white, sudsy look to it.

For a moment, we halt, huffing, puffing, and gaining breath. A quick glance into her tired and weary eyes and you can tell she's about to be spent, she's done, and she wants to go home.

We're both pretty much worse-for-wear and ready to collapse.

"You gonna make it?" I ask, panting and holding palms against my knees.

"I should ask you the same thing." Mocking my display of fatigue and leaning a shoulder into mine.

"Look…" I say, looking around, fires blazing, concrete crumbling and somewhere out there the undead crying. "When we get outta here, I don't care where we go, but I just want you to know…"

An abnormal crash interrupts my awkward sounding speech.

"The hell was that?" She gasps, standing up straight.

I aim my gun, taken from its holster, down toward the corner of a parking garage that stands not even fifty feet from the road that leads right to our freedom; Our way out.

A splash of grey and black flash from the side of the steel beams and forever vacant vehicles and an inhuman roar echoes; Demonic, evil, menacing.

"No…" Meryl begins pounding fists against my upper-arm, showing definite signs of despair and anger. "No, no, NO!" A tear glides down the side of her face like she's giving up; She knows for sure that it's all over.

"Don't freak out now." Clutching her by the arm, "Stay with me, babe, I need you."

She nods, as if those words were all that she needed to hear and grabs for her shotgun.

"Come out, come out, you piece of shit." I taunt, showing no fear, only determined anger.

Expecting some little monstrous dog-thing to come hurdling out from the corner, I aim close to the ground, keeping a safe distance, pacing backward a few feet.

An enormous brown and vermillion colored claw grips out from the side and crushes the fragile structure within its palm. Much bigger, much, much bigger than either of us could have ever expected or imagined.

Tall as the garage itself, the impish creature steps outward, hunching downward, standing almost humanoid, but more like a bear on its hind legs.

Its teeth yellow and serrated, eyes sunken and blackened, it screeches with another deafening roar.

"Fuckin' what?!" Saliva shoots from my mouth. "Fuck me!"

My brain boils like a pan of eggs, not seeing any clear option here; I've worked myself overtime and now I'm drawing a huge blank.

Its mouth opens again and liquid flame spills from its jaw, turning pavement into molten tar.

"Dante!" Shaking me, trying to move back. "What're you waiting for?! SHOOT!"

I think for a split second. "Where's our backup from the bridge?!" Yelling, "Why aren't they firing on this thing?!"

A good question, but an obvious answer trails behind; Not something I had wanted to consider.

"Who cares!" She begins emptying shell after shell, blasts flashing in the corner of my eyes as I stand in devastated astonishment.

Its feet begin to move, charging forward against charred Earth; Bullets merely tickling its seemingly armored skin.

I've gotta think of something fast, whether I'm able or not. I've gotta come up with something or neither of us are going to live to see the light of day again. I'm not losing someone else, not again.

Just behind the monster, with blades pointing directly up, is a downed Blackhawk, jutting crooked and dug in deep within a small area near the road and the highway.

"Meryl!" I grab her by the hand, forcing her to drop her weapon and follow my lead, diagonally and zigzagging around the melting ground.

The beast stops dead and stares down at us with an almost confused look on its face, growling, opening wide and preparing to spit once more.

"What are you doing!?"

Firing at its face, the bullets just bounce and a hand clamps down right behind us as we move and more fire spills out, its heat tearing at the clothing on our backs and burning like the hot sun, spilling down.

Ground rumbling, it turns as we dash by, getting closer, I can see it now.

The sound of a roar passes through us like a wave and again it charges.

Still holding on tight, I pull her and myself directly into the choppers mutilated cockpit, next to a limp and sorrowful looking corpse of what was, presumably, left of the United States Air Force.

Balling ourselves up into a fetal position, I cover her body with my own and press my lips against her frayed and dirt encrusted hair and we close our eyes together, impending doom leaping forward.

24

Point Blank

Back when we were kids, Jack and I made a pact. If either of us ever lost our way or strayed from the beaten path we'd originally set out for ourselves, we gave the other full permission to do whatever necessary to pull one or the other back into reality – to remember who we were, what we are and where we come from.

That seems so distant now; I can't tell you what I'd do to stop this.

In the police force, back in Harrisburg, those were the days. An older ranking officer had once told me, "If ever you seek revenge, remember to dig two graves." Probably a quote he'd stolen from a movie or a book, but it makes sense.

I feel sort of lucky so far, at least.

Although, we were both drunk at the time. Alcohol and its bitter and cold refreshing taste, I miss that.

Now my brain slips back into the situation, out of the cage I built within my mind to block out all the madness and all I want is for it to be over, to sit back with a smoke and a beer, clanging glasses together and celebrating victory.

But there is no victory in this, there never will be.

I didn't hear the crash, the slice, the sound of piercing flesh that you'd expect, but my sweaty palms still hold Meryl, tight.

I'm alive.

"Is it dead?" She whispers, moving just slightly, wriggling beneath my arms.

Thunder cracks across the sky in a brilliant white and little rain drops begin to fall against the glass of the choppers circular window.

My eyes feel as though they're beginning to lose focus and for a moment I feel almost like I'm not even here. Off in some distant land watching from a monitor to see what happens next.

We open our eyes completely and directly in front of us sits a disgruntled and gnarled looking monstrous face, with its tongue oozing out of its impaled and smashed head.

We could speculate as to how something this size managed to squeeze through a sliver of a wormhole, inside of a bank vault somewhere back in Manhattan, but the only thing that matters now is our final task.

The end of my pistol presses up against its nose and I rise from the wreckage, letting out a hand to pull Meryl up and onto the uplifted pavement.

"Come on, it's almost over now." I say, with a glimmer of hope in the tone of my voice, as if the light at the end of the battered and desolated tunnel is just ahead.

I hadn't even stopped to wonder why, out of all the other people in the city, her and I were pretty much the only ones left standing. Against almost impossible odds, two rise from the ashes of a fallen society and their cries of desperation fall on deaf ears.

The Earth shakes periodically, like an aftershock, with wind blowing heavy and rain slowly increasing in speed.

Holding her by the hand and not letting go, never letting go, we push onward toward a bridge that sits just below a red gleaming sun that beams across the sky like a beacon.

Finally.

Our trek across this damned city seems to have taken years.

Years of contemplation and careful execution.

Along the way, you lose a few voices, a few followers. You see things you'd never imagined possible and experiences you'd thought were left for anyone else but you and they come anyway.

Our day of reckoning finally arrives and all either of us do is pray that it's less than underwhelming and tragic.

A long, hard and beaten road home – The ramp up to the Verrazano-Narrows Bridge is endless as we walk with heavy steps and heavier hearts.

"Dante…" Meryl speaks. "What was it you were going to say earlier?"

"Don't worry about it." I respond. "When we're outta here, somewhere far away, maybe safer, maybe not, I'll tell you…"

Her head hangs to the side in disappointment, but then her hand reaches for her pocket and pulls out two, small familiar objects.

"No, you didn't." I grin, as she hands over a single cigarette and my ol' zippo.

"Hahahaha!" I laugh uncontrollably, with tears of joy just ready to burst from my eyes. "You really are something else!"

Striking a flame and inhaling deep, I let out a sigh of comfort and relief, letting my guard down, the same as hers.

What could possibly be left that would really pose any more of a threat?

The wrong question to ask yourself and the wrong thing to do, when still entrenched in enemy territory, whether you believe you're about to escape, or not.

You're always safest, right before you die.

Savoring every single puff as we stroll, the front of the bridge emerges and what the two of us lay eyes on absolutely steals our breath and a stinging, punctuating burst of warmth and adrenaline shoot directly up my spine.

"Fuck." Is all I can say, cigarette falling to the ground, feeling pointless. "Just… Fuck it all."

We arrive at the edge of a destroyed bridge, vomiting off into the water. They'd definitely been found and ZeroFactor had struck here, most likely, long before we even came remotely close to arrival.

Meryl falls to her knees and my focus gazes into a shard of glass hanging from a shred of a wrecked vehicle reflecting the barrel of a forty five that glimpses through rising flames.

Would you give up tomorrow, just to have today?

A voice from behind speaks. "You know, in my dreams, I've dreamt of a paradise, a dying breed, swirling, spinning and swimming in their own, self-created ocean of greed."

I turn slowly, with heavy heaves of breath and she's standing there with a gun pointed at me and behind stands Jack, with a knife to the neck of someone we'd lost – Rob.

"You…" Aiming the end of her weapon at Meryl. "Perky-chick, standup with your hands behind your head and turn around slowly."

Doing exactly what she asks, Meryl turns, speaking only two words. "Fuck you."

The rain patters down harder than ever.

"You know D…" Aiming at me, again. "You've been one hell of a pain in my ass."

Jack walks forward, grinning, head shaved in a zigzag form. Rob's facial expression looking desperate, helpless, waiting for me to make some sort of last ditch move that would assure our safety and send these bastards back to whatever depths of hell they'd crawled out of.

"And don't think for one second that I'll even allow you to escape this." Nuhm points at her scalp with the other hand. "I'm sure by now you know what I am and what I'm capable of."

"What's that look for, Dante?" Jack notices the ever-increasingly angry look on my face, teeth grinding and chipping away at each other. "You really think human beings would be allowed to continue as they were?" Dragging his knife slowly across Rob's neck. "All you gotta do is see the truth."

"To hell with your truth." I say.

"I've felt like this for a long, long time. People..." He grunts, "People fuckin' sicken me. But hey, there's a lot less of 'em now, huh?"

"You can't just eradicate human life, what gives you the right..."

"I have the right." Nuhm demands, "I've seen the very true nature of humanity."

"Keep pointing that gun at me bitch..."

"Or you'll what?" Giggling, "It's true you've come out on top, even after being trapped within my little fortress, but these are only games. It ends here."

"You like them zombies?" Jack asks, "I noticed you two playin' around with 'em earlier. Little present from..."

Nuhm finishes his sentence. "Yours Truly, leader of the New World Order, the ZeroFactor movement."

"At least let Rob go!" Meryl pleads, tears beginning to streak down the sides of her face, rain beading through strands of her hair.

"Well..." The evil nutcase curls her lip and looks upward in thought. "I do have somewhat of a proposition."

"Not interested." I spit.

"If you'll allow me to speak." She snaps, "I'll let your little friends go, but your life is mine."

"No!" Meryl bursts out in a fit of hysterics.

"Kill me, you mean?"

"It's only fair." She says.

"I don't care for your explanations and excuses as to why you think you're justified for all of the things you've done." My eyes shift downward. "If you're asking me to trade my life for their freedom though, yeah, sure, so be it."

This is my duty, leader and protector.

"Dante!" Meryl cries with pouring tears that blend with drops of rain. "Don't!"

"It seems that there's no other way." Feeling empty and forsaken.

"Then it's decided." Jack pushes Rob to the edge of the bridge next to Meryl and the two of them walk forward.

Nuhm De'Ara presses her gun against my forehead as Jack approaches the two of them.

"D, you stupid bastard, what…" Rob tries an attempt at convincing me otherwise.

"Forget it, both of you. I want you to get out of here. I want you to rally all that are left and I want you to stop this."

My final request.

"That's not likely going to happen." Nuhm smirks with a snarl, giving Jack a nod.

"I hope the two of you can swim!" Putting his booted foot in front of Meryl.

"Wait, NO!" I shout.

"DAAANTTTEE!!" Meryl screams in echo as Jack shoves her, then Rob, over the edge, laughing in crazed satisfaction.

"I fuckin' swear!" Grimacing at her as she backs up just a few feet.

"Don't want any blood on my outfit." Pulling back on the pistols automatic hammer. "Last words, you got any?"

"You better fuckin' kill me, 'cause you're both goddamn dead – Even Jack, you're no brother of mine."

"Humph." He crosses his arms. "I think he's said quite enough."

"Bye, bye, Dante Marcellus. You almost made it, eh?"

In slow motion, the muzzle flashes and a bullet leaves the chamber, sparking and bursting right for me. Then, with a snap, cold rushes through my veins. Two shades of black swirl, twist, then snap, the colors drip and sink away. When it's all over, when I think I'm dead, the rain is all I can hear.

In that little moment, before transition, I know; I now know everything that's happened. Why I'd gone comatose and why I had such a hard time remembering.

A gunshot to the head can sort of do that to a person, I suppose.

She should've killed me.

25

These Final Words

Pittering, pattering, splashing against my eyelids, blinded by a sharp yellow tinge that peels away at them; I feel the downpour of a place in time that has no predetermined future – The present.

I think of the bridge, Eight Three Northbound and I think of it bursting into crumbling concrete and Julianna's eyes piercing through the darkness of the water.

Most of all, I think of how clear things are now, considering I no longer struggle with my memory.

She most definitely should've killed me.

Before opening my eyes, before I'm even able, I wonder of Rob and Meryl – Especially Meryl; A stale, gut churning reminder of my failure and what could have possibly happened to them and how Meryl had managed to survive, going off as some rogue assassin.

Rob – I really let you down, didn't I?

It's time to stop asking myself questions. It's time to take charge and responsibility.

"Open your goddamn eyes already."

I know that horrible voice anywhere.

Raindrops still fall, warm and sticky with humidity – Strange for the Winter season – My eyelids crack open to a sky filled with clouds of grey and a Sun tainted by a deathly orange and red.

Tilting my head downward from its thrown-back position, the first sight I see are the tops of buildings in the Harrisburg area, all ablaze in ember and flame, including the domed top of the capitol building.

"Where the hell?" I speak, with a mouth full of dryness and tingling dehydration.

Coming into clear view now, I see the end of my own gun pointing directly at me.

"This seems…" And there she is. "All too familiar." Grinning sinisterly and pushing aside hair that covers half of her face.

My teeth bare and grind. "I remember…"

Looking down at my body, against the concrete top of a building, I see that I'm bound by nothing, yet leaning over the edge, just slightly.

"Do you now?" Placing her foot just over my abdomen as she speaks and pulling me upward. "It's really been a long journey, D…"

She dons a pair of tight black velvet pants and a dark green military jacket that barely covers an exposed chest.

"You've aided me quite more than I ever thought you could." Stepping back and releasing me from her foothold. "Now, this time, since I no longer have any need of you, you'll surely be dead."

"And why the hell didn't you kill me the first time?" I look around and realize that we're atop the old Harrisburg Hospital building, tall and black if viewed from the distance of the bridge.

Shooting her eyes back toward me. "I thought I had, but when we found that you'd gone comatose instead…" Checking an attachment on her wrist for a moment. "We devised a special little plan, much greater than what I'd originally had in mind…"

"And that involves me, how?" Sneering, catching the edge of my wrists around something sharp and metallic.

"I know what you think; I can see deep inside of your mind and I knew exactly what you were planning." Giggling, "And it won't matter if you plan on attempting to strike me with that shard of metal below your hands there…" Walking up to me, knife suddenly in her opposite hand, "I'll know before you even move."

"You knew about PaxCorpus and my project that I'd planned to preserve the remaining survivors of humanity?"

She nods, dragging the edge of her knife across her tongue.

"Then why'd you allow it to happen?"

"I'm glad you asked." Leaning a shoulder against the wall of a small rectangular air duct. "I, or we, figured it'd be much easier to exterminate you morons, if you were all organized in little proxies across the United States."

She's using my own plans against me – My heart sinks and stomach turns upside down.

"And that little voice, that thing, constantly speaking to you, guiding you…" Pointing at her skull again. "Temporal interference, your little helping hand won't be intervening anymore."

That explains it, the silence, at least.

Then something else occurs to me, something I'd almost completely left out of my thought processes, something important that maybe I should've thought of immediately, feeling almost guilty for not doing so.

"How'd you find me? How'd I get up here and what the fuck did you do with Julianna?!" Burning with fiery rage now, growing like a mountain, deep inside.

She laughs with hands on her knees, breasts spilling out from behind the unbuttoned cloth of her jacket. I almost stand up and attempt to tackle her before she regains composure and says, "You're going to absolutely love this part…"

My mind jumps back and forth, unable to come to a clear explanation.

"I should really…" Adjusting her head slightly and touching her hand to an unseen spot on the back of her neck. "Thank you, for the ride, at least."

It all unravels like a tangled ball of yarn. Her face shifts and morphs right before me and I see a face I'd kissed and the woman I'd made love to, promised my heart to, for slightly less than six years.

I feel myself turning upside down – I feel the rush of heat to my head and the liquid gathering at the corners of my eyes. I feel rage, anger, confusion, pain and bewildered despair.

"I thought, once, a while ago…" Eyes dark and cloudy. "That maybe I'd fallen in love with you…" Shaking her head and chuckling that mad sounding laugh again. "But those sort of feelings are petty and to be left behind. Sort of a Stockholm syndrome thing, I guess. You really are quite the man, though."

"You can't do this!" I begin yelling at the top of my lungs, wanting to throw myself in her face. "You can't FUCKING do this!"

A combat boot strapped to her foot hits me in the chest and it throws me back down.

"I thought I'd tear you down, from the inside out, right under your nose, watching your every move as you did everything that I wanted."

Puts a whole new meaning to sleeping with the enemy.

"And that little cunt, hunting down every one of my most efficient men and women, executing them like she's some arch-angel on a righteous path of vengeance; She won't be here to save you. No one will, I'm afraid."

Everything was a lie; It was all a goddamn lie. I feel disgusted with myself, as good as dead. I can't put this into words.

"You've got nothing left. All these stupid people, your friends, and…" With her left hand in quotations, "Your wife-to-be… Gone."

Looking up at her again, that face; Julianna's fuckin' face. "You may as well just fucking kill me then. Put that gun to my head and blow my brains out." Angry and out of reasons to care, to continue.

"Oh, I intend on doing just that, but I thought maybe you should see Jack one more time. He'll be here soon."

Shaking violently, eyes twitching, I sit and watch as she walks to the opposite side of the building, taking a look over the edge.

"You really should see this." Grinning in satisfaction. "It's beautiful."

"You're insane." I growl through saliva that drips from my mouth, sticky and stale.

"Insane?!" She gasps, as if surprised. "You've seen what they did to me." Pointing with my gun as if it's her index finger. "They mutilated a woman I don't even know anymore and turned me into this half-dead, cybernetic…" Shifting her eyes in rapid thought. "THING!"

Her finger barely squeezing the trigger. "Don't you fucking call *me* insane!"

"You can't just take the actions of a few people and place the blame on an entire civilization…"

"Sure I can!" Snapping back. "You remember what it was like before all of this. Simplistic goddamn animals droning on, day in and day out, with their iced mocha shit, double-quarter cheeseburger whatever. Herding like fucking sheep the moment something violent or tragic happens!" Stomping a foot down directly between my legs. "Reproducing and spreading disease, causing pain and suffering, for WHAT?!" She asks.

"For the betterment of mankind?!" Calming down just slightly and backing off again to the edge. "This – What I've done – It's for the best." Breathing heavily, fuming. "Don't you call me insane…"

I stare upward to the sky and the rain, watching as it soaks down into my hair and onto my skin. "You're no better than the bastards who fucked you up…"

"That is it!" She turns to me from across the rooftop, holding the pistol tight and ready to squeeze. "You think what you're doing is good?! There is no good, there are only lesser evils! I've had enough of you." Squinting, "It's been a wonderful ride, but now…"

She wanted to pull that trigger; She wanted to put me down permanently. Trailing away in slurred words, her chest opens up wide, exposing metallic looking ribs and torn synthetic flesh; She jolts back toward the edge.

I jump up and run toward her dying body.

A gunshot from nowhere ends everything with no remorse or even a second of warning.

Staring blankly into the sky, her mouth hangs open and I want to hold the woman I loved. Torn in two by feelings of hatred and sorrow, I shake my head with my fists and see the truth.

Ripping my gun from her hand, I say, "Farewell to who you were; To hell with what you are…" Pushing her limp carcass over the edge, I walk away.

Not watching.

Not caring; No more.

Now it's all over – The struggle to remember; The fight; The anguish. Now, what's left is nothing but a gaping hole, torn in the middle of my life. Nothing left to do, nothing left to care for or even about – I stumble, placing my weapon into the waist of my pants, and I head down – Down into the depths of the hospital and into the destruction that was once a safe haven – My kingdom.

These streets, the scorching rain and the violence that tears in and out of every crevice, as far as the eye can see; They welcome me with open arms – I collapse, exhausted and dead inside, my knees catch rocky pavement and I embrace my fate – My inevitable end.

26

The Impossible Truth

A heat wave pushes through me and my arms fall to my sides.

From the middle of the Susquehanna, Three Mile Island, its sirens begin to wail a depressing sound – A meltdown is surely imminent.

"Perfect." I mumble through my lips, eyelids fluttering around.

Bodies are strewn all throughout the streets and somewhere out there gunfire rings, shatters and echoes.

Probably the remaining ZF troops, unaware of their leader's demise, I think. Who cares.

Don't give up, Dante.

The voice, with the death of Julianna – Nuhm De'Ara – it returns.

"Why the hell not?" I ask. "There ain't a fuckin' thing left."

You're overlooking something. Don't get caught up in emotion. There's still much left to be done. Your story doesn't end here. Not now, not anytime soon.

"And yet, I still have no idea what or who you are…" Holding my position on the ground, down on my knees.

And it still doesn't matter; I still don't know, anyway.

"Whatever…" I pull the pistol from my waist, cock back its hammer and place the barrel into my mouth.

Take that thing outta your mouth or I swear…

"What?!" I laugh. "You gonna stop me?! HOW!?"

Oh, I could. But I think your focus should be on the edge of the road there, directly in front of you.

Over the pavement, just atop a rippling haze of heat, a matte-black armored bank truck suddenly appears, driving right for me.

"The hell?" Arching eyebrows in confusion and removing my gun from my face.

Who do ya think fired that final shot?

And it clicks. Sometimes I can be blinded and stupefied by my own overwhelming emotion or lack thereof.

The vehicle screeches its tires to the side, passenger door slinging open and revealing a tubby looking, bald man, with a long grey beard, just sitting there at the steering wheel, staring at me.

"Get in." He says. "Name's Ed."

"Should I know you?" Still not moving.

"Considering that I'm your only ride out of this city and I've got your girlfriend here, who just saved your ass, no less." He looks to the back of his truck. "Yeah, you should, at least, *want* to know me."

The double doors at the rear of the vehicle fly open and out whisks a fucking sight-for-sore-eyes – And they're definitely sore.

"Meryl…" My tongue loosely allows her name to escape my lips.

She walks right by me, with that wiggle in her step, rifle over her back, wearing a nostalgic outfit, with digital grey and black camouflage striping down her legs; A black wife beater and her hair silky brown, longer than it used to be – She turns.

A patch covers her left eye and a scar slides down the right side of her bottom lip – She smiles and offers me a hand.

I just sit there and stare at her for a moment.

"Don't worry, D, I'm me, no one else." Her voice soothes ringing ears and chokes back a waterfall of tears.

Reaching out, I stand slowly, not taking my eyes off of her and she gazes into mine.

I move inward and our lips touch again, filling me with life anew.

"What…" Holding her by the arms and releasing from a long awaited embrace. "What happened to you?"

"I should ask you the same." She smiles, inches from my weary face. "Come on and get inside. We've gotta get outta this place before it's turned into a smoldering, irradiated crater."

"Yeah, we're about to go into a nuclear meltdown…" For some reason, I still don't feel that urgency that I probably should – Sirens blaring loud, over and over.

Putting a finger to my lips. "Relax. I'll take care of things from here."

She returns to the back of the truck, whispering something to someone unseen and I pull myself into the seat next to this Ed guy.

"How touching." He winks and turns his head to the side. "Shut the door."

I allow myself to fall back into the cushy seat; Comforting, worn leather.

"Hey, retard," another voice I thought I'd never hear again, "have a drink."

I look back to see Rob, just as he used to be, holding a canteen gushing full of water.

Grasping for it, I pop off the cap and take down five healthy gulps.

"Sorry." He says. "No smokes."

Breathing slowly for a moment, allowing myself to hydrate, I look to him again, handing him the canteen.

"Forget about it, shit's bad for me anyway." Still confused. "So where'd you guys come from, how'd you know I was here and Rob!" Surprised, "The hell you been up to?!"

Glancing at Meryl again, I notice her sitting there with her back arched to the doors, just nonchalantly staring at me, with that lustful gaze in her eyes I can remember seeing atop that convenience store in Brooklyn.

"Man, you wouldn't believe…"

I didn't even notice the vehicle beginning to move.

"…The shit we've been through."

Mocking the movements of an Olympic swimmer, "We fuckin' swam our ass's outta that bay all the way to goddamn Staten Island!"

"Christ…" I grin, feeling only an inkling of happy.

"You mean I dragged your sorry ass to the island." Meryl pokes, jokingly.

"Yeah, yeah." He continues, "And then this dude here, Ed, just cruising the streets, looking for refugees or something, picks us up!"

"And what?" Feeling almost slightly more conversational and crossing arms. "You three've just been wandering the country for six years?"

"Sort of." Ed speaks, with his deep bellow of a voice. "We were helping with survivors for a while…"

Rob interrupts. "And then we told people about your PaxCorpus idea and suddenly, or, well in a few years, we had surviving encampments all over the United States…" Putting his hand on my shoulder. "Thanks to you, for pulling us through that city."

Brushing him away. "Yeah, but I started this one here, Pax was my baby, hell, I didn't even know how I'd come up with it, for the longest time and now look…"

"It's true we just lost a lot of people here, Dante, and it is saddening, to no end…" Meryl leans upward. "But there are more encampments – Hundreds more."

Things fall silent for a moment.

"Then…" She continues, "I started discovering the locations of these ZF bastards and where they kept their strongest leaders." Kicking her feet up. "Well, then it was basically just marks on a chalkboard."

I look at her face again. "And in the process, you lose an eye?!"

Her remaining eye shifts to the side, facial expression morphing from enthusiastic to mournful.

"This is more recent." Putting a few fingers to her face. "They knew we were attempting to track down Nuhm De'Ara's location and they captured us." Gulping and shifting her palm to her forehead. "They never had a chance to do anything to these two, but they did horrible, horrible things to me…"

Rob notices that the overall mood is suddenly ten times more depressing.

"But then, like…" He jumps up, "We escaped, we found her location and learned that you…" Getting uncomfortably close to my face, "Were, in fact, *not* a dead-man, but in the same freakin' place!"

I palm his head and push him back like a basketball. "The bitch masqueraded as a soldier and fooled me for six years…"

"But that's over now." Meryl interjects, seeming as if she doesn't even want to hear details. "We can finally get something done without these assholes interrupting things."

"Right." I say, having a bit of trouble absorbing all of this new information.

Ed notices the, still, slightly troubled look on my face and offers some of his own wisdom.

"What these two are trying to say is…" Pausing for a moment, licking his lips, one hand on the steering wheel, the other combing fingers through his beard, as he dodges debris in the road. "You need to stop living in the past, Dante, leave it behind and just grab hold of the future. 'Cause it's comin' fast."

I look down for a moment, sighing heavily. "I suppose you're right."

"Atta boy!" Rob jiggles his hand on my shoulder.

"Would you stop touching me?!" I shout, half irritated.

He laughs and falls back into his money-bag chair and Meryl then moves into my ear, whispering.

"Later, when all of this is over and we're outta here, I have something to show you." Touching her tongue to my ear. "I'll let that simmer for a while."

"Pfffft." Rob scoffs, "Why you get all of her attention?"

"Alright, enough chatter." Ed's voice pounds in seriousness. "We're here."

"We're where?" I ask, looking out of the window – The headquarters building.

"We're here to show these fucks we mean business." Slamming the emergency brake and pulling the keys from the ignition. "Lock 'n load!" Yelling and grabbing for a shotgun; Meryl an automatic rifle; Rob an AK-Forty

Seven and I reach for my pistol, wondering where the other could have possibly gotten to in all of this mess.

Meryl, before pouncing out of the back, hands the second one to me. "Found this earlier, thought you may want it." Along with a belt-strap full of magazines. "You got enough energy for this?" She asks, head lowering with her eyebrows to the bridge of my nose.

"Hell yeah." I respond, half too tired to even stand, but determined enough to kill off a bunch of terrorist mother-fucks.

27

One Bullet at a Time

Walking side-by-side, undetected and unexpected, Ed delivers a briefing in speech mode.

"Alright, Gentlemen and Lady." Resting his shotgun over his shoulder. "We have a little under an hour before TMI goes up…"

I look at him, about to ask how he would know such a thing.

"Our intelligence says they've strapped the entire base with high explosives; It'll be one helluva meltdown." Taking his weapon in hand as we come up close to the building. "These bastards are in our territory now, let's teach 'em that fucking with us, no, PaxCorpus – The last hope for humanity – Is a grave, horrible mistake."

I half expect him to whip out a cigar, just for effect.

Standing at the steps to the front door, the building is only a former shadow of what it was; Only a few days ago. Shattered windows, collapsed walls and that stupid symbol graffiti all over it.

Rob steps in front of us and puts his left hand, palm-side down, out.

I sigh, thinking. "Seriously, man, seriously?"

Ed places his hand on top of Rob's. Meryl, slightly reluctant, places hers in next.

I roll my eyes.

"Come on, D." Meryl whispers and winks. "For morale, at least."

My hand goes in on top of Meryl's, Rob does a three second countdown. "Three, two, one, BREAK!"

We charge, ready for our sweet revenge – Ready to kill – Weapons aimed high, Ed kicks and blasts his way through the first blockaded door.

Meryl and Rob rush inward, going left and right, two shots go off and I walk inside to see the desk of George, with no body to be found – No sign of violence or struggle.

"Hmmm…" I ponder to myself, shifting eyes toward the identical, adjacent to each other staircases. "Watch, they could just come down…"

"We got this man!" Rob interrupts me with a shout.

"Who in da fuck is that?!" A loud voice comes from behind a wooden, riddled with holes door, on the first floor.

"Down!" I command, with a hand motioning south.

Six new holes poke through and open it swings, with a small smoking canister.

"Cover your eyes!" Meryl puts her head down and a flash of white fills the room for no more than a second.

Walking through all confident with a semi-automatic rifle in hand, a butch and stocky looking woman with a shaved head calls out. "Come out, come out, ya dirty little fucks!"

Another burst from her rifle into the ceiling signals warning, pieces of rubble flaking down atop our heads.

"Alright, I've had enough of this." Rob reaches out from a column that he stands behind and provides cover fire – I stand up straight, with both pistols and leap over the desk that Meryl and I had taken cover behind, firing shot after shot.

Surprised, bubbles of gelatinous goo popping from her chest; Each bullet strikes an even more fatal shot than the last.

"Sit the fuck down." Placing my boot on her face, I splatter the back of her skull against the tiled floor before she even has a chance to react or cry for any mercy.

"Holy hell." Ed stands up from his crouch behind the stairwell. "Where'd you two meet this guy again?"

They look at each other and back at Ed. "In a very dark place in a troubled time. He's alright though, trust me." Meryl smiles.

"Cool." Nodding with wide eyes.

"Aaauuggghhh!!" A tiny little guy comes screaming through with a machete in the air, quickly dropping to the barrel of Ed's gun.

"Anyway." He says. "Let's move."

The next room, large and like a circular auditorium, is something we're not prepared to lay eyes on.

"And what in the hell is this?" Ed takes point, getting the first look at our surroundings.

A floor painted in blood and decorated with human entrails, leading to a small electronic console in the center. From the ceiling and walls hang cages of long dead bodies and chandeliers stuck with body parts and organs – Of course, across every window, barred, bullet-proof and reinforced, the ZF signature.

Meryl covers her mouth and grabs her stomach. "I'm gonna fuckin' vomit." She chokes.

"You know…" Rob waves a hand in front of his face. "I'd say, 'what died in here?' but, yeah, hmm…"

Strangely enough, there aren't any other soldiers or people, for that matter, to be seen.

I might be able to identify a few of the corpses that aren't completely torn apart – Still wondering what had happened to Ray and Paul – If they weren't so disgustingly mutilated.

"Guys…" I avert my eyes for a moment. "We gotta find every single one of these motherfuckers before they get out of Harrisburg. I'm not letting this go."

The aforementioned console, in the center of the room, begins to buzz and hum.

Ed points with the end of his weapon. "Look."

We all turn to its sparkling and flashing blue light as a six-foot tall holo-image emerges from a crystal like object in its base.

Forming into a slender human-type appearance and fading from blue to red, its face materializes atop the body of a woman and a voice greets us.

"Welcome." she says, face coming into clear luminescent view.

"Nuhm!" I jolt forward with both hands on the machines panels, which suddenly arise from the ground.

"If you're standing here, in this room…" The holographic video shakes and almost loses its signal. "Then I am presumably dead." Slapping her hands together. "Congratulations!"

"I don't like this…" Meryl backpedals, eyes glaring fearful at the dead woman's image.

"You 'n me both." Ed turns around and gets himself a good second look at the room.

She's dead, I tell myself, and this is just some kind of recording.

"The building you're standing within was once a safe haven for Pax Units." Her image lifting arms into the air as if presenting a gift. "Now, as my last farewell to you, I present the Z-Arena!" The sound of some automated audience clap echoes to the sound of her voice.

"The what?!" I say, blood pressure levels rising.

Before she speaks again, doors slam down with metal barriers and giant looking mechanisms.

Laughing with every bit of her insanity, "You have sixty minutes to survive waves of my personal death-squad, in five minute intervals. There'll be tricks!" Pointing a finger to the other side of the room. "There'll be traps!" Locking in on my eyes as if this is really her and she knows it's me, Dante. "And most of all, there will be blood!"

"Oh shit, shit, shit!" Rob panics. "Whose bright fuckin' idea was this again?!"

"Shut up!" Ed snaps, beard swishing to the side.

Meryl grabs me by the arm. "We gotta get outta here, I can't be here!"

"There are six doors…" Nuhm explains. "Each opening and increasing in numbers every three hundred seconds, but you can escape earlier than that, if you have the guts…"

Everyone turns from their hysterical cries and they stare blankly at the hologram.

"Your vital signs and brain-waves have been registered by my systems." A gun appears in the grasp of her left hand. "If one of you kills the other, you may leave." Aiming its barrel at me and she winks. "You can't trick the system, don't even consider it. One of you dies by, say, Dante's hand, and the waves will stop, doors will unlock."

"Hell no!" Rob shouts in disbelief.

"Dante." Tightening her hold on me. "I'm getting that feeling, that claustrophobic feeling. You gotta get me outta here!"

"I'm thinking, dammit!" I look around, I ponder, the ceiling, the windows, doors, all protected. "Damn it all to hell!"

"Nobody shoots anyone other than whatever comes through those doors, got it?" Ed says, as if he doubts the rest of the groups' intentions and loyalty to each other.

"No shit!" I shoot back at him.

"Have fun!" Nuhm's image prepares for a closing line. "Remember – one hour or death! Until next time…"

She fades from view, systems powering down as emergency flood lights that line the walls, begin to flash.

Our faces light up in white and orange as we all look for some type of cover – Behind the room's center console, separated by office furniture and a stair-like collection of theatre chairs.

Stomping feet and the scraping of claws echo through the adjacent halls.

Rob's head whips back and forth. "They're coming at us from all angles!"

"Like we don't already know that!" I stand, both guns aiming at two separate doorways. "Back to back, now!"

Four of us – Six of them. We put our backs together and stand facing the incoming danger as the mechanisms slide each opening upward, all moving in coordination with each other.

A soldier comes through each, guns blazing, and they shut, locking themselves once more and the smallest bout of yelling can be heard from behind.

Moving in a circular pattern and squeezing fingers against triggers, just barely dodging the whizzing bullets and pieces of wall and stone; One goes down, then two.

"I'm out!" Meryl announces from directly behind.

I double tap her on the shoulder and lean back as far as my spine'll allow me to go and she ducks down – Two more fall – Rob and Ed finish the remaining psychos.

"Five minutes!" A voice shouts from a hidden speaker.

"Holy shit!" Rob stumbles and grabs his leg in pain. "I'm hit!"

"Ed!" I point. "Take care of that!" Pulling each magazine from the pistol in each hand, both half spent. "Meryl, you good?" I ask, kneeling down as she breathes heavily, blinking slowly.

"I'm fine." She says, monotone, stuffing a fresh banana clip into her rifle.

The walls shake and my eyes dart upward, the fixations on the ceiling ready to give way.

Then my eyes find their way back over to Rob, Ed wrapping his wound in cloth and squeezing a small syringe into the vein of his arm – Exhaling, his eyes dilate.

"This is too goddamn nuts." Standing up again with the help of Ed's hand. "I'm good to go now, I guess."

I can't see us making it through this alive, even if we make the time limit, but we've at least gotta try – We can't all just die.

"I've an idea…" Facing the three of them. "These chandeliers above us are ready to break. We lure them here and I'll take care of the rest."

Ed nods in agreement, but decides to question me anyway. "You really think we can keep this up for just under an hour?"

My lips almost move, but Meryl takes the place of my words.

"Not to mention the fact that in the exact same amount of time we'll be nuclear fucking waste."

With his palms out and head shaking, Ed strikes a bulb. "That too!"

"Just bear me with me, I'll come up with something." I assure them, but I'm anything but assuring on the inside.

I hadn't fought this hard for survival, not for six years, just for all of it to end suddenly over some horridly sick game – I've been shot, sliced, stabbed, blown up more than once and now I'm going to be done in by a dead woman and her little "going away" present of a few hired guns – No goddamn way.

I wonder where my little voice has gone.

"Alright, up." I command. "Same formation as before, we blast whatever comes through these doors." Aiming with my head to the two closest. "And we take cover here, hopefully forcing the other four toward the center of the room."

"Whatever." Rob shrugs, moving with the rest of us to the East side of the room. "We're dead, this is it."

The next wave begins. Six bigger, angrier looking men emerge from their little hidey-holes, dressed in thick black armor with shining face plates.

We manage to drop the first two as planned, with at least a few pops of random gunfire and we all swivel around simultaneously. I aim to the sky as the last three move in on us – Lurching slowly with pounding footsteps, preparing to pull their triggers – My mind lapses and scurries around – My eyes almost fall shut and I stumble.

Meryl turns her head and shouts, the white of her teeth at the corner of my eye. "Dante! The hell are you waiting for?!"

I blink and focus again, discharging two rounds and moving for cover.

The fixtures fall and crush Nuhm's, apparent best, into puddles of crunchy goo and again the room falls silent.

The guys, Rob and Ed, put their backs to the wall and begin to reload with whatever they have left and Meryl moves in close.

"What was that?" She whispers. "You're running out of stamina, aren't you?"

I shake my head, sweat dripping down from strands of hair. "No, it's fine. I'm fine."

"You sure about that?" Asking again, she doubts the truth in my voice, tired and silently begging for an end to the fucking madness.

Something scrapes at the metallic doors, reminding me of that little trip to the moon, in that glassy elevator with all the blood that gushed on through.

"You hear that?" Rob puts an ear to the surface of one of the doors.

"That ain't no gun wielding terrorist." Ed states, a little dumbfounded, not having heard such a thing before, most likely.

Falling short of the five minute timer, the doors launch open like rockets and six, clawed and creeping fast demonic creatures leap outward – Walking fast across walls and ceiling.

"Ah shit!" He yells.

I regain my composure as fast as I can, firing blindly at the rooms entire structure, while the other three swiftly jump into action.

"The fuck!?" Franticly aiming and barely shooting, Rob scrambles to the ground and watches, eyes darting around at each shadow of a creature.

Meryl charges to the center of the room and pounces onto the center console, firing like mad – Heaven hath no fury.

I move toward her, emptying clips from both pistols and dropping one of them completely.

Screaming in guttural terror, Ed bursts from his head as one of the monstrous beings rip neck and bone apart.

"EDDDD!!" Rob yells a horrified scream. "NO!" Blasting the murdering bastard to the ground.

"Fuckin' goddammit!" I exclaim, remaining pistol freshly loaded, three of us remaining. I burst into a sprint with all of my energy and circle the room in a blaze of gunfire, taking down each brown and redheaded, long tongued, leaping freaks.

Rob falls down to his knees, holding hands up in sorrow. "No…"

Meryl lowers her weapon, eyes gaping in terror at the sight of a dead man she'd known and confided in for years.

"I'm sorry…" I say to the two of them at once. "There wasn't a damn thing I could do."

Rob pounds a fist on the ground and accuses in furious anger. "This is HER fault!"

"Now you just wait a minute." Putting a palm toward him. "We all decided to come here."

"Meryl's right." Watching him carefully; Watching his sanity fall to pieces. "If anything, it's all our fault."

"Fuck you." He snarls. "He was like a father to me."

"Five minutes." The voice echoes in cold reminder.

With his forearm, he wipes tears from his eyes and rips Ed's shotgun from his dead fingers and swiftly points it at Meryl.

"We're getting out of here, now!" He decides, cocking back on the barrel.

"Rob, you lower that fucking gun." Hesitating to point my own at him.

"Go to hell, you can join her!"

Sparks fly and before I can react, Meryl's body lunges to the ground in mangled betrayal.

"You bastard!" Clenching teeth, hands shaking, as he turns for me in unexpected surprise as the doors around unlock and the lights go off.

I empty what's left of my pistol's clip into his chest and kick his slack-jawed body to the ground.

A sweltering breeze rolls in and I throw myself down, blood drenched.

"No, dammit, NO!" Slapping my palms against the temples of my skull, "I won't walk out of here alone, I WON'T!"

Something or someone laughs from somewhere inside of the building and the doors lock down and latch themselves shut again.

"Five minutes." The announcers voice returns.

Head and chest feeling tingly, I smack down onto my back. "Fuck it."

Then my head begins to spin, eyes feeling swimmy – Everything goes black and I open my eye lids.

28

From Dusk till Dawn

"Hey." Ed says from the driver seat of the armored truck. "Welcome back." Smiling a cheesy grin, teeth stained yellow.

"Have a nice nap?" Rob pats me on the shoulder.

I rub my eyes with balled fists and yawn. "What the hell?"

"You must've been having one hell of a nightmare." Meryl puts a hand on my head and rubs it through each strand of hair. "But this can happen; Post traumatic situations considered."

Asking not a single person in particular. "So how long was I out and when did it happen?"

"About the time Rob started bitching…"

"Hey!" He says with a grin, laughing. "Yeah man, you kinda just snapped out like a light, didn't even warn us."

Switching to serious mode. "We're about a little over fifty miles away from Harrisburg, should be relatively safe from the explosive nuclear blast."

"Explosive?" I remember from the dream, his mention of high-explosives and Three Mile Island.

"Yep." Meryl leans forward. "Those idiots planted more plastic explosives than a single vehicle could possibly even consider carrying."

"I see…" Wondering if that dream was really a dream or some crazy-ass premonition of things that may have been, if we'd stayed.

Ed speaks again. "It's over now, go ahead and rest some more, I know a place we can stop at for the night."

We glide silently down a road, cluttered by brown and dead trees, cracked apart pavement and every so often, a run-down abandoned small-town house.

"Five seconds!" Rob announces.

They all grab hold of something and I lift my eyes to the rearview, Harrisburg's tallest buildings barely visible off in the distance past the bounds of a few mountains.

The ground vibrates, the vehicle rocks and like a bass-drum kick to the face, an enormous, yellow and greenish mushroom of a cloud erupts, some fifty five miles behind us, glowing and blinding in the mirror and I shift my eyes away.

"Whoo!" Rob cheers.

"Calm down." Ed grumbles from just above his beard. "There used to be people living there, you know."

He realizes his not-so-thought-out over excitement and plops down.

My past, everything, gone in a flash; An instant.

"Oh well…" I say. "We'll move on…"

In mostly silence, for the remainder of our ride, I stare, forehead against the window. Just staring at tiny pieces of the Earth, still untouched and untainted by things we'd still have to deal with, even with ZeroFactor, now, hopefully, falling apart, having lost their leader and all.

There's still plenty of evil to fight – To eradicate.

How in the world we're even going to accomplish that is far beyond me. I mean, you go ahead and give me a call when you can think of a way to shut down a wormhole and eliminate hordes of the undead, which never seem to friggin' die.

"We're here." Ed brings the vehicle to a halt and I have a flashback for just a moment – My dream – A twitch picks at the corner of my eye.

"Where's here?" I ask, hoping to hear something more like a comfy ass bed and a mountain of cigarettes.

We sit in front of a small, run-down and hidden-by-rubble motel on the edge of nowhere.

To the West, the Sun sets and it glows brilliant across the tops of mountains, reflecting off of the front of the building and the shade-drawn windows that line it.

Ed kicks open his door, yawns with a hand to his mouth, which then slides down through his beard. He grabs for his shotgun that rests between his seat and the emergency brake and says, "Take your own rooms or what-have-you…" Exhausted and blinking one eye at a time. "I'm going the hell to sleep. Just remember to keep those doors locked up tight."

With that, he disappears behind a brown-steel door and not another sound is made – Probably passed out just as his hand left the knob.

The rest of us, strung out and staring each other, still sit in the truck, feeling mostly awkward.

"Well…" Rob breaks the silence. "Uhm, I guess I'll go take a room for myself then." Easing his way through the double-doors of the rear, meandering around before deciding on a place – That perfect little spot to rest his face.

I look back for a moment and then forward again, unlatching my door, stepping out and stretching my legs in a series of cracks followed by a gaping yawn. The sun dresses me in a shade of yellow and I just gaze at it for a moment, in wonder and disbelief – Everything's gone – I still can't convince myself of the truth.

Meryl emerges and I blink a few times, looking over in her direction; She reaches out a hand to me.

"Follow." She says and I reach my fingers for hers, glancing one more time toward Harrisburg – Its explosive glowing cloud still hanging in the sky.

We walk to a door on the far opposite end, away from the other two and she presses lightly against a metal creaking opening, swinging with ease to her touch – She leads me inside.

"Now…" Parting the curtains only slightly, to allow the gaze of the sun to spill through. "It's time for you to relax."

The bed in the middle of the room looks mostly untouched, with ruffled white sheets, flat pillows and across from it, one of those televisions you'd use change to view.

Kicking boots from her feet, she throws herself down onto the mattress, with a bounce and with legs in the air she removes her littered-with-holes socks.

"Come on." Sitting upright. "Don't just stand there like you're scared or something – We've been through a lot, you and I."

A little reluctant, heart and stomach still paining and churning from the recent, upsetting events – I advance and pull a sweaty and dirty ass shirt off of my chest, sitting down beside her and looking mesmerized into her eyes.

"It's been hell." I say with a cough and a grunt that clears my throat.

"Shh…" Putting a finger to my lips, she tears off the shirt she'd been wearing for who knows how long and reveals two perky, uncovered breasts, pointing at me with the smallest, pink nipples I've ever seen.

Laying hands against my clammy chest, she leans in and forces me backward, taking my mouth into hers. I suddenly feel invigorated, as if given a second chance or a new life – A second wind of passion I thought had been buried long ago.

Sliding fingernails down, she unbuckles the belt of my blood and bodily fluid encrusted pants and slides them down onto the ground before removing her own.

"Meryl, wait." I stop her as she slides her beautifully long and silky smooth legs from each pant-hold. "I don't know if I can do this…"

Ignoring me, she twirls around; Her ass looking the way I'd always imagined it'd be, in the flesh. All those times I'd daydreamed of the hot chick from the other unit back in the NYPD and then on through the trenches of hell.

Leaping like a cat back down into her crouched position over my body, she takes her tongue and teeth to my neck, furiously, before taking me in completely, moving her hips in an upward circular motion and down straight, with a flesh-packing pound.

She moans like a banshee and gasps and I grab her by the waist – Throwing torn emotion to the wind – Forcing my tongue into her mouth, she closes her eyes.

Like a burning fire, we ravage and destroy each other, with her nails digging into my skin, my pelvis pounding hard against hers, bruising skin and weakening bone – A mix of pleasure and pain. We engulf each other in an energy filled inferno I'd not experienced in a long time.

Teasing me with the soaking wet lips of her cunt, she moves up, pushing my two pistols off of the bed and kneels down on all fours.

"Finish me." With a tired, breath of a whisper. "I know this is what you want."

I grab hold of her ass and squeeze until they're red and I slam myself into her as if beating the life out of someone who'd wronged me in ways you couldn't possibly imagine.

She vibrates, swollen, up against me, shaking almost violently and slowly falling from excitement into heaving breaths, gasping for air. We slide down and directly beside each other, sprawled out and goddamn ready to sleep for a decade.

Placing a hand across my body, she pecks my cheek and whispers directly into my ear. "You know, I've always loved you."

I let out a slight grin, feeling a little unsure, a little uneasy, but if I don't say something I'll completely ruin the moment. Hoping I don't regret the words about to come out of my mouth, regardless of all of the insanity and the betrayal – I let 'em loose, thinking, 'what the hell?'

"I love you, too."

Darkness wraps around the room, devouring all light as the Sun sets completely, she reaches for a sheet and pulls it up to our heads and asks. "What was it you wanted to say to me, six years ago?"

"That I'd never leave you behind; I'd do all I could, all within my power to protect you…" I say with a whisper of words, long awaiting their release.

She smiles, feeling no need for further conversation, closing her eyelids and falling directly into sleep.

I lay there for a while, staring into the ceiling, wondering of things from the past and things to come.

Have I really made it this far?

Have I seriously lost this much?

A final moment of clarity in a situation that resembles something normal; Something not planned or lied about – No deviation or hidden ulterior motive.

For once, despite the anger and anguish, the death and the loss, I'm free of the emotionally cut off person I'd been most of my life.

I've finally found what and where I'm supposed to be.

Sleep now, you've got a journey of a life ahead of you.

29

A Long Time Ago

A cloudy white mist rolls in and I hear a countdown…

"Five!" A voice shouts and I'm staring into a tall glass of golden liquid.

"Four!" They announce, a hand sliding a small box in front of me on the darkly brown colored, wooden counter of a bar.

"Three!" A buzzed and swaggering Jack puts an arm around my shoulder.

"Two!" There's a crowd around me and the lights above are just barely bright enough to see what's going on.

"One!" Everyone shouts in glee. "HAPPY BIRTHDAY!"

Behind me, there's a small little area with speakers sitting upright adjacent to each other, a guy working at a computer and a nervous looking woman holding a microphone, bursting into song. "Happy birthday to you!" She slurs. "Hap, happy biiirfday to you!"

"Man, how's it feel to be a quarter damn century?!" Jack's head bobs inward and I'm chugging down the rest of the liquid from the glass in front of me, bottom up toward the low-hanging ceiling.

"Feels like it's gonna be a damn hangover tomorrow morning!" I slam the empty mug down and the unsteady bar shakes, drinks swimming around in their glasses all around us.

"Hah!" Pushing the gift closer to me. "I'm sure the chief'll be happy about that. Come on, open the present."

My hands fumble around at the shiny red wrapping, wondering what the hell could possibly be within its rectangular shape.

"This isn't entirely something from me." Quickly putting his left, sweaty hand over the opening I've made. "It's something Dad left behind before he disappeared a while back. Had your name on it, somewhere deep in Mom's closet."

A mustached, tall and skinny guy walks up to me on the opposite side. "Wutcha get man?" Sergeant Fortney asks. "I hope it's a pair of panties." Plopping down on an empty stool. "We all know how you like ta play dress up when no one's around."

"Man, shut your face." A fist lightly pumps against his shoulder. "Bartender!" I shout. "Three of your strongest! Stat!"

"Comin' right up." An aggravated and not entirely entertained man, dressed in black with a scowl across his face and a gloomy look in his eyes, acknowledges. "This on your tab?"

"Mine!" Jack moves forward toward the buzz-kill of a bartender. "It's all on me!"

"Sure." He says, filling three shot glasses halfway, first, with a brilliant looking red liquid and then almost spilling over the edges with a dark, syrupy liquid. "There you go."

The three of us do it at once, sliding the shot glass down into the mug, thrusting both fluids into my mouth and gasping outward with a breath of fire.

"Okay." Jack coughs. "Now open the damn present!" Sliding his glass to the other side of the counter.

The woman from before begins to sing some sappy Country song; Something about losing her man and slashing his tires, I don't know.

"Alright, alright…" Tearing away quick before anything else interrupts, Jack staring in anticipation and Fortney with his head in his palms, obviously too drunk to care.

What sits inside, haphazardly placed, is a shiny new gun, black and two empty magazines sitting beside it.

"What?" Astonished, I take it in my hands. "You're lucky we're cops or that guy over there'd be callin' us!" Twisting it around, engraved on its side, it says. "To my number one son, let this be both your shield and your judgment."

"And hey!" Jack points with a shaking finger, "it's not just any gun," I notice a slew of people staring. "It's a Colt Nineteen Eleven, best handgun ever made. I remember Dad mentioning something about it a long time ago. He always had that obsession with fine firearms."

"Well, uh…" Placing it gently back into its box, "I wish he were here to have maybe given it to me himself…"

"Me too man, me too…" His arm grabs tighter around my shoulder. "Come on, follow me outside and bring that with ya."

We stumble up from our stupor and he slams fifty bucks down onto the counter, box in my hand, we push through a crowd of inebriated bodies and out into a street, emerging from a small niche of a bar on the corner of Bridge Street.

A sign overtop reads. "Carnahans."

The street light, just before the sidewalk, glows down, bright with a feeling of pins and needles against my skull.

"Gah!" I exclaim. "Let's walk, too fuckin' bright here."

We meander to a traffic light that sits green with a two-tone blue and red ricer chugging by with its fart-can, little white-kid, thug wannabe as a driver. Blaring that thumping Hip Hop migraine causing noise. Shaking a fist in his direction, I remind Jack, "I'm gonna arrest that guy tomorrow, don't let me forget!" I laugh and the light goes red, signaling our ability to cross to the opposite side by a few houses and a car wash.

"Hey!" He pulls me in a different direction, all wiggling around over each other as if our feet are coordinated. "You remember that park?"

A large green field that's black under the night sky; Jack and I had gone fishing here as kids, you know, with all those fish with more corn in their bellies than anything else.

"Fuckin' right I do." My blurry, jiggling vision attempts to focus. "You know, I took some chick here back a few years ago, we were dating."

He laughs and with a belch. "I remember you telling me about her, some little pothead with more arrogance than brains…"

I hiccup and we walk in wet grass, the humid spring air rolling in over through the early morning. "Yup! There's a kid's playground way back there…" I wave with my free hand. "It was a night kinda like this one, she'd climbed into the jungle gym and for a while we just stood there making out, well, 'til I fucked her brains out."

"Oh man!" Finger in his throat. "You sick fuck! Those poor, poor children…"

"Needless to say…" Standing by a creek with flowing tar looking water, I light up a smoke and together we fall into the seat of a giant grey stone. "She's even less brainy now."

"Only crazy thing like that I've ever done…" He begins, hand pressing against my arm. "I was with this Jesus-freak of a woman, maybe ten years older than me and I was attending church with her…"

"Whoa, whoa." I chuckle, almost knowing exactly what he's going to say. "That's definitely worse."

"Hold on, lemme finish the damn story!" Retracting to a leaning position with hands between his legs. "Wait, wait…" You can tell he's on the verge of alcohol induced vomit. "Alright, I'm good, anyway, she had told me she was a virgin and she'd never been with a guy, said she thought that I was the one…"

"Yeah, you, the one." Hysterically laughing now, bumping shoulder-to-shoulder, puffing away. "She must've been a real winner, what, thirty some-odd years old?"

"DUDE! Seriously." Waving smoke out of his face, "There was a closet in the back and there I showed her maybe one hundred twenty seconds of nervous, ass-pounding sex."

"No wonder they call ya minute man, man." Flicking a half burned cigarette into a white bubbling patch in the stream. "You totally desecrated sacred ground there."

"Sacred, shmatred, you and I both know that shit doesn't make any difference." Head moving from side to side, "If there is a God, he'd have high-fived me."

"True." Looking up toward the moon and its chicken-pocked surface. "I always imagined God as more of a bro, like a college frat douche that runs around drunk all the time, tellin' everyone how much he loves them."

"Really now?" Hand against his head and the sound of chirping crickets beating at my eardrums.

"Honestly though…" Turning to a more philosophical tone. "If there's a God, he or she would defy both gender and race." I put a hand out in gesture. "It would be able to see all dimensions at once, the tenth one, if I'm correct and it'd be able to see the infinity of the Universe, all together and the Earth?"

Jack looks at me in a stumped kind of stare, blank and dead-as-stone.

"We'd be just a speck of dust, blown away someday maybe by a waft of a fart from this gigantic entity we'll never really know anything about, if it exists."

"That's deep man." Glassy eyes looking down. "But I gotta tell you something…"

He's changing the subject; I think I know what's coming.

"I know in a coupla months you'll be heading out to Manhattan for that SWAT team thing or whatever, leaving the simplistic life of Harrisburg behind and putting your life on the line even more than you already do…"

"Wait, wait." Fist balled with my index out. "It's not the simplicity I'm leaving behind; It's the goddamn crooked bastard cops and the mafia gov'ner. You think there'd be a shooting a day if more than two people actually tried to do something about it?"

"I don't know…" Shaking his head, "I don't bother myself with that, ya know, it's how people get shot, themselves." Reaching for my pack I'd laid on the ground and pulling a smoke out for himself. "I'm coming with you…" Flicking his thumb against his finger, suggesting that I light it for him.

"What?!" Shouting with an echo that anyone else in the area can probably hear. "What do you mean you're coming with me?" I strike a flame and he inhales. "You know what it takes, right? The stress and the difficulty it involves?"

Unknowingly ashing on my shoe. "Yeah, of course, but man, aside from Ma, you're the only family I got left…"

Kicking it away out of sight. "So you're worried then?"

"I don't know." Orange lighting up a drunkard's face. "I just think you need someone that knows you, out there, maybe watching your back?"

I would tell him I don't need anyone to watch my back, but he's my brother, after all.

"I'm guessing I can't stop you?" Questioning him, knowing what his answer'll be.

"Nope." Smashing the cigarette into an uplifted swatch of mud. "We're shipping out together."

Looking away, I breathe out with a hum, just imagining all of the things that could possibly happen with two brothers working side-by-side in an Emergency Response Unit; The possibility of failure or even death – These things happen.

What if there's some sort of crisis and we get split up – Maybe something along the lines of the nine-eleven attack.

Maybe I worry too much.

"Yo, Bro." Arm back around me. "I can tell you're thinking of craziness, don't worry about it, just imagine all the hot New Yorkian chicks out there, just waiting for us!"

My expression goes from serious to grinning in hilarity. "Did you just fuckin' say 'New Yorkian'?!"

"Hell yea man!" His teeth glow white against the light of the moon. "And I hear they go nuts for badass cops up there."

"Yeah." One eyebrow up. "Just like they and all the other people do here."

"You ever even been to Manhattan?" He asks. "It's no Harrisburg."

"No." Lighting another smoke, buzz falling and slowly bringing me back to a semi-sober state. "I've been to Brooklyn, one mess of a place to be, especially during rush hour, but never Manhattan. This is something new for me, the whole thing is."

"Well…" Standing up, "Same here. But I've been thinkin'"

Here we go again, Jack thinking and all. He changes subjects more than I change pairs of pants.

Walking together again, toward the squad car parked in an alley away from everything else. "People, nowadays, they just don't give a shit."

"What do you mean?" I look at him through squinting, muddy vision.

"I mean, they're just so oblivious." Stopping to watch a couple of people driving by shouting at some lonely looking woman walking with her head down along the littered sidewalk. "In an apocalypse sort of situation, they'd kill you before offering you a hand."

"You know what I think?" Patting him on the back before we reach the handle of the door to a poorly maintained vehicle. "I think you watch too many movies."

30

The Beginning of the End

"Wake up you two, goddammit!" Rob pounds relentlessly at the door. "Get the fuck outta bed, now!"

My eyes burst open to a blue shadowed room, sitting upward, I reach over the bed for my pants, fumbling around till I'm almost half decent, struggling to get to the door and the knob.

"Jesus Christ, hurry!" He shouts impatiently.

"ALRIGHT!" I yell back at him.

Meryl jolts upright, dazed and confused. "What the hell's going on?!"

"Get your clothes on and weapons ready, I think we got some trouble."

Standing fully clothed after about fifteen seconds of the two of us wandering around and deciding who wore what, we look again into each other's eyes – I cock back the barrel of each pistol and turn from our gaze, kicking through the door to see Ed and Rob moving fast toward the truck, a very large mob of undead closing in on us from every direction – Running all gangly and hungry for flesh.

"Ah, how the shit?!" I turn back once more to be sure Meryl's still behind. "Move, move, MOVE!"

We meet the two of them at the vehicle to find Ed pounding his forehead against the steering wheel. Meryl's head pokes out beside mine and Rob stands nervously, gun in the upright position and jittering back and forth.

I place a hand on his shoulder. "What's up, Ed? Stop beatin' yourself!"

"We're out of goddamn fuel." He says, defeated. "I had half a damn tank when we all slept last night."

"No good man, no good!" Rob panics.

"What're we gonna do?!" Meryl aims for the crowd, ready to fire.

I look at her, then Rob and Ed. His fifty year old, stocky frame shifting out of the driver seat, he grabs his shotgun, cocks back on the barrel and says, "It's pumpin' and thumpin' time."

About the Author

I began writing this book mid-2008. And it wasn't until I'd messed up 20,000 words of the original story, that I finally figured out *what* it was going to be. I assure you, if ever you stumble upon the original, original draft, you'd run screaming for your life.

Many hours and many nights of lunch breaks have been spent writing this craziness, so I really hope you had a good time riding with Dante.

And fear not, the sequel is already in the works. If you've finished reading this any time after February 2011, you can probably find updated information on the sequel, whatever it may be called, on my personal website (linked at the beginning of the book).

So congrats! You didn't go insane! Now, if you'll excuse me, I've got zombies to kill and things to blow up.

Connect with me Online
Twitter: http://www.twitter.com/paxcorpus
Facebook: http://www.facebook.com/paxcorpus